TRADE SECRETS

David Wishart

CRÈME de la CRIME

This first world edition published 2015
in Great Britain and 2016 in the USA by
Crème de la Crime, an imprint of
SEVERN HOUSE PUBLISHERS LTD of
19 Cedar Road, Sutton, Surrey, England, SM2 5DA.
Trade paperback edition first published 2016
in Great Britain and the USA by
SEVERN HOUSE PUBLISHERS LTD.

British Library Cataloguing in Publication Data

Wishart, David, 1952- author.
  Trade secrets. – (A Marcus Corvinus mystery)
  1. Corvinus, Marcus (Fictitious character)–Fiction.
  2. Murder–Investigation–Fiction. 3. Rome–History–
  Empire, 30 B.C.-476 A.D.–Fiction. 4. Detective and
  mystery stories.
  I. Title II. Series
  823.9'2-dc23

ISBN-13: 978-1-78029-080-5 (cased)
ISBN-13: 978-1-78029-564-0 (trade paper)
ISBN-13: 978-1-78010-726-4 (e-book)

All Severn House titles are printed on acid-free paper.

Severn House Publishers support the Forest Stewardship Council™ [FSC™],
the leading international forest certification organisation.
All our titles that are printed on FSC certified paper carry the FSC logo.

MIX
Paper from
responsible sources
FSC® C013056

Typeset by Palimpsest Book Production Ltd.,
Falkirk, Stirlingshire, Scotland.
Printed and bound in Great Britain by
TJ International, Padstow, Cornwall.

DRAMATIS PERSONAE

(Only the names of characters who appear or are mentioned more than once are given. The story is set in May, AD 41.)

ROME

Annia: Gaius Tullius's widow.
Annius, Quintus: Annia's brother.
Bathyllus: Corvinus's major-domo.
Clarus, Cornelius: Corvinus's son-in-law; a doctor in Castrimoenium.
Festus, Lucilius: a potter.
Gemella, Tullia: a friend of Perilla's, and Gaius Tullius's sister.
Hermia: Titus Vecilius's wife, and one of Tullius's women friends.
Lippillus, Decimus Flavonius: Watch Commander friend of Corvinus's.
Marcia: Lucilius Festus's wife, and another of Tullius's women friends.
Marilla, Valeria: Corvinus's adopted daughter; Clarus's wife.
Memmius, Gaius: the Aventine Watch Commander.
Meton: Corvinus's chef.
Mysta: Corvinus's grandson's nurse.
Perilla: Corvinus's wife.
Petillius, Titus: Corvinus's cat-loving neighbour. His wife is **Tyndaris**.
Picentina: a lady's maid. Her mistress is **Publilia Clementa**.
Poetelius, Publius: Tullius's business partner.
Timon: Annia's major-domo.
Tullius, Gaius: the victim; part-owner of an import-export business.
Vecilius, Titus: a glassworker.

Vibius, Titus: the owner of a pottery business; one of Tullius's former suppliers.

OSTIA

Agron: Corvinus's long-time friend; the owner of a cart-building business. His wife is **Cass**.

Arrius: an Ostian quay-master.

Cispius: an ex-colleague of Gaius Manutius.

Correllius, Marcus: an Ostian businessman, stabbed outside the Pollio Library in Rome.

Doccius, Publius: Correllius's deputy.

Fulvina, Caesia: a friend of Perilla's; the owner of a seaside villa.

Fundanius, Publius: a business rival of Correllius's.

Mamilia: Correllius's widow.

Manutius, Gaius: Vinnia's ex-husband.

Mercurius: Correllius's slave.

Nigrinus, Titus: captain of the *Porpoise*.

Nigrinus, Sextus: Titus's brother.

Pullius, Marcus: a businessman whom Correllius had arranged to meet outside the Pollio.

Rubrius, Titus: a local butcher and wineshop regular.

Siddius, Gaius: a crane operator at the docks.

Vinnia: a wineshop owner.

ONE

Fascinating things, babies. So long as you keep a respectful distance, that is, because the little buggers can be really devious. Witness the existence of projectile vomiting.

Which was currently relevant: as of the evening before, we'd got Marilla and her doctor husband, Clarus, over on a visit from Castrimoenium, plus of course the grand-sprog, young Marcus Cornelius, born at the start of the Winter Festival so now pushing five months old, as promising a little bruiser as ever dirtied a nappy and presently ensconced on the atrium couch opposite snoring his socks off against his grandmother's shoulder.

'You want to hold him for a while, Marcus?' Perilla said. 'I have to go upstairs to change. They'll be here in an hour.'

True; it was the lady's monthly poetry-klatsch morning, when her literary pals met to juggle their anapaests, and this time she was hosting. Not exactly my scene. By the time the cultured hordes rolled up for their cakes and honeyed wine I'd be long gone.

'No, I think I'll pass,' I said. 'I'll leave it to the experts.'

'Oh, come on, dear! He's perfectly harmless! And I'm no more an expert with babies than you are.'

True again; it'd become obvious pretty early on that Perilla couldn't have kids herself, and we'd adopted Marilla in her early teens when her bastard of a real father took his well-earned final nose-dive down the blunt end of the Capitol. Even so . . .

'No, I'm OK,' I said.

'Coward.' Perilla stood up carefully, prised young Marcus loose, and handed him to Marilla on the other couch. 'You really should take your grandfathering duties more seriously.'

'Yeah, well, I'll wait until things reach the conversation stage.'

Clarus, on the couch next to Marilla, grinned. 'Corvinus, he won't even be able to put two words together for another two years at least,' he said. 'And handling an actual conversation will take just a little longer.'

'Really?'

'Trust me.'

Jupiter! It was a different world, this!

'So what are your plans for today, dear?' Perilla said to Marilla. 'You're very welcome to join us if you like. Albia Tertia's giving a short talk on the funerary epigrams in Cephalas's *Anthology* with her own translations, which should be quite fun. Tertia's always good value.'

I glanced at Clarus and caught the wince and slight look of desperation. Right; not a literary man, by any means, Cornelius Clarus, unless you could call medical treatises literature. Particularly the ones featuring illustrations of dissected body parts. Marilla wasn't exactly a fan, either, to put it mildly. I could've told Perilla she was on a hiding to nothing for a start, but she was probably only being polite.

'No,' Marilla said carefully. 'No, we thought we might do a few touristy things while we're here. Clarus has been to Rome before, of course, lots of times, but we've never really got round to it. I thought today we'd take a boat trip from the Sublician Bridge upriver to Augustus's Mausoleum. And Clarus wants to go to the Pollio Library. They've got a rare manuscript of Erasistratus he'd like to take a look at. But that can wait for another day.'

'On the sensory and motor nerve systems,' Clarus elaborated.

'Is that so, now?' I said.

'It's fascinating stuff. He also has a lot to say about bodily degeneration due to sudden or chronic diseases.'

'Really.' Gods! Some people had a weird definition of 'touristy', let alone what constituted good reading material. Still, everyone to their own bag. Me, I'd be spending the time more constructively with a leisurely shave in my usual booth off Market Square, followed by a few hours propping up the bar at Renatius's with the other punters, soaking up the booze and generally putting the world to rights.

'Are you taking young Marcus?' Perilla asked. 'On the boat trip, I mean.'

'No, we'll leave him behind with Mysta,' Marilla said; Mysta was the nurse. 'It'll make a change, getting away on our own for a while, particularly since Clarus is busy most of the time. Besides, he's had a bit of diarrhoea these last few days, so it might not be a good idea.'

It was my turn to wince: ah, the joys of parenthood. Still, she'd brought the glad news out deadpan, so I assumed she was pretty much hardened to small unpleasantries like that by now.

'Very well, dear,' Perilla said. 'I'll see you later. Have a nice time.' She turned to go. 'Oh, and you too, Marcus, if you really do insist on going out.' The barest sniff as she made for the stairs; Perilla doesn't altogether approve of me passing up an opportunity to broaden my cultural horizons, particularly when the alternative choice of venue is Renatius's wineshop on Iugarius where most of the punters are plain mantles at best, with a fair sprinkling of freedmen. Me, I've always thought that was a definite plus: reasonably close to the centre as Renatius's is, the purple-striper brigade wouldn't be seen dead doing their drinking and social networking there. The wine was good, too, which set the cap on it.

Marilla stood up, still holding the sleeping Sprog.

'I'll get changed as well,' she said to Clarus. 'Marcus seems to be flat out, so I'll put him in his cot and tell Mysta what's happening. Give me ten minutes?'

'Sure.'

She left. Clarus was grinning.

'What's so funny?' I said.

'Oh, nothing.'

Uh-huh. Me, I can tell how many beans make five, and I'd seen the look of panic on his face when Perilla handed out her invitation change to one of relief.

'You hadn't any plans for the morning at all, had you?' I said.

He shook his head. 'No. Or nothing definite, anyway. It's only our first day, after all. That was pretty fast thinking on Marilla's part.'

'You're learning, pal. Both of you. Although Marilla's had a lot more practice.'

The grin widened. 'Simple self-preservation,' he said. 'And man's a learning animal. Mind you, the tourist thing's true enough, in general terms. The visit to the Pollio, too, but like Marilla said that can wait.' He settled back on the couch. 'So. How are things in Rome under the new regime?'

'Pretty quiet, all things considered. Certainly no ructions. It's early days yet, sure, but Perilla thinks Claudius will make a good emperor, and from what I've seen I'd tend to agree. Particularly after Gaius.'

'You've met him? His wife's a cousin of yours, isn't she?'

I kept my face straight. 'Messalina. Yeah. We haven't had much to do with each other in the past, mind.' And we'd have a hell of a lot less, in future, if I had anything to do with it; that lady I wouldn't touch with gloves and a ten-foot pole. 'He's a nice enough guy in himself, Tiberius Claudius, if you make allowances. There again, me, I'd settle for sanity.'

Too right I would: Gaius's last six months had been hairy, for all concerned, me included. Perilla had made the right decision after all: Rome and the empire were better without him.

'How's the sleuthing going? You never did tell us how that Surdinus business you were working on before the Festival turned out in the end.'

I shrugged. 'It went OK.' I wasn't going to elaborate: Clarus was close-mouthed as they come, but there were some things it was better – and safer – for him not to know. Him or anyone else, for that matter. 'More or less. Not one of my best.'

'You get whoever did it?'

'Yes. In a way.'

He grunted; a very intelligent guy, Clarus, and he knew obfuscation when he saw it. Well enough to drop the subject, certainly.

'Anything on at the moment?'

'Uh-uh,' I said. 'Not that I'm complaining. Having a bit of quality time to myself will make a pleasant change.'

Which, in retrospect, was a pretty silly thing to say. Considering the number of evil-minded gods hovering around with their ears pricked, it was just plain asking for trouble. But then I always did have a big mouth.

It was well into the afternoon when I rolled back in, by which time the poetry gang had usually dispersed to their respective homes, leaving the Corvinus household a blessedly poetry-free zone.

Only this time, as it transpired when I came into the atrium holding my customary welcome-home wine-cup, they hadn't. There was one of them left.

Bugger.

'You know Tullia Gemella, Marcus?' Perilla said. She was looking a bit chewed.

'Ah . . . yeah.' I gave the lady sitting across from her a nod. An overstatement there: I knew the name, sure – one of the recent and extremely keen recruits, with a thing, according to Perilla, for lyric pieces involving shepherdesses, rustic swains, and a general atmosphere of bosk – but I'd never actually seen her in person. The adjectives 'large' and 'imposing' sprang to mind. Also the phrase 'a strong personality': even although the lady hadn't opened her mouth yet, she just radiated self-possession, confidence, and a knowledge of her own considerable worth. So must Hannibal have looked when he was faced with the Alps and muttered: *'I'll bloody have you lot for a start!'*

Well, it explained Perilla's chewed look, anyway; in the time between the end of the poetry-klatsch meeting and my arrival, Things must've been Fraught.

'Pleased to meet you, Tullia Gemella,' I said. 'I'll just—' I turned to go.

'No, don't leave, dear,' Perilla said quickly. 'We've been waiting for you to get back. Gemella wanted a word.'

'Yeah? What about?'

'Her brother's been murdered.'

I'd been taking a sip of the wine, and I almost swallowed the cup.

'What?'

'Two days ago.' Add an unlikely 'prim' to the list: Gemella's tone and manner suggested that the guy had committed some sort of social faux pas. 'At least, that's when his body was found.'

I went over to my usual couch and lay down. Hell. Hell and damnation. So much for the quality time idea.

'Gemella happened to mention it at the meeting,' Perilla said brightly.

'The silly fool got himself stabbed,' the lady said. 'In Trigemina Gate Street, of all places.'

The knee-jerk response was, *Oh, dear! I'm sorry to hear that,* but I stopped myself just in time from making it.

'You like to elaborate, maybe?' I said.

That got me a frown that suggested I'd just committed a social faux pas myself, but that she was prepared under the circumstances to overlook it. 'Certainly,' she said. 'Shortly after sunset, two days ago, my brother Gaius Tullius was found stabbed to death at the Shrine of Melobosis in Trigemina Gate Street. Or rather, just off the street in question, because the shrine is a little way down an alley to one side. The body was discovered by a courting couple.' She coughed. 'Or so the local Watch told us. Seemingly the shrine is quite a popular venue with people of that sort.'

'"Us"?'

'Actually, his wife, to be precise. And she told me, the poor girl. Now I should say at the start, Valerius Corvinus, that I'd very little time for Gaius myself, brother or not, but he was family, and I understand from Rufia Perilla here that murder is quite a hobby of yours.'

The faintest of disapproving sniffs that suggested she put that on a par with screwing goats, but I let it pass; I'd be taking it up with the loose-mouthed lady later.

'His wife being?' I said.

'Her name's Annia. You'll want to talk to her, no doubt. She and Gaius have a little pied-à-terre in Ardeatina Road, just past the Capenan Gate and overlooking Asinianus Gardens.' Another sniff. '*Not* the best address, I know, and a long way from the centre, practically out of town altogether, but she seems to like it, which is the main thing.'

'So what was your brother doing in Trigemina Gate Street? That's the other side of the city.'

'Ah,' she said carefully. 'I'm afraid in that regard I have no information to give you. He had his reasons, I'm sure, which may or may not, unfortunately, have been legitimate, Gaius being Gaius. Certainly he'd have business contacts near the river. Who and where precisely they might be I have no idea, but of course his partner would be able to tell you that.'

'His partner?'

'Gaius was a businessman, a merchant, rather, part-owner of an import-export business dealing mostly in glass and pottery. His partner's name is Publius Poetelius. They have a small office on the Sacred Way near its Market Square end. Again I can't give you precise details, but I'm sure anyone will be able to point you in the right direction if you ask.'

'Fair enough,' I said. 'OK, lady. Now tell me what you're not saying.'

That got me the frown again, in spades.

'I beg your pardon?' she snapped.

'You say you didn't like the guy, and that his reasons for being in Trigemina Gate Street might or might not have been legit, "Gaius being Gaius". To me, that's pretty conclusive. Your brother was some sort of crook, right?'

She bridled. 'Certainly not! Or at least not as far as I'm aware.'

'So what, then?'

Spots of colour appeared in her ample cheeks, fighting their way through the rouge.

'Nothing of great import, at least in a criminal sense,' she said at last. 'He . . . spread his favours. Where women were concerned, I mean.'

I had to stop myself from laughing. Gods! So might a particularly prim Chief Vestal look and sound when asked in court to provide a detailed eyewitness description of a flasher.

'You're saying he had a mistress?' I said.

The spots of colour deepened. 'My brother was not one to do things by halves, Valerius Corvinus. Let alone quarters or eighths. I'm sure you understand me, but if you don't then again I suggest you consult his partner on the matter. I expect Poetelius can tell you far more about that aspect of Gaius's character than I can.'

'Did his wife know?'

'I'd be very surprised if she didn't, poor woman, but I wouldn't care to comment further on the subject.' She stood up. 'Now I really have taken up enough of your time. The rest is up to you. Perilla, my dear, thank you so much for a most enjoyable meeting. A pleasure, as always.'

And she was gone. Perilla and I were left looking at each other. The lady was having the decency to look sheepish, as well she might under the circumstances.

'Who the hell's Melobosis?' I said.

'One of the Oceanides. Not a particularly prominent nymph. I didn't know she even had a shrine in Rome.' Perilla cleared her throat. 'Look, I'm sorry for landing you with this, Marcus, particularly when we've got Clarus and Marilla staying, but Gemella was quite . . . pressing.' Yeah, that I'd believe. Like half a ton of marble. 'And she really is genuinely upset, far more than she seemed. Of course, if you'd rather, I can tell her you can't help.' She paused, frowning. 'Or perhaps sending her a note to that effect would be better.'

I grinned; it wasn't often the lady chickened out of a head-to-head: *strong personality* was right. And despite what I'd said to Clarus, it'd be nice to be looking into a clean, straightforward murder again; it might get the nasty taste of the Surdinus affair out of my mouth, for a start. 'No, that's OK,' I said. 'I can have a word with the wife, at least. See what she says. It's really her business, after all, because Gemella's only the guy's sister. I'll do that tomorrow.'

Which is what I did.

TWO

Next morning I left Perilla to snooze on as usual – not an early-morning person, the lady – and went down to breakfast on the terrace. Clarus and Marilla were up already, Marilla tucking into her usual light breakfast of omelette, cheese, olives, dried fruit, bread rolls, and honey, with young Marcus gurgling away and blowing bubbles in his basket beside her.

'You're around early, Corvinus.' Clarus was like me: a straightforward breakfast-roll-dipped-in-olive-oil man. 'Going somewhere special?'

At dinner the previous evening I'd been careful to avoid, at Perilla's insistence, any mention of Tullia Gemella's visit. Clarus would've been interested, certainly, but that would've been as far as it went. Marilla was another matter. Adopted or not, she's a lot like me in many ways: she'd've insisted on the full gory details, as far as I could give them, and she'd've wanted to be involved. Oh, sure, I was under no illusions, and neither was Perilla: being Marilla she'd find out eventually what was going on, and pretty soon at that. But I wasn't going to precipitate things, because if I did then the lady had made it abundantly clear that she'd have my guts for garters.

'Just a bit of business,' I said. 'Someone I have to see in Ardeatina Road.' I reached for a roll. 'You got anything special planned yourselves?'

'We thought we might do the Pollio,' Marilla said. 'Take Marcus with us. It's a lovely day, and I can sit in the Pollio garden with him while Clarus does his thing inside with Erasistratus. What sort of business?'

'Nothing important. Just someone I have to talk to.'

'Oh?' Marilla put down the knife she was holding. 'About what?'

'Come on, Princess! I said it's not important, just—'

'Corvinus, you never have business. Certainly not at this

time of the day. It's a murder, isn't it? Or something like that, anyway.'

Bugger. 'Why should it be a murder?'

'Because you're not telling. And your left eyelid twitched.'

Hell. This I didn't need, certainly not at breakfast: motherhood hadn't affected the lady's ability to recognize fudging when she heard it, anyway. And when she did she was as efficient as a ferret down a rabbit hole.

'Look, Marilla,' I said. 'I told Clarus yesterday that I'd nothing like that on at present.' I turned to Clarus. 'Right, pal?'

'True.' Clarus dipped a piece of his roll in the oil, eyes lowered; he was definitely learning, was Cornelius Clarus.

'There you are, then.' I poured some of the oil from the flask onto my own plate. 'So just clam up and eat, OK?'

'Hmm.' She picked up the knife again, and I breathed a quiet sigh of relief. Then she put the knife down. 'Even so—'

Fuck.

Bathyllus, our major-domo, buttled over with a fresh supply of rolls. Saved by the domestic.

'Would you like an omelette this morning, sir?' he said.

'Uh, no, that's OK, Bathyllus.' I dipped the roll I was holding into the oil and stood up. 'Actually, I'm a bit pushed for time. I'll just take this with me. Have a nice day, kids. See you later.'

Jupiter, that had been close! I made my escape. Quickly.

I was going down the steps when I saw the cat. Or what had been the cat. It was lying on the pavement right next to the house wall, halfway between us and the neighbours' property; neatly laid out, like someone had put it there. I went over to look. Pure white Parthian, groomed to its carefully manicured claws, about as far from your average scrawny street moggie as you can get, and definitely now an ex-feline.

Oh, bugger. Admetus.

To say that we didn't get on with our immediate neighbours was an understatement. The situation at present wasn't one of outright war, sure, but if we'd been countries both sides of our common border would've been fortified in depth and guarded by six legions on constant alert and a battery of artillery kept at hair-trigger readiness. And cats figured largely among the areas of possible friction. Where a love of cats was concerned, Titus Petillius and his ex-housekeeper-now-wife, Tyndaris, were the ailurophile's ailurophiles, and the fact that a few years previously our temporary house guest, the hellhound Placida, had nailed Admetus's sister had consigned Perilla and me to leper status. If even the slightest suspicion were to arise that the brute's death lay at our door metaphorically as well as literally then, if it meant getting rid of us, the Petillius household would welcome a leper colony as neighbours with open arms and a standing invitation to dinner.

Something had to be done. And quickly. I bent to pick the cat up. Bathyllus could arrange for it to be buried in our garden, and Petillius would be none the wiser . . .

'Murderer!'

I straightened. The man himself had just come out of his front door. He was standing on the top step, goggling, finger pointing accusingly.

Oh, shit.

He came towards me. I backed off.

'Uh . . . Look, pal,' I said. 'I just found it, right? Someone must've dumped it there.'

He was glaring at me like Medusa on a bad-hair day.

'Cat-killer!'

'I'd nothing to d—'

'By the gods, if there's any justice in Rome you will pay for this!'

'Oh, come on, pal! It's only a cat! And like I said I only—'

Mistake. Make that Medusa with a grade-one hangover, an abscessed tooth, and an extra supply of snakes. He was deep purple now and about a hair's breadth from apoplexy. Without another word, he snatched the limp body out of my unresisting grasp, turned, and marched back into the house, slamming the door behind him.

Yeah, well; that could've gone better. It seemed that the truce was well and truly over. Still, there was nothing I could do about it at present; we'd just have to hope that the guy would calm down enough to listen to reason. And that in the interim there'd be a herd of flying pigs.

I went back inside, apprised Bathyllus of the situation, then
set off again for the Tullius place.

Ardeatina Road is our side of town, but about as far down as
you can go without running out of city; a fairish hike, but
pleasant enough on a good May morning. Tullia Gemella's
description of the house as a pied-à-terre was just about right
– it was one of those places built for the cheap end of the
market, for punters who feel themselves a cut above a tenement
but can't afford the fancy prices asked for hillside properties
– and with the cypress branches round the door the place
wasn't too hard to find: the funeral would be over by now,
sure, but the household would still be in mourning. I knocked
on the door, introduced myself to the door-slave, and was
taken into the pocket-sized atrium.

Annia, the dead man's widow, wasn't alone. There was
another guy with her, and when I came in they were deep in
urgent conversation. Then Annia saw me, and put a hand on
the man's wrist. He looked round.

'Uh . . . I'm sorry,' I said, stopping on the threshold. 'You're
busy. Maybe I should come back later.'

'No, that's quite all right.' The lady smiled. No looker,
Annia, not by a long chalk, but she was no mouse either, I
could see that straight away. Tullius's widow had *poise*. 'This
is my brother Quintus.' Yeah, I could've guessed that: similar
age – early thirties – same chunky build and heavy features.
We nodded to each other. 'Gemella told me you'd be coming,
or that you might be, rather. And why, of course. I'm very
grateful.'

Not that she sounded it, exactly. I suspected that arms had
been seriously twisted here. Or at least responsibilities firmly
pointed out.

'I'll leave, dear,' Annius said. 'We can discuss things another
time.'

'That's OK,' I said. 'In fact if it's all right with your sister
I'd rather that you stayed. Maybe you can fill in some of the
corners.'

He frowned. 'I'm afraid that isn't likely. Certainly not about
the actual circumstances of Gaius's death. We didn't get on

at all, we had almost no contact other than what was strictly necessary for family reasons, and frankly I think my sister is far better off without him.'

Well, that was certainly frank enough, especially as an unsolicited starter, and I noticed that he was in an ordinary plain mantle, not a mourning one. I winced, mentally: what had happened to the tag 'Of the dead, nothing but good'? The interesting thing, though, was that when he'd come out with that little speech the lady hadn't batted an eyelid, and although she was wearing a mourning mantle herself she didn't look all that cut up, either. All of which, plus that lukewarm expression of gratitude, went to suggest that husband, Tullius, might have been, but he hadn't left much actual grief behind him.

'Besides,' Annius went on, 'I couldn't have stayed much longer in any case. I've some business to attend to in town. And Annia may talk to you more freely without a brother's intimidating presence.'

'No problem,' I said. 'Pleasure to have met you.'

'The pleasure's mine.' He got up from the couch. 'Annia, I'll drop by tomorrow again, if I may, and we'll take it from there. Meanwhile if there's anything you need you know where I am. Corvinus.'

I gave him a parting nod, and he left.

'Sit down, please,' Annia said. I did, on the couch her brother had been using. 'Now. What can I tell you?'

'Practically everything, lady,' I said. 'All I know from your sister-in-law is the when and the where, plus the fact that your husband co-ran an import-export firm.' I wasn't going to mention the womanizing angle; that'd have to come from her, with due prompting if need be.

'Did she give you his partner's name? Publius Poetelius?'

'Yeah, I got that.'

'Good, because I'm afraid I can't help you much on the business side of things. My father was in business, as indeed Gaius's was, and Publius's, for that matter – they were all close friends, which explains our various relationships, and we've known each other since we were children – but it's an area of my husband's life I know very little about.'

'So, uh, what area do you know about?' I was tactful.

She smiled and looked down at her hands, folded in her lap. They were smooth and well-manicured, but they wouldn't't've been out of place on a wrestler.

'You mean the women, of course,' she said. 'Oh, yes, I'm sure Gemella will have mentioned that aspect, so we may as well get it out of the way.' There was a bright tightness in her voice. 'It's been going on for years, practically since the start of our marriage. Which was, if you're wondering, just over ten years ago. I know some of the names, but not all; Gaius tended to change his girlfriends almost as often as he changed his mantle, and the list would be a very long one. The two most recent, in chronological order, were a Marcia and a Hermia.'

I blinked and sat back. 'You're pretty well-informed, lady,' I said.

'Oh, Gaius wasn't particularly concerned to keep his activities secret. Or not from me, at any rate; I don't think his women were aware that they were only one of a series. Or indeed that the position of mistress might be filled by more than one incumbent at the same time.'

'Did you mind?'

'Of course I minded,' she said calmly. 'Although perhaps not in the way you might think. I'd been asking for a divorce for years, but Gaius wouldn't agree to it.'

'Why not?'

'For the most obvious reason of all. My father was far wealthier than Gaius's and he gave me a good dowry. Most of it's in property, tenements on the Aventine and in Circus Valley, a shop or two here and there, that sort of thing. Nothing too grand, but the rents form a substantial part of our income. If Gaius had divorced me through no fault of mine, I'd have had most of it back. Gaius needs working capital for his business. Liquid capital, in the form of specie. Without the rents coming in on the first of every month he'd have a serious problem with cash flow, and in the export line a healthy cash-flow situation is vital.' I must've looked a bit fazed because she smiled. 'Yes, I know. I said I wasn't up on the business side of things, and I'm not, because Gaius wanted it that way, but I didn't say I was a complete ignoramus. I told you, all of us are from business families. Money and trade have been the standard topics of conversation at mealtimes as long as I can remember. I'm no stranger to either.'

'Is your father still alive?'

'Oh yes, and flourishing. Not Gaius's, though; he died several years ago.'

'So why did you marry him?'

She smiled. 'Because I was nineteen, late for marriage, and a fool. Because he was the best-looking man I'd ever met, and the smoothest talker, and that counted with me in those days. And because my father – my mother died when I was two – was totally against it. That's often a clincher where young women are concerned, particularly with stubborn ones who know their own minds, or think they do, which I was.'

'But you brought him round?'

'I brought him round. Against his plainly expressed and perfectly valid reservations. I told you: I was a fool.'

'No kids?'

'One, a year after the marriage. A girl. She died at birth. None since, for – again – the most obvious reason.' She shifted on her chair. 'I think we've exhausted that topic, Corvinus. Can you ask me about the murder now, please?'

Fair enough; that side of things – in detail, anyway – wasn't really any concern of mine, and she was politely and quite rightly reminding me of the fact. 'Your sister-in-law said it happened in an alleyway off Trigemina Gate Street,' I said. 'The west side of the city, near the river. Any significance in that?'

Was that a blink? I couldn't be sure. 'No,' she said slowly. 'Not that I know of. It's an industrial area, obviously, lots of warehouses, wharves, and factories, so he probably had business there. Certainly it's not at all unlikely. But that's all I can say, except that he didn't mention a visit to me, which as I told you would have been completely in character. You'd do better to ask Publius.'

The surviving partner. Yeah, I'd get round to him. 'He didn't happen to mention anything out of the usual run of things at all?' I said. 'In the days leading up to his death, I mean?'

She considered. 'Actually, there was one thing,' she said.

'And it's something Publius may know nothing about, unless Gaius told him, which he may well have done.'

'Yeah? What was that?'

'An accident, six days ago. Or, in retrospect, it might not have been an accident at all, so perhaps it's worth mentioning. Gaius told me about it when he got home.'

'Go ahead, lady.'

'It happened in Ostia. Gaius had gone down there to supervise a shipment. He was walking along one of the wharves past a crane when the netful of amphoras it was lifting slipped its hawser. He said he'd been lucky.'

Yeah, I'd agree with that. Lucky was right; those buggers are pretty big and heavy, especially when they're full, and there isn't much room on an Ostia wharf to dodge a netful of them. And six days ago would put it three days before the murder. My interest sharpened.

She was watching me closely. 'Is it significant, do you think?' she said.

I shrugged. 'Could be. It's something to check out, anyway. Did he give you any more details? Like which wharf it was, exactly?'

'No. But you should be able to get the relevant information from Publius. Even if Gaius didn't mention the actual accident itself, Publius would know the number of the wharf the shipment was going from, and that would be enough to start with.'

Right. Me, I'd be surprised if Tullius hadn't told him, because it isn't every day you're nearly flattened by falling amphoras, and little details like that tend to get mentioned when someone asks you how your day went. In which case he might be able to tell me a bit more.

I stood up. 'Fine. Thank you, you've been very helpful. Is there anything else you can tell me before I go?'

'No. That's all, I'm afraid. Everything I can think of for the present, at least.'

'Yeah, well, if something else does occur to you I'm easy enough to find. We're on the Caelian, first side street off Head of Africa Road before the Appian Aqueduct. Or you can get in touch through Tullia Gemella, of course.'

'I'll do that, of course. And thank you for coming.'

'You're welcome.'

I left. Maybe I should've signed off with a polite expression of my condolences for her loss, but it didn't seem appropriate somehow. Certainly from all appearances she wouldn't've wanted them.

Frankly, mind, from the way Tullius was rounding out at present I didn't blame her.

THREE

OK. So where to next? The places I needed to go were the office on the Sacred Way to talk to Tullius's partner, Poetelius, and Trigemina Gate Street itself, to check out the murder site; plus I had to pay a call on the Thirteenth District Watch Commander, who had his station on the slopes of the Aventine opposite the Circus. I couldn't do all three today, not comfortably, anyway. I tossed a mental coin and it came down Poetelius.

I got to the Market Square end of the Sacred Way just after mid-afternoon, with a short stopover at a wineshop for a badly needed cup of wine and a plate of cheese and olives. The office was on the second floor of one of the old properties you tend to get a lot of on the Way, rubbing shoulders with the new stuff that went up under Augustus; a stiff climb up a rickety wooden spiral staircase that looked like it'd been home to the same families of woodworm and beetles since Sulla was in nappies. If Tullius and his partner ran an export business then we clearly weren't talking market leaders here.

Office space was pretty cramped too. There were only four clerks, but they were sitting practically on top of each other at a couple of desks that virtually filled the available floor space, and the walls were completely lined with record cubbies.

'Afternoon, pal,' I said to the nearest clerk. 'The boss around?'

He hesitated. 'Which one did you want to see?'

Yeah, well, I'd've been surprised if Tullius was on offer, but I appreciated his tact. When I said Poetelius, he looked relieved.

'Then there's no problem, sir. Just go straight through.'

I gave him a nod and squeezed past.

Poetelius was sitting at a desk in what was basically a glorified broom closet. He put down the wax tablet he'd been reading and looked up.

'Good afternoon,' he said. 'What can I do for you?'

A youngish guy, not much older than Annia; I'd've put him mid-thirties, max. No sign of a mourning mantle, but maybe it'd put the customers off. Certainly there wasn't much else about him that might indicate he'd suddenly found himself bereft of a close friend and partner and was taking it badly, but I was beginning to recognize that that was par for the course where Gaius Tullius was concerned.

'Valerius Corvinus,' I said. 'Your late partner's widow, Annia, maybe told you I might be dropping in. Or it could've been his sister Tullia Gemella.'

'Actually, it was both. The messages reached me yesterday evening.' We shook. 'Yes, Corvinus, I was expecting you. Pull up a stool.'

I did; there was one – just one – tucked out of the way below the desk. When I sat down I was so close to the door that I could lean back against it.

'Now,' he said. 'What can I tell you? I should say that Gaius's death came as a great shock, but on the professional rather than the personal level. Please don't feel that you have to be delicate in any way.'

Straight in and up front, just like Quintus Annius, albeit a smidgeon more tactful. I blinked; truth be told, prime rat though the guy seemed to have been, I was beginning to feel more than a little sorry for Gaius Tullius. First his sister, then his wife and brother-in-law, now his business partner. It'd be nice, somewhere along the line, to come across someone who wasn't as happy as not to see him dead.

'Fair enough,' I said. 'So. First off. He was killed in Trigemina Gate Street. Was there any reason he should be in that part of town?'

Poetelius hesitated. 'You mean for business purposes?' I nodded. 'Yes, there was. Two of our suppliers have factories there. Lucilius Festus has a pottery and Titus Vecilius a glass-works. He could have been visiting either of them.'

'"Could have"?'

'He didn't mention it to me beforehand, no, but there wouldn't't've been anything unusual about that. Except that it was officially a holiday, of course, the Festival of Mercury, so the office was closed. Gaius generally handled the personal-contact side of the business. He was much better at that than I am. I deal mostly with the legal and accountancy side of things, plus the correspondence with our overseas customers.' He smiled. 'To tell you the truth, that's quite enough. I'm rarely out of the office from one month's end to the next. Not that I mind; it's what I'm good at. We work' – he caught himself – '*worked* very well together.'

'So the business is doing OK?' I said.

'Not too badly, considering.'

There'd been a small but noticeable hesitation there. Uh-huh: I knew an evasion when I heard one. 'Look, pal,' I said. 'You told me not to be delicate, and I'm taking you at your word. I'm not a potential customer sussing you out. All I'm interested in is who knifed your partner, and I'm right at the start here. What information's relevant and what isn't, I don't know yet, but if I don't have all the facts originally I can't make the distinction later. And that might mean I miss something that'd turn out to be vitally important. You understand me?'

He frowned. 'Very well. I'm sorry, I'll expand on that. Tullius controlled the purse-strings. Or rather, he controlled the money he got through Annia every month which acts at need as a float.' He must've noticed me blink at the last word, because he went on patiently: 'It can take months between the time we pay the supplier for a consignment and ship it and the time we get the money back plus our profit. Oh, yes, the customer pays a deposit, naturally, a large one, but there's always an initial shortfall which has to be filled. And in the meantime we have other orders coming in which have to be treated in the same way. Then there's the risk – the constant risk – of shipwreck. If a ship carrying a cargo of ours goes down then we bear the loss, and of course that can be very substantial. Which is why, like everyone else in the trade, we don't normally put the whole of a large order into the one ship. All this means that having an export business is rather like walking a tightrope. Get the balance right, build up a clientele of enough regular customers to keep things moving along smoothly so you're always in profit, and you can do extremely well. The business funds itself. But you need a safety net, in case things go wrong or there are unforeseen expenses. Which is what Gaius provided.'

'So what's your problem?' I said. 'The safety net or the tightrope?'

Poetelius didn't smile. 'Very good, Corvinus. The tightrope. I told you: Gaius effectively controlled the company's finances. He also, by extension, had the final say where suppliers were concerned. I drew up the contracts and worked out the profit margins, certainly, but he did the actual hiring and firing. We've been having complaints from customers recently about the quality and general saleability of the goods we're sending them. Some – quite a number, in fact – have taken their business elsewhere, which means the momentum's gone, or going at least. To change the metaphor, we've been living on our fat.'

'So what you're saying is that Tullius was choosing the wrong suppliers.'

'Yes. Or rather, from a list of possibles, not choosing the best available.'

'And why would he do that, now?'

Poetelius's eyes shifted. 'Gaius wasn't really a businessman, a proper one, I mean. His judgement was flawed, and he made mistakes. That can happen to anyone in the trade from time to time, of course, but in Gaius's case it happened too regularly not to matter. And as I said the final decision regarding suppliers was his.'

'Come on, pal! Give! There was more to it than that, right?'

A pause; a long one. 'Yes. Yes, there was. But I'm afraid I can't—'

'Did it have anything to do with his women?'

Poetelius looked startled. 'You know about them?'

'Yeah. From both his sister and his wife, so you're not breaking any confidences. If that's what's worrying you.'

'Very well.' He took a deep breath. 'Just as an example. I mentioned we had a supplier – a pottery supplier – called Lucilius Festus.'

'With a workshop in Trigemina Gate Street. Right.'

'Yes. Our previous supplier was a man named Titus Vibius. He produced good stuff, popular with the customers, and he was reasonably priced and reliable. A year ago when the contract came up for renewal Gaius decided to award it to Festus instead. Oh, I've nothing against Festus. He's a good man and a fine potter. But he isn't in Vibius's league.'

I was beginning to get the picture here. 'On the other hand, he's got a good-looking and compliant wife. Or a daughter, maybe.'

Poetelius nodded. He was not looking happy. 'Wife,' he said.

'Would that be Marcia or Hermia?'

His eyes widened. 'Who told you?'

'Annia. I said, pal: there's no need to be coy. The lady knows already.'

'Marcia, then.' He hesitated. 'And Hermia is the wife of Titus Vecilius.'

'Who has a workshop in the same street?'

'Yes. He's even more recent, within the last couple of months. Although to be fair he's at least as good as the man we used before, if not better.'

Uh-huh. 'Do the husbands know?'

'Oh, yes. I'm absolutely sure they do.'

'How so?'

Poetelius hesitated again, for longer this time. Finally he said:

'Because they both came here, separately, four days ago, out for Gaius's blood. Fortunately he wasn't in the office, or the situation would've been even more unpleasant than it was. I told them I'd pass on the message, which I did.'

'Four days ago? The day before the murder?'

'Yes. Mid-morning in Festus's case. Vecilius an hour or so later.'

Jupiter! '*Both* of them? The same day?'

'That's right.'

'They say how they knew? That Tullius was carrying on with their wives, I mean?'

'No. And I didn't ask. My main concern was to get them calmed down and out of my life. I didn't go into the matter with Gaius, either, when he turned up.'

Yeah, well; it looked like we had two prime suspects at

least with motive in plenty for zeroing the guy. A visit to Trigemina Gate Street was definitely a priority. But, gods alive! Two angry cuckolded husbands in the one day! Either the bastard had been really, *really* unlucky or someone was out to get him.

Which reminded me.

'Uh . . . By the way,' I said, 'Annia said that Tullius mentioned an accident he'd had six days ago in Ostia. He tell you anything about that at all?'

Poetelius's face clouded. 'No. Gaius was in Ostia that day, certainly, supervising the loading of a crate of glassware. But he never mentioned any sort of accident. Not to me, anyway.'

Odd. Still, we could think about the ins and outs of that one later. I told him what the lady had said.

'It should be easy enough to check,' he said when I'd finished. 'Just give me a moment.' He reached over to the records cubby on his left and pulled out one of the thin beechwood sheets. 'Here we are. The glassware was being loaded into the *Circe*, berthed at Quay Twenty-five A. If there was an accident involving a crane nearby, the quay-master would know. They're pretty strict about that sort of thing at Ostia, for obvious reasons.'

'Fair enough.' I stood up. 'Oh, maybe one more thing, just for completeness' sake. You mentioned a guy named Vibius.'

'Titus Vibius. Yes.'

'You happen to have an address for him?'

Poetelius frowned. 'Of course. But why would you want to talk to Vibius? Like I said, he isn't one of our suppliers any longer.'

I shrugged. 'Call it dotting the i's and crossing the t's, pal. I told you, I'm only at the gathering-information stage here.'

'Very well. His yard's opposite the Emporium, facing the end of the Aemilian Porch.'

Same part of town, in other words, further along Trigemina Gate Street, beyond where it turned away from the river. Interesting. Maybe I'd drop in on Vibius while I was at it. Tomorrow looked like being a busy day.

'What about Tullius's brother-in-law?' If I was going to be thorough, I might as well go the whole hog. And I hadn't missed how quickly the guy had clammed up when I'd walked in on him and Annia earlier that morning.

'Quintus? He lives somewhere on the Esquiline, I think. I don't know where exactly, but Annia would be able to tell you. He and Gaius haven't had anything to do with each other for years, certainly not in the line of business. I don't think I've seen him since the wedding.'

'Isn't that a bit surprising? I mean, Annia said that your fathers – yours, hers, and Tullius's – were good friends and that you'd known each other since you were children. If he's in business himself then I'd've thought—'

'Gaius and Quintus never liked each other even as children, Corvinus. And when Annia' – he hesitated – 'chose to marry Gaius he broke off all connection with him. Not that I was all that sorry myself. Gaius had his faults, certainly, but I'm afraid I had about as little time for Quintus as he did. He was a smug, self-opinionated prig as a child and he's carried these qualities into adulthood.'

Happy families, indeed, both in the immediate and the extended form. Well, as the guy had said, if necessary I could check on his address with Annia. I said my goodbyes, and went home.

FOUR

There was a definite tang of woodsmoke in the air of our street when I got back, plus a faint smell of roasting meat overlaid with a touch of incense and perfume. I glanced in passing at the Petillius wall, from the garden behind which rose a thin spiral of smoke.

Bathyllus opened the front door as usual as soon as I'd got my foot on the first step.

'Hi, little guy,' I said, taking the obligatory wine-cup. 'What's going on next door?'

'That'll be the funeral, sir. Or the tail end of it, rather.'

I goggled. 'The *what*?'

'The funeral. Admetus's, sir.' No one can look and sound as bland as Bathyllus when he wants to. 'It was held a few hours ago.'

Jupiter! I took my wine through to the atrium. No sign of Clarus and Marilla yet – they were obviously making a day of it – but Perilla was lying on the couch with her usual book. I kissed her, went over to the couch opposite, and lay down.

'What's this about a funeral?' I said.

'Bathyllus told you, then?' She laid the book aside. 'Oh, yes. Properly conducted and complete with flute player. I watched it from upstairs. It was quite impressive, really, particularly the eulogy.'

Gods, this was surreal! 'Couldn't they just have dug a hole in the garden for the brute and planted a rose tree on top? I mean—'

'I suspect it was done for our benefit, dear, to make us feel guilty. And of course because the body cremated was a cat's, the usual rules about funerals having to be held outside the city limits don't apply. What on earth prompted you to pick him up in the first place? It was simply asking for trouble.'

'Yeah, well, I didn't expect to be nailed by the male equivalent of an avenging Fury two seconds later, did I?' I took a morose swallow of the wine.

'How did he die, do you know?'

'No idea. Probably ran under a passing cart when he was out last night killing mice or screwing the local queens. You make contact at all? With next door, that is?'

'I tried. Their major-domo slammed the door in my face before I could get a word out.'

Ah. Well, I hadn't really expected anything else. We'd just have to wait this one out and hope that hell froze over soon.

'So. How was your day?' she said. 'Did you talk to Annia?'

'Sure.' I gave her the basic rundown. 'The case looks open and shut, easy-peasy. The only real question is which of the outraged husbands did it.'

'You believe that?'

'There're a couple of curious points. But on the whole it's the most likely explanation, yeah.'

'What sort of curious points?'

'The question of why the guy went anywhere near Trigemina Gate Street only a day after both of his lady friends' better halves had threatened to rip his head off, for a start, particularly on a public holiday when there was no need, business-wise. That was just asking for trouble. Me, I'd've kept well clear. Probably permanently.'

'Mm.' She was twisting a lock of hair.

'Then there's the Ostian incident. That doesn't make sense. The guy told his wife, but not his partner. Having a load of amphoras dropped on you isn't something that'd slip your mind. And it's worth at least a passing mention.'

'You're sure the thing happened at all?'

'How do you mean?'

'It's a theoretical possibility. Your only source for the story is Annia herself. She could have made it up.'

'Why the hell should she want to do that?'

'I don't know. I said: it's just a possibility. Or, of course, Tullius's partner might have been lying when he said he knew nothing about it.'

'That's just as crazy. Again, why? Particularly since he gave me all the information I'd need to check it.' I took another gulp of the wine. 'In fact, everyone I've talked to so far – including the brother – has been pretty much up-front about things. They're happy enough that I'm trying to trace the killer and willing enough to cooperate, but equally none of them're making any secret of the fact that they think a world without Tullius is a far better place. At least, that's the impression I've been getting so far.'

'Never mind, dear. No doubt it'll all work out in the end. So what about tomorrow?'

'I thought I'd call in at the local Watch station, see what they can tell me. I don't know the guy there, but he's bound to know Lippillus, so that should help.' Decimus Lippillus was an old friend of mine, head of the Public Pond Watch. 'Then I'll have a word with the two husbands, find out what their stories are. Talk to the wives as well, if they're around. There's another guy, too, a Titus Vibius, lives in more or less the same area, who might bear a substantial grudge. I'll call in on him while I'm at it.'

'What about the Ostia side of things?'

'That can wait. Oh, sure, I'll go down there in another day or so, check it out, probably drop by at Agron's while I'm in the neighbourhood and split a jug of wine.' Agron was another old friend, an Illyrian with a cart-building business.

'One thing about this case, lady: we're not short on leads. It makes a nice change.' There was the sound of voices from the direction of the lobby. 'Ah. That's the kids back.'

It was; a moment or two later, Clarus and Marilla came in with the nurse Mysta holding the well-wrapped-up Sprog. Perilla smiled at them.

'Just in time for dinner,' she said. 'Did you have a nice day?'

'Oh, yes.' Marilla was beaming.

There was something very wrong here; or not *wrong*, exactly, just distinctly odd. Clarus was looking definitely shifty, while Marilla looked like the cat who's finally nailed the canary.

'OK,' I said. 'So tell us about it. You know you want to.'

'Take Marcus upstairs,' Marilla said to Mysta. 'I'll be up in a minute.' Mysta left, and she turned back to me. 'We've got a murder for you.'

I stared. 'You have a *what*?'

'Or not exactly a murder. Although it comes to the same thing, really. At the Pollio.' She settled down on the third couch. Clarus cleared his throat and sat down next to her.

'You're kidding!' I said. I glanced at Perilla. She was staring too.

'No, it's true enough,' Clarus said.

'I thought you'd be pleased.' Marilla was still beaming.

'Now look here, Princess—' I began.

'The man was stabbed. Only he was dead already. And when I told the Watch officer who we were he said he knew you, so—'

Gods! 'Look, Marilla, let's just have this in order, OK?' I said. Perilla had her mouth open to say something, but I held up a hand and she closed it. 'You're saying someone was killed – murdered – at the Pollio Library, right? While you were there. And that you were involved.' Jupiter, I didn't believe this! She'd only been in Rome five minutes. And the Pollio, for fuck's sake! *No one* gets themselves murdered at the Pollio! 'Take it slowly, a bit at a time.'

'All right.' She glanced at Clarus. 'I told you. I was sitting on a bench in the Pollio gardens with Mysta and Marcus, waiting for Clarus to finish; you know that bit at the side, near the Danaid Porch, with the fountain and the benches?'

'Yeah,' I said. 'I know it.'

'Anyway, there was this man on another bench a few yards away, who was there when I arrived. I thought he was asleep, only it turned out that he wasn't. Clarus arrived, and we were just getting ready to go when he sort of toppled over. Clarus went to check that he was all right, of course, and he was dead. He'd been stabbed in the back. Only—'

'Only he was dead already,' Clarus said.

'How do you know that, pal?' I said.

'You want the clinical details, Corvinus?'

'Ah . . . no.' Gods! 'No, I'll take your word for it.'

'There was hardly any blood. From the looks of things, he'd had an apoplexy. He'd been dead for at least an hour.'

'So why—' I began.

'Marcus, dear . . .' Perilla murmured.

'Anyway,' Marilla said, 'Clarus went inside and told them, and they sent for the Watch. We had to stay, of course, because there'd be sure to be questions—'

'Naturally you did,' I said. Chances were, under the circumstances, you couldn't've pulled the little lady away with grappling hooks and a team of oxen. Bugger!

'And when the Watch officer arrived it turned out that he knew you. A Flavonius Lippillus.'

'Lippillus? He's in charge of the Public Pond district. What was he doing over on the Palatine?'

'I don't know. But you can ask him yourself when you see him. I said you might be interested, and he didn't seem to mind. He'll be at the Palatine Watch station on Tuscan Street, if you'd like to call in. I said you'd do that tomorrow.'

Hell; this I didn't need! And Perilla wasn't looking too happy either, to put it mildly. Which was understandable: there we were being careful to keep the young lady's nose out of one murder, and she'd gone and stuck it into another off her own bat. Got me involved, too. One case I could handle, but two at the same time was pushing things.

'So all in all,' Marilla finished, 'yes. We had a very nice day, thank you.'

Perilla had her mouth open again, but luckily at that moment Bathyllus shimmered in.

'Dinner, sir?' he said. 'Meton says he's ready whenever you are. No real hurry, though.'

Well, that was a nice change, anyway: our touchy chef normally had dinner timed to the second, and he took it very personally if we didn't eat to order. At least that side of our domestic arrangements seemed to be going smoothly at present, if nothing else was. Which it decidedly wasn't.

Fuck. Double fuck.

'No, that's OK, pal,' I said, trying not to look at Perilla. 'We'll go through now. What's on offer?'

'He's made a special effort, sir. Snails sautéed with fennel followed by roasted pigeons in a sweet onion sauce. With a custard tart and preserved fruits to follow.'

'Oh, marvellous!' Marilla said. She likes her food, does Marilla, and Meton's always had a soft spot for her.

My stomach growled: the plate of cheese and olives I'd had for lunch in the wineshop had been hours ago, and there hadn't been much of that, either. Not that, from the look on Perilla's face, it was going to be a very comfortable family meal, despite Meton's efforts. 'Sounds great,' I said, getting up quickly.

At least the Watch officer concerned had been Decimus Lippillus; all I had to do was pay the guy a short visit, explain the situation, that I was otherwise engaged at present and was keeping well clear. He'd understand, sure he would, and if she didn't like it then Marilla would just have to lump it. Besides, if she thought she had a vested interest – which, to be fair, she did – then keeping the lady off my back would be difficult in spades.

Still, it was odd. And getting mixed up with two unconnected murders – or whatever you liked to call the second one – inside ten days was really pushing the boat out. Those evil-minded gods hovering around with their ears pricked were really working their socks off this time round. One way and another, the next day was going to be busy, busy, busy.

For the present, though, I'd settle for the roasted pigeons.

FIVE

I was up betimes the next morning: Trigemina Gate Street is a fair way from the Caelian, on the south-west edge of the city where most of the big workshops and warehouses are so as to be handy for loading and unloading cargoes to and from Ostia, and if I wanted to fit in a visit to the Palatine Watch-house on Tuscan Street as well – which I didn't, really, but there you go – I'd have to get my skates on. Plus there was the head of the Aventine Watch to see, re the details of the actual murder as far as he knew them.

Like I say, busy, busy, busy.

Added to all this, I wanted to be gone before Marilla put in an appearance, because the lady would take it as her natural right to tag along on the promised visit to Lippillus, at least. And that, considering it was going to be a thanks-but-no-thanks call, I could do without. The chances were there'd be serious ructions when she found out in any case, but at least it'd be a fait accompli.

Besides, so far she didn't know anything about the Tullius business. How long we could keep to that happy state of affairs I didn't know, but the longer the better.

So I grabbed a roll with a slice of cheese between the two halves to eat on the way and headed towards Tuscan Street.

I was lucky: Decimus Lippillus was at his desk in the Watch Commander's office.

'Hey, Marcus!' he said when I came in. 'I've been expecting you. How's the lad?'

'OK.' Lippillus and me went way back, almost pre-Perilla: a good twenty years, in other words. Despite that, he still looked like he had a year or so to go before his first shave and adult mantle; not just because of his height, or lack of it, either. Even so, midget and fresh-faced kid lookalike or not,

Decimus Flavonius Lippillus was the best Watch Commander in the city, bar none. 'How's Paullina?'

'Flourishing. Putting on weight, but there you go.' Lippillus's common-law wife and former stepmother Marcina Paullina was African, twice his size and a real honey. 'Perilla well?'

'Yeah, she's fine.' I pulled up a stool and sat. 'What're you doing here at Tuscan Street? They kick you out of Public Pond?'

He laughed. 'In a way. Old Titus Fannius retired last month and the City Prefect decided to move me. It's a promotion, sure, but one I could do without. The air on the Palatine's a bit rich for my taste.'

'So. Tell me all about this murder over at the Pollio. Or stabbing, rather.'

'*All* is stretching it, Marcus, because we know practically zilch. The dead guy was an Ostian by the name of Correllius. Marcus Correllius.'

'*Ostian*?'

'Yeah. A businessman, seemingly, according to his slave. And no, you're right; it wasn't murder, not according to that smart-as-paint doctor son-in-law of yours, although that wasn't for the want of trying on the part of the guy who put the knife in. What's his name? Clarus?'

'Cornelius Clarus. Yeah. He's the local doctor down in Castrimoenium.'

'So he said. Smart cookie, that. Well, he's saved us a bit of work, anyway, and I'm grateful for that, at least. You can have the case if you want it, the whole boiling, with my blessing.'

Bugger; this didn't sound good; I was glad that Marilla wasn't here. 'Hang on, pal,' I said. 'Death was from natural causes, fair enough. But if the guy was stabbed, then—'

He was shaking his head. 'Marcus. Watch my lips here. I hate to say this, but it's a question of the constructive use of Watch time.'

'How do you mean?'

'I mean that we'll probably have to stamp this one "Unsolved".'

'Come on! That's ridiculous!'

He held up his hands, palm out.

'Yeah, I know, I know!' he said. 'I don't like it any more than you do. OK, a crime's involved, absolutely, no argument, and personally I'd love to take the thing up. But I'm short-staffed, I'm up to my eyeballs already. Between ourselves, old Fannius left things in a bit of a mess that it'll take me months to sort out, and finding the guy who's shoved a knife into someone who's already a corpse comes pretty low on the list of priorities. Besides, I told you: the man was over from Ostia, and that's the best part of a day's journey each way for a start. Plus it's technically beyond my jurisdiction, and I'd have to clear any investigation with the Ostian boys, or set up some sort of liaison arrangement. Frankly, there're just too many complications. To tell you the truth, I was relieved when your Marilla suggested you might like to take it up.'

Shit; I was being ganged up on here. First Marilla, now Lippillus.

'Truth is, pal,' I said, 'I've got enough on my plate myself to be going on with. Guy by the name of Gaius Tullius, killed a few days ago in Trigemina Gate Street, and I'm right at the start of things. When she volunteered me, Marilla didn't know that.' Not that, knowing the lady as I did, it would've made a blind bit of difference, mind, but still . . .

Lippillus frowned. 'Damn. Well, it can't be helped. I'll do what I can, of course – *am* doing what I can, with what resources I can spare – but I can't promise much. You want the details anyway? Just in case?'

'Sure. So what've you got?'

'Not a lot so far, and it all comes from the slave he brought with him. Like I said, the guy's name was Marcus Correllius, and he was an Ostian businessman.'

'What kind of businessman?'

'Mercurius – that's the slave – didn't say, but he gave me a contact address. Private house, on the Hinge to the south of Ostia's Market Square. That's a pretty expensive area, seemingly, so chummie wasn't short of a silver piece or two.'

'The slave wasn't in the Pollio garden at the time of the murder, presumably?'

'No. Correllius had sent him away, told him to come back

in a couple of hours. Which he did, just after your Marilla
and her husband found the body.'

'Uh-huh.' Curious; you'd've thought his master would've
wanted the bought help to be on call. 'So what was he doing
at the Pollio in the first place? Correllius, I mean?'

'A business meeting. Mercurius didn't know the details, just
that the meeting was with a guy named Marcus Pullius.'

'In *Rome*? And at the Pollio? Why the hell not in Ostia?'

Lippillus shrugged. 'No idea, and like I say the slave didn't
know either. But it's not all that strange. Most Ostian businessmen have dealings with people and companies based in
the city, and who did the travelling would depend on the
circumstances. As far as the Pollio goes, it's a common enough
meeting place. Well-known, central, easy to find if you're from
out of town like Correllius was.'

Yeah, true: even so, if this Pullius were local himself –
which, presumably, he was, or why Rome at all? – and a
businessman in his own right, then surely he'd have an office
where they could've met and discussed things in privacy and
comfort. And if Correllius was as big a wheel as his private
circumstances suggested then he was no hick from the sticks;
he'd know his way round Rome well enough. So why choose
a park bench to meet, for the gods' sakes?

'Who's this Marcus Pullius, then?' I said. 'He come forward?'

'No, we haven't seen hide nor hair of him. And Mercurius
didn't know anything about him, either. He'd never seen the
guy before, never even heard the name.'

Odder and odder, and the whole thing was beginning to
stink to high heaven. Even if, contrary to all indications, Pullius
wasn't the actual perp and had just decided for reasons of his
own not to get involved, if he'd been important enough for
Correllius to have travelled all the way from Ostia to see then
I'd've expected his slave to know something about him. Unless
he did and wasn't telling, of course, and that made things
more interesting still.

'This Mercurius doesn't seem to know very much,' I said.

'Yeah. I noticed that at the time. Of course I did. He seemed
to be straight enough in himself, mind. And he was certainly
upset.'

'You trying to trace Pullius?'

Lippillus grinned. 'Don't teach your grandmother to suck eggs, Corvinus! Of course I am, as far as I'm able. But no luck so far.'

Hell; leave it. 'Fair enough,' I said. 'Were there any witnesses? To the actual stabbing, I mean?' Unlikely, sure: I knew those benches outside the Pollio, and it would've been easy enough for someone to step up behind an ostensibly sleeping man, do the business, and be off and away unseen in a matter of seconds. Particularly if he'd all the time in the world to wait his chance.

'That's something else we're working on. Nothing so far, certainly no one who was currently using the library, because I asked. Naturally, I did. And remember, it could've happened any time up to an hour before the body was found, so any witness would probably have been long gone. That's assuming they knew they *were* a witness in the crime sense, which under the circumstances they probably wouldn't.'

Bugger; I was getting hooked, despite myself. Even so, like Lippillus, I'd got other, more important, fish to fry at present; like it or not, I'd just have to leave things as they were and pass on.

'OK, pal,' I said. 'You'll keep me informed like you said, just in case?'

'Sure. No problem. So what's this Tullius business? Trigemina Gate Street, you said?'

'Yeah.' I gave him the details. 'I'm on my way over there now.'

'That's Gaius Memmius's patch. He's Watch Commander for the Aventine. A good lad, Memmius, and a good officer. He'll help you if he can. Just mention my name.'

'Thanks,' I said. 'I'll do that.' I would, too: as with everything in Rome, having a friend in common made things a lot easier, and not all Watch Commanders appreciated a civilian outsider poking his nose into Watch affairs. 'You got time for a cup of wine somewhere? It'll have to be a quick one, because I'm pushed this morning.'

He laughed. 'You kidding? I didn't even have breakfast this morning, or any morning this month. I told you: I'm up to my eyeballs.'

'Another time, then. Sorry I can't help more.'

'That's OK. Offer's open, and like I said I'll send you word of any developments. Look after yourself, Marcus, and give my regards to the family.'

I left.

So; next stop the Thirteenth District Watch station on the Aventine, near the Temple of the Moon.

I was lucky; not only did Watch Commander Memmius know Lippillus well, but he'd mentioned my name to him a couple of times in the past, which made things a lot easier: like I say, some commanders, particularly the ones who owe their jobs to the fact that they're drinking cronies of the City Prefect, can be pretty snooty.

I gave him the spiel, for what it was worth so far.

'That's right.' He rested his elbows on the desk in front of him. 'Tullius was found just after sunset four days ago at the Shrine of Melobosis in an alleyway off Trigemina Gate Street. Single stab to the heart. The bugger wouldn't've known what hit him.'

'Was the body hidden at all?'

'No. That was odd, because it could've been, easily, because the shrine's pretty overgrown. Whoever Melobosis was, she didn't have all that many worshippers.'

'One of the Daughters of Ocean. Or so my clever-clogs wife tells me.'

'Is that right, now?' He grinned. 'You learn something new every day. Anyway, the guy was lying presumably where he fell, out in the open. The kid who found him had just taken his girlfriend inside for some privacy, and they tripped over the corpse in the darkness. A bit of a put-off, that, under the circumstances. Inconvenient, too. The youngsters had been using the shrine for their evening bouts of privacy for quite a while, and now the girl won't go near the place.'

'No one saw anything, I suppose? Saw the victim or the perp going in, I mean?'

'No. Not that I've been able to find out. The alley's a dead end, and most of the buildings in the area are offices that are only used during daylight hours. Also, of course, the fifteenth being Mercury's festival, they'd've been closed all day anyway.'

So barring a visit by a casual worshipper to the shrine itself – which seemed unlikely, from what Memmius was saying – the body could've lain undiscovered there since the previous night. Bugger!

'You happen to know anything about two of the local residents? Or almost local. A Lucilius Festus and a Titus Vecilius.'

Memmius frowned. 'Why do you ask? You have a reason to think one of them did it?'

'It's a possibility. *Just* a possibility.' I had to go careful here: Memmius was a nice guy, and what with the Lippillus connection he was amenable enough, but he was still official, and I'd no proof. 'They had connections with the dead man, and they both have businesses on Trigemina Gate Street itself, that's all. I'm just checking angles.'

'Fair enough.' He leaned back on his stool. 'Me, I'd discount Festus. From what I know of him, which isn't much, and that's the point, he's the quiet family type, solid citizen, never in any trouble that I've ever heard of. He married a young widow from out of town ten or twelve years back whose husband died leaving her with a two-year-old kid, and he can't see past her. Vecilius, well, him I do know, professionally. He's certainly got a temper, and he's a bit too fond of the booze for his own good. Big lad. He's crossed our path a few times, beat up a stevedore a couple of months back for making what he thought were suggestive advances. To his wife, not to him. But I don't think he'd go the length of murder.' He gave me a sharp look. 'Of course, if his wife *was* involved that might be a different story. Was she?'

'Yeah. Probably. Festus's as well.'

'Is that so, now?' Memmius whistled between his teeth. 'Both of them, eh? He must've been an active lad, our Tullius.'

'So it would seem.' I got up. 'Anyway, thanks for your help. I appreciate it. You mind if I nose around a bit, ask a few questions, have a word with Festus and Vecilius?'

'Go ahead. It's a free city.' We shook. 'Just keep me posted, that's all. And give my regards to Lippillus when you see him next.'

'I will,' I said, and left.

OK. A quick visit to the scene of the crime, just to get the details clear in my own mind, then it was the two husbands. From what Memmius had said about his propensity for jealousy and violence things weren't looking good for Vecilius, sure, but I was an old enough hand at this business by now to suspend judgement. The same applied to Festus: even solid citizens could lose the rag if the circumstances were right, and I knew from Poetelius that he'd lost it far enough to make at least verbal threats. We'd have to see how things went.

The Shrine of Melobosis was more or less what I'd expected: a small, narrow enclosure twenty or so feet square halfway along the dead-end alley with a high wall in front, sandwiched between three-storey buildings to the sides and rear. No way in, in other words, except through the rusted iron gate in the alleyway itself. I pushed it open and went inside.

It wasn't quite as overgrown as I'd expected, particularly in the middle round the altar itself and at the sides which showed signs of at least sporadic attention, but there was a lot of dense cover at the back: plenty of self-seeded bushes and tall weeds that looked like they'd had everything their own way for years. Like Memmius had said, odd: if the killer had wanted to hide the body and delay its finding he could've done it easily; in fact, it was strange that he hadn't and just left the guy lying there, given that he'd also probably had all the time in the world to tidy up after himself. Apart from that, it was the perfect place for a private rendezvous, as witness the courting couple's choice of it as an evening venue: off the beaten track and tucked well away from things, completely hidden by its walls from the alleyway itself when the gate was closed, shut in on every other side by buildings, and from every indication almost totally unvisited; the little lamp in front of the central altar was dry as a bone, and there were no signs of any offerings, not so much as a withered flower.

Chummie had been taking a bit of a risk, mind, all the same. Once inside the gate, he'd have no problems, sure, but the before and after of the murder were another thing entirely.

The place's very isolation could work against him, because despite the day being a public holiday and the area round about being pretty much deserted as a result, if there had been anyone to see him going in and out he might well've been remembered. Maybe in the event someone had seen him, at that; but, given that any potential witness would quite understandably have thought no more about it, the chances were we'd never know.

I shivered. Some of these holy places – the ones that've been set aside as holy – have an atmosphere of calm cheerfulness about them that you can feel straight away as soon as you go in. This one didn't: it was just sad. Sad, sunless, uncared for, and deserted. The atmosphere had nothing to do with the murder, either; that was just how things were. I wondered why the nymph was here in the first place – after all, we were well away from the coast, and she was a Daughter of Ocean – but no doubt whoever had been originally responsible for setting up her altar had had their reasons. Still, it seemed a shame she'd come so far just to be ignored.

There were a few wild flowers growing by one of the side walls. I picked them, laid them beside the oil lamp, and went back outside, closing the gate behind me.

So. Time to interview the suspects. I came out of the alleyway onto the main drag and stopped the first guy I met, a slave wheeling a barrowful of sandals.

'Excuse me, pal,' I said. 'You happen to know where I can find Lucilius Festus's place? The pottery? Or failing that Titus Vecilius's glassworks?'

'Yes, sir, of course. Both.' He grounded the barrow and pointed. 'Festus has his yard up by the Gate, Vecilius's is the other direction, halfway between here and the Emporium. Left-hand side, you can't miss it.'

'Thanks.'

'No problem.' He trundled off.

Not far away, then, either of them: the Trigemina Gate was only a couple of hundred yards to the right, while the Emporium was a scant half-mile further down the road. Six of one, half a dozen of the other. OK. We'd start with the least likely candidate. Festus.

There was only one pottery on offer before the Gate, so that had to be the one. I negotiated my way through the stacked pots in the yard and went into the building behind it where a dozen or so slaves were working the wheels, turning out what looked like everyday low-grade tableware.

'Any chance I can see the boss?' I said to the nearest one.

'Who wants him?' A big guy in a tunic was coming towards me, wiping his hands on a towel. Festus, obviously.

'Name's Valerius Corvinus,' I said.

'Customer? Only we're working on a big order at present, I'm afraid, so we're fully committed. We may be able to supply you from stock, mind, if you'd like to take a look around. Depends on what you need.'

'The order would be for Gaius Tullius, would it?' I said.

The hand-wiping stopped. Pause; definite pause, and the polite manner went down a notch.

'For his partner,' he said shortly. 'Tullius is dead.'

'Yeah, I know,' I said easily. 'That's why I'm here. I'm representing the widow.' I paused, myself. 'So, ah, how come you do? Know that the guy's dead, I mean.'

He shrugged. 'No big deal; it's fairly common knowledge round here. Someone shoved a knife into him in Melobosis Alley, right?'

Fair enough. At least we were through the preliminaries stage and I could go straight for the throat.

'I understand you had a run-in with him the day before he died,' I said.

'Really? Then you understand wrong, friend. I never saw him, more's the pity, not then, anyway. The last time I talked with that bastard was about a month ago. And that was about pots.'

'You sure about that?'

He glared at me. Then he grunted and turned away. 'Come into the office,' he said over his shoulder. 'I don't discuss my private business in front of the bought help.'

'Office' was dignifying things: the cubbyhole was even smaller than Poetelius's, a few square yards of floor space at the rear of the shop separated off by lath-and-plaster walls and a curtain. Festus pulled it aside and stood back.

'Sit down,' he said. 'I'll stand.'

I sat on the only stool next to the little folding table that served as a desk. He pulled the curtain shut behind him.

'Now,' he said. 'If you've got any accusations to make you go ahead, make them to my face and I'll spit in your eye.'

'Calm down, pal,' I said. 'No one's accusing you of anything. All I want is your side of the story.'

'What you want and what you'll get are two different things. Let's have one thing clear from the start. Whoever killed Gaius Tullius did me and the rest of the world a favour.'

'Yeah, that seems to be the general opinion, so no argument from me. And I'm including his wife in this.'

That got me another long look – a surprised one, this time – and another grunt. 'OK,' he said at last. 'I'm sorry. Maybe I was a bit sharp, and I've nothing to hide or be ashamed of. Ask away.'

'First off. You went round to his office the day before the murder. How long had you known he was' – I hesitated, but there was no way round this – 'seeing your wife?'

'I only found out that morning. There was a letter shoved under the door when I came down. It was addressed to her, but I didn't know that until I opened it.'

'A letter from who?'

He shrugged. 'It wasn't signed. It just said that Tullius was dropping her and taking up with some woman called Hermia.'

'Third person?'

His face clouded. 'Come again?'

'I mean, the letter wasn't from Tullius. Whoever wrote it said *he* was dropping her, not *I* am, and gave the guy's name.'

'Uh . . . yeah.' There'd been a pause while he worked that one out; obviously not the sharpest knife in the box, Lucilius Festus. 'Yeah, that's right.'

'OK.' Well, unless Tullius was idiot enough to do his dumping in writing and deliver the note in a way that was just asking for trouble, the alternative explanation wouldn't've made much sense, particularly since it named the other lady. Still, it was just as well to check. 'You knew who Hermia was?'

'No. I said. She was just a name.'

'So what happened then?'

'What do you think? I got Marcia downstairs and showed

her the thing, let her read it for herself. There were . . . words.
I told her I was going to see Tullius, and she'd better not be
in the house when I got back. Then I left.'

'She didn't deny having an affair with the guy?'

'She didn't bother trying. The truth was plain on her face.'

'So where is she now?'

'Her mother has a cookshop by the Capenan Gate. She went
there with the kids. At least, I assume she did.'

'Uh-huh.' Well, I could trace the lady later, if need be.
Meanwhile: 'What about the day of the murder itself? Tullius
was in this part of town. You didn't see him?'

'You kidding? If I'd known he was sniffing around and seen
him, I'd've broken the bastard's face for him.'

'So where were you, exactly?'

'Where would I be? I told you: we've a big order to fill. I
was here in the yard working.'

'All day?'

'Sure all day, barring a couple of hours in the afternoon
when I went to pay my respects at the Temple of Mercury.'

Oh, yeah; the festival. Mercury's the god of business, so
it's usual on his feast day for anybody with commercial interests to visit his temple near the Circus, give the guy his annual
pinch of incense, and offer up a prayer or two to keep him
sweet for the coming year. Convenient. Festus could be lying,
sure, but if so it was a plausible lie. Unfortunately, given that
about half the working population of Rome were doing the
same and Mercury's temple was about as packed as the Circus
itself on a race day, it was also virtually impossible to check.
Bugger.

Even so—

'There anything else you can tell me?' I said.

'That's it. That's all there is.'

I shrugged and got up. 'Fair enough. Thanks for your help.'

'You're welcome.' I turned to go. 'Oh, and Corvinus, if that
was your name. One last thing.'

'Yeah?'

'Just so you're absolutely sure where I stand. I hope Gaius
Tullius is burning in hell.'

SIX

Vecilius's glassworks was a low building that covered most of a short block, with a two-storey house taking up one of the corners. I glanced up at the window as I passed. A young woman's face looked out for a moment, then just as quickly disappeared.

Uh-huh.

I went inside, and the heat hit me like a sledgehammer. Jupiter, how could people work in this? Even with the clerestory ventilation, it was like walking into an oven, with three or four open charcoal furnaces going full blast and half a dozen slaves in sweat-soaked tunics doing complex things with lumps of molten glass stuck on the ends of long blowpipes. A guy carrying a tray of perfume bottles walked past me, and I stopped him and asked for the boss.

'Over there, sir.' He nodded towards the far corner of the room.

I went across, being careful to keep well clear of the blowpipes. Vecilius – presumably – was working on a tall vase set on a revolving wheel, dipping a metal rod into a clay pot of molten glass on the brazier beside him and trailing a thin thread of green in a spiral down the vase's length. I waited until he was finished and had set the rod down. Then I said:

'Titus Vecilius?'

He turned. He was a big guy, broad rather than tall, with huge hands, hairy arms and a good three days' worth of black stubble.

'That's right.'

I indicated the vase. 'Nice. Delicate work like that must be tricky.'

He shrugged. 'It's simple enough if you've a steady hand. What can I do for you?'

'Name's Valerius Corvinus. I'm looking into the death of Gaius Tullius, on behalf of his widow.'

He gave me a long stare. Then he cleared his throat, spat, and took a drink of water from the cup beside him.

'Is that so, now?' he said.

'You knew he'd been murdered?'

'I'd heard. Three or four days ago, wasn't it? It couldn't've happened to a nicer guy.'

That came out flat. Well, as with Festus I wasn't unduly surprised; a murder practically on your doorstep doesn't happen all that often. I was getting used to the reaction, too. 'Look. Can we talk about this outside? It's pretty hot in here.'

'I've work to do. And I've no time to waste on Gaius fucking Tullius, dead or alive.'

'You'd enough time for him the day before to go round to his office and threaten him through his partner, pal. Now do we talk, or do I draw my own conclusions? Your choice.'

He swore under his breath and walked away from me towards the exit. I followed.

It was blessedly cool in the open air. Vecilius had stopped just outside the door.

'OK,' he said. 'Five minutes. What do you want to know?'

'How you knew that your wife was having an affair with Tullius, for a start.'

'My wife wasn't having no affair with no one!'

'Fine. Suppose you tell me what the real situation was.'

'Look. I leave the house after breakfast that morning and come in here as usual, right? Only half an hour later I realize that I've left a customer's instructions for a one-off set of table glassware at home. So I go back for them. I find this crazy bitch laying into my wife, Hermia, claiming that she's pinched her boyfriend, Tullius, and threatening to scratch her eyes out. So I grab her by the waist, bundle her outside, and shut the door. That's it, that's the whole story.'

'So what did your wife say?'

'That Tullius had been sniffing around, sure, trying it on. But that she'd told him to get lost.'

'And you believed her?'

He gave me an ugly look. 'You saying I'd any reason not to?'

'Uh-uh.' I shook my head. 'I don't know anything about it one way or the other. Who was the woman? You know her?'

'I didn't at the time, but I do now. A friend of Hermia's, or she had been up till then. Name of Marcia. Slut!'

'So you went round to Tullius's office to, ah, discuss things.'

'Damn right! If I'd found the bastard I would've punched his lights out, but I didn't. As it was I told his partner, Poetelius, straight that if he showed his nose around here again they'd have to cart him off on a stretcher. They would've done, too.'

'And did he? That you know of?'

'No.'

He was lying, I'd've given good odds on that, but I valued my teeth too much to say so straight out; in his present mood the guy would've clobbered me.

'So where were you the next day, the day of the murder?'

'Here, in the workshop.'

'All day?'

'Of course, all day. Sunrise to sunset. I've a business to run.'

I shrugged. 'OK, pal, keep your hair on. No problems. Thanks for your help.' I turned away, then as if I'd just thought of it I turned back and said, 'Can I speak with your wife, maybe?'

'She's out.'

'That's a pity.' I glanced up at the window where I'd seen the woman's face. 'That your house, by the way?'

'Yeah. So?'

'Handy. Living just next to the shop, I mean.'

'Yeah, it is. Now fuck off. That's all you're getting.'

'Sure. Thanks again. You've been really, really helpful.'

He didn't answer. I walked on down the road, in the direction of the Emporium. When I turned to look back, he was still watching me.

OK. So we'd just have to leave Hermia for another time. It was getting on for noon. I still had Poetelius's disgruntled ex-supplier Vibius to see, but before that I thought I'd check out the local wineshop situation. I reckoned I deserved it.

I found one just short of the Emporium itself, where Trigemina Gate Street takes a bend past the Aemilian Porch. Not a particularly upmarket establishment, but then it wouldn't be in this part of town, where the clientele would be mostly workmen and stevedores from the wharves. The place was empty at present. Bad sign, but maybe we hadn't quite hit the lunchtime spot.

'Morning, sir,' the guy behind the bar said. 'What can I get you?'

I glanced up at the board. 'A half jug of the Graviscan would do nicely, pal. And some cheese and olives, if you've got them.'

'No problem.' He busied himself with pouring from one of the big jars in the rack beside the counter. 'Down here on business, are you?'

I knew an opening and a talkative barman when I saw one, but I waited until he'd set the jug and cup with a plateful of cheese, olives, and bread in front of me and taken the money before I said, 'More or less. At the Vecilius glassworks.' I took a tentative sip of the Graviscan. Not bad, but a long way from the best I'd ever tasted. 'You know him? Vecilius, I mean?'

'Sure. He's one of my regulars. Too much of a regular at times, although I shouldn't be complaining about that.'

'Likes his wine, does he?'

'He can sink a fair bit of an evening, but it's more what comes out of his mouth than what goes into it.'

'A bit of a troublemaker, you mean?'

The guy chuckled. 'He's that, all right. Touchy as a bear. You wouldn't want to get the wrong side of him, sir, particularly where his wife's concerned.'

'That so, now?' I took another sip and a bit of the cheese.

'Not that I blame him for it. She's a good-looking woman, Hermia, and he was lucky to land her. She knows it, too, if you catch my drift, but then she's got him wrapped round her little finger. Still, where Vecilius is concerned she's a subject best avoided.'

Joy in the morning! I'd got a real gossip-monger here. Mind you, it was lucky there were no other customers or he might not've been so chatty. Even so, it'd be a mistake to push too hard. I didn't comment, just nodded, drank some more of my wine, and got on with the olives and cheese. The silence lengthened. Finally, I crossed my fingers in the hope that he hadn't heard anything about the murder and said casually:

'Strangely enough, he was telling me he had a bit of a run-in with an admirer of hers the other day. Or a would-be admirer, rather.'

'Vecilius?' The guy gave me a sharp look. 'Did he, now? Well, well, you don't say.' He pulled up a high stool and sat directly opposite me, like a Suburan housewife settling in to dig the local dirt over the wall with her neighbour. 'Three or four days back, would that be?'

'Yeah.' I tightened the crossed fingers. 'Yeah, it would, actually. He say anything about it?'

'Not as such. Not the run-in side of things. But he was in here in the morning, practically first thing, sinking wine like it was out of fashion and spouting off. The way he does sometimes.'

My interest sharpened. So much for Vecilius's claim to have spent all day, sunrise to sunset, at the glassworks.

'That usual for him?' I said. 'Morning drinker?'

'Nah. He's a worker, Vecilius, I'll say that for him. Careful, too; he'd have to be, in his line. A glassworks is no place to be when you've had one over the odds. Normally it's just the half jug at the end of the day, maybe a whole one if he's something to celebrate or the company's good.' He filled a spare cup from a jug on the counter and took a contemplative sip. 'Tullius, would that be the guy's name, now, by any chance? Hermia's admirer's, I mean? *Gaius* Tullius?'

Heavenly choirs sang, but I kept my face straight.

'It could've been,' I said. 'Something like that, anyway. Three days back, did you say?'

'No, it was four for certain. The monthly delivery arrived just after he left.'

'Vecilius left?'

'Sure.' He chuckled. 'About this time, it was. My suggestion: he'd had two full jugs, and he was practically legless. But he was back an hour later to finish the job.'

'Still talking about this Tullius?'

'No. Never said a word about anything, in fact, just took his jug and cup into the corner there and drank his way through it. Then he passed out and I had a couple of the lads take him home.' He grinned. 'That's Titus Vecilius for you. Not the man to do things by halves.'

'Right. Right.' Shit! I'd got him! Not only had Vecilius lied about being at the workshop all day, the day of the murder, but after getting thoroughly canned and cursing Tullius six ways from nothing he'd gone walkabout for an hour. And when he'd come back the subject of Tullius had been shelved. Like, I suspected, the poor bugger had himself . . .

Titus Vecilius was so much in the frame you could've hung him on the wall of the Danaid Porch.

The barman had picked up a rag and was wiping the counter in an absent-minded way. 'This Tullius, now,' he said, sucking on a tooth. 'Correct me if I'm wrong, sir, but wasn't that the name of the stiff the Watch picked up knifed in Melobosis Alley?' He gave me a sly sideways look. 'If so then your mentioning him off the cuff, like, and showing a bit of interest in Titus Vecilius's movements is quite a coincidence, isn't it? Tullius was a friend of yours, perhaps? Or maybe you've got some other vested interest in finding out who knifed him?'

Bugger.

'Uh-uh,' I said. 'No connection. I'd never met the man, just heard the name. It could be the same guy, sure, but if so then like you said it's just pure coincidence. These things happen.'

'Sure they do. All the time.'

Well, I supposed the chances of the local wineshop owner *not* knowing about the murder had been pretty slim, after all. I was just lucky the gossipy bastard also had a nasty, muck-raking streak a yard wide. Even so, I'd no desire at this point to complicate matters. I finished my wine at a gulp and stood up.

'Thanks, pal,' I said. 'Be seeing you.'

'Pleasure. Call again.'

I went out. I'd talk to the third supplier, Vibius, sure, while I was in the area, but at this point I suspected that it'd just be a matter of dotting the i's and crossing the t's. I'd got my killer cold.

Case over. Done and dusted.

*   *   *

Like Poetelius had told me, Vibius's pottery was further along the road, past the Emporium and opposite the end of the Aemilian Porch. Just as at Festus's place, there were the usual bread-and-butter amphoras and rough clay storage jars piled up in the yard outside, but when I went in most of the racks held the sort of items you'd only find in shops specializing in upmarket tableware and fine decorative goods. Pretty expensive shops at that: from what I could see, the stuff was first-rate, pick-of-the-range formal dinner party rather than everyday domestic standard for the dishes, and birthday-present quality for the vases. Yeah; Poetelius had said that the guy was a master craftsman, in a different league from Festus altogether. Losing the contract to an also-ran when you were producing work like this must've rankled.

It didn't seem to have hurt him in the longer term, anyway. The place was busy enough, with five or six slaves bringing up one-off pots and jars on the wheel and a dozen more working at the benches packing moulds and glazing or painting the biscuit-fired pieces. I paused to watch one old guy in a freedman's cap who was using a tiny brush to paint the lid of a cosmetic box no more than three inches long and wide with a scene involving nymphs and satyrs. Lovely stuff.

Finally, he put the brush down and turned towards me.

'Yes, sir?' he said. 'What can I do for you?'

'I was looking for the owner,' I said. 'Titus Vibius. He around at present?'

'I'm afraid not. But if you're a customer then perhaps I can help you myself.'

Ah, well, I couldn't be lucky every time. 'No, it's a private matter. You have any idea when he'll be in? Or where I can find him?'

'That I don't know. But you could try his house, sir, on the off-chance that he might be there. Down the road a little on the Porch side. The one with the red-painted door.'

'Thanks, pal.' I left him to his finicky work and went back out into the street.

I found the house – like Vecilius's, a two-storey property with a garden to the side – and knocked. A couple of minutes later, it was opened by an elderly slave.

'Yes, sir?'

'The master at home?' I said.

'He is. Who shall I say?' I gave him my name, and then repeated it louder when he cupped his hand to his ear. 'Thank you. The master's in his study, sir. If you'd like to come in and wait, I'll fetch him for you.'

No lobby and atrium here – the place wasn't big enough – but it was a lot more spacious than a tenement flat in the town proper would be; one of those older upper-working-class houses you get on the outskirts, with two or three rooms off a central corridor ending in a staircase leading up to the first-floor landing. The slave opened the door on the left.

'In here, sir,' he said.

'Who is it, Silvius?'

I looked up. A girl, maybe fifteen or sixteen, was leaning over the balustrade. Quite a looker: brunette, and from what I could see of her with quite a nice figure.

'A Valerius Corvinus, miss. Come to see your father.'

'Oh.' She disappeared, and I heard a door close upstairs.

'Sir?' The slave was standing aside, waiting.

'Uh . . . right. I'm sorry.' I went past him into the room.

'The master won't keep you a moment. Make yourself at home, please.'

He shuffled off, closing the door behind him.

There was a couch and a couple of chairs, which was about all the available floor space could manage; simple, but good quality. I sat on one of the chairs and looked round. The same description applied to the decor; nothing flashy, but one wall had a very nice fresco of deer in a wooded landscape, and the others were plain-colour-washed with a frieze of acanthus at the top and painted-in panelling at the bottom. In the corner opposite me was a small table with a pottery vase full of narcissi, in the same style as the vases I'd seen on display in Vibius's workshop. Someone had good taste; probably his wife.

A couple of minutes later the door opened again and a guy in his early fifties came in. Tall, thin, slightly stooped, grizzled hair, dressed in a lounging-tunic.

'Valerius Corvinus?'

'That's me.' I stood up.

'What can I do for you?' Vibius waved me down again and sat on the other chair. 'If it's business, you'd do better talking to my foreman at the workshop. He handles most of the orders these days.'

'No, it's not, actually. Or rather, not that kind of business.' I went through my usual spiel. 'I'm acting for a lady by the name of Annia, Gaius Tullius's widow.'

His eyes widened. 'Widow? Tullius is dead?'

'Yeah. You didn't know?'

'Why should I? And in what way are you "acting for" her?'

'Tullius was murdered. Four days ago, in an alleyway near the Trigemina Gate.'

'Merciful heavens!' Well, the surprise seemed genuine enough. And he was right; there wasn't any reason why he should know. 'Who did it?'

'That's what I'm trying to find out. Like I said, I'm going around asking questions on his wife's behalf.'

'So why talk to me? It's more than a year since I saw him last.'

'So I'd heard. No hassle, I'm just being thorough, and it won't take long. You got ten minutes to spare?'

'Certainly. More, if you need them. But I'll tell you now that you're wasting your time. There's nothing I can say that will help you.' He paused. 'And I'll tell you something else, Valerius Corvinus. If and when you find out who the killer is, you bring him round here and I'll be honoured to shake the man's hand.'

I blinked; there'd been real venom behind the words, not just casual dislike, and coming suddenly from this gentle-looking, soft-spoken guy it put me off my stride.

'According to Tullius's partner, Poetelius, you used to be one of the firm's main suppliers,' I said.

'That's right. For ten years, or thereabouts, practically since they set up in business. I supplied Tullius's father, too, before he died.'

'Care to tell me what happened? Why you decided to part company with them?'

'It's simple enough, and the parting company was no doing

of mine. Fourteen months ago the contract came up for renewal. Tullius told me he was awarding it elsewhere. End of story.'

'He give you a reason?'

The barest smidgeon of hesitation. 'No. No, he didn't.'

'And you weren't expecting the decision?'

'No, again. In fact, just a couple of months previously he'd talked about doubling the existing order. That made things even worse.'

'How do you mean?'

'We were working flat out as it was. With double the order I couldn't deliver fast enough and still guarantee the same quality, so before the new contract could be signed I had to expand – buy more slaves, suitably skilled ones, install an extra kiln, order and pay for extra materials, make a dozen other improvements. That doesn't come cheap, especially when it all has to be done on only two months' warning. I wasn't exactly living hand-to-mouth at the time, but I didn't have nearly enough ready cash to meet the expense, which meant I had to borrow.'

I was getting the picture here. Money-lenders aren't known for their generous and philanthropic natures, and the interest rates for a big loan advanced at short notice would be crippling; Vibius would've had to pay through the nose. 'And then Tullius suddenly cancelled the contract, right?' I said. 'Leaving you with a debt you couldn't service.'

'We could, just, although it wasn't easy. I had other customers, of course, Tullius's firm wasn't the only one, but their order was the biggest on our books by a long chalk, and because it had been coming in regularly for the past ten years we'd got into the habit of relying on it to keep things turning over. It takes time to build up a replacement market, and the sudden fall in sales and the wait to bring them up again nearly broke us. Certainly it swallowed every copper piece I had in savings. We're over the worst now, but things are still difficult, and will be for years to come.' He gave me a straight look. 'Which is why, Valerius Corvinus, you will not catch me shedding any tears for Gaius Tullius. And now, if that's all you need to know' – he stood up – 'I'll let you go about your business. I'm sorry, but I can't wish you luck.'

I stood up too. 'Right,' I said. 'Thanks for your time.' I paused, my hand on the door handle. 'That your daughter, by the way? The girl upstairs.'

He frowned. 'Yes. Yes, it is. My daughter, Vibia.'

'She's a lovely-looking girl. You and your wife must be proud.'

A pause. 'I am, certainly. My wife is dead.'

'I'm sorry to hear that.' I opened the door. 'Thanks again. And my apologies for disturbing you.'

'Don't mention it.'

I left.

Interesting, yes?

SEVEN

I got back to the Caelian well before dinner time, to find Perilla in the atrium babysitting, with the Sprog on the couch beside her and Mysta in attendance; evidently the currently sprogless Clarus and Marilla hadn't rolled in yet from whatever junketing they were indulging in today, which suited me fine, because I could fill the lady in on recent developments. Not, I knew, that the blessed status quo would hold for much longer; at the very least, when I told Marilla – as I'd have to straight off, because she was sure to ask – that I'd turned my nose up at her murder the shit was going to hit the fan in no uncertain terms. So a bit of quiet before the storm was welcome.

'Oh, hello, Marcus, you're back,' Perilla said. 'Look, he can almost sit up on his own now. Isn't that marvellous?' Then, to the Sprog: 'Who's a clever boy? Grandad's home.' The Sprog blew a respectable raspberry at me and tried to stuff the little wooden horse he was holding into his mouth. 'He's getting on *really* well for his age. And I think he might be teething.'

'Is that so?' I lay down on the couch opposite and set the full wine-cup that Bathyllus had given me on the table. It's always amazed me how even when they've no kids of their own women turn into hands-on experts inside of five minutes where babies are concerned. That, and pick up the gooey voice which seems to be an essential part of the communication process.

'Do you want him for a bit?' Perilla said.

'Uh-uh. Not me.'

'He won't break, dear. And he's really very amenable.'

'Yeah, I'm sure he is.' I eyed the Sprog warily. He'd evidently got the horse's head just where he wanted it and was giving it a thorough gumming while he stared back at me with fascinated interest. 'Even so.'

'Well, have it your own way. Actually, though, he is feeling a bit moist underneath, so I think he might need changing.' She turned round to Mysta. 'Would you, Mysta? You can bring him back down again later when your mistress gets home.'

'Yes, madam.' Mysta collected the Sprog from her and carried him off, holding the wooden horse in place. Perilla smoothed her tunic – I was sure I saw a damp patch there; a lucky escape, then – and turned back towards me.

'So,' she said. 'How was your day?'

'Pretty successful, all told,' I said. 'I talked to the husbands. Vecilius is our boy.'

'You're sure?' Perilla said.

'He said he'd been at the workshop all day, which was a complete out-and-out porky. There was at least an hour unaccounted for, which would've been plenty of time to commit the murder.' I told her what the wineshop owner had told me. 'Chances are he came on Tullius sniffing around again and knifed him.'

'But, Marcus, that doesn't make any sense.'

'Oh? Why not?'

'First of all, Tullius would have to be a complete fool to go anywhere near Vecilius's wife, particularly since he knew that Vecilius knew about the affair. Secondly, how would Vecilius have got him into the shrine? Tullius would've known that to agree to a private encounter off the beaten track would be simply asking for trouble.'

'You got a better suggestion?'

'No, but—'

'Then clam up. Look. The scenario's simple. Vecilius has spent the morning shifting the booze in the local wineshop and sounding off about his wife's lover. He gets thrown out and on his way home he sees Tullius near Melobosis Alley.' Then, when she opened her mouth to protest: 'OK; maybe he *was* a complete fool. The point is he was there, whether you like it or not, and the logical assumption – which would be Vecilius's as well – is that the guy was tomcatting. Vecilius straight-arms him, takes him to the shrine for a private word, there's a frank exchange of views, and Tullius ends up stiffed.

Vecilius goes back to the wineshop and gets properly stewed. Now me, I can't see what the problem is here.'

'All right.' Perilla sniffed. 'Have it your own way. Only it is a little obvious, isn't it?'

'Jupiter and all the gods, lady!'

'Yes, I know. But let's assume for the sake of argument that Vecilius wasn't the killer. What else have you got? What about the other outraged husband? You spoke to him, too, yes?'

'Sure. Lucilius Festus. He seemed pretty straight.'

'Could he have done it? In terms of opportunity, I mean?'

'Maybe. I had a talk with the local Watch Commander, and the body could've lain there the whole day, so we've no time slot. Festus claimed he took a couple of hours off in the afternoon to go to the Temple of Mercury.'

'And did he?'

'Possibly. But my chances of checking are zilch, because half the merchants and tradesmen in Rome were paying their respects that day. The place would've been heaving.'

'What was he like as a person?'

'I said: he seemed pretty straight, solid family type. Not the murdering kind. That was Watch Commander Memmius's view, too.'

'Hmm.' Perilla was twisting a strand of her hair. 'Perhaps all the more reason, then, if he'd found out Tullius had seduced his wife. How long had he known, by the way?'

'Seemingly Marcia – that's the wife – got an anonymous letter shoved under the door the day before the murder, and he'd intercepted it. The day he and Vecilius went round to alter the guy's face for him at his office, in other words.' I told her the story. 'Me, I don't think we need look far for the person who sent it. Annia told me she knew the two women's names, and if she was pushing for a divorce – which she was – then stirring things might've seemed a good idea.'

'Or it might have been Poetelius.'

'*What?*'

Perilla shrugged. 'It's just as possible, in practical terms. He knew the situation as well. And he knew where Festus and Marcia lived. Did Annia know that?'

'Why the hell would Poetelius want to blow the whistle on

Tullius? Particularly since it'd set two of the company's suppliers at a partner's throat.'

'I don't know, dear. I only said it was a possibility, which it is. Who else did you talk to?'

'Titus Vibius. The supplier Festus replaced.'

'Anything there?'

I frowned. 'Maybe. He hated Tullius, that was for sure, and in the way of business that made sense, because the bastard nearly bankrupted him.' I told her about the cancelled contract. 'Even so, and even if that were a good enough reason in itself for murder, which I doubt, the timing'd be all wrong. After all, it was past history, over a year ago, and the guy's business is more or less back on an even keel these days.'

'Does he have a wife?'

I shot her a glance. 'No. He's a widower. He has a daughter, sure, a real looker. I wondered about her at the time, but I doubt if she's a factor.'

'Why so?'

'Because it wouldn't fit the pattern. She's barely more than a kid, and from what we know of Tullius's tomcatting activities he went for older, married women. Besides, like I said, there's the question of timing.'

'It's another possibility, though, isn't it?' She was still twisting the lock of hair. 'Myself, I'd like to know how long Vibius's wife has been dead. And how she died.'

I stared at her; gods, the lady had a more suspicious mind than I did. Fortunately. 'Uh . . . good point,' I said. 'Well done. OK, filed for reference.'

'So what are your plans now?'

'I'll try to have a word with the two wives, see what they have to say. Vecilius's Hermia'll be tricky, sure, because the house is bang next door to the workshop and I can't see chummie being too cooperative, or too friendly if he knows I'm calling. Marcia's easier: she's gone off to her mother's near the Capenan Gate, or she probably has. And there's the Ostia side of things to check out as well. Lots to be going on with.' I took a swallow of the wine. 'So. How are things on the domestic front? Any developments in the Petillius saga?'

'Absolutely none. I passed Tyndaris in the street this morning and got a frozen glare. Oh, and according to Bathyllus the household had a visit afterwards from a monumental sculptor. I suspect the next stage will be a small tomb in the garden.'

Fuck. The gods save me from OTT cat-lovers. Well, if the silly beggars wanted to throw their money around that was their concern. We'd just have to keep our heads below the parapet and hope things calmed down.

'Well, if we're lucky the whole thing will just—' I stopped; I'd heard the front door and the sound of footsteps crossing the lobby.

The kids were back. I took a deep breath and a hefty gulp of wine; chances were I was going to need it.

'Hi.' Marilla came in, with Clarus in tow. 'What time's dinner? We're starving.'

'Another hour, I'm afraid, dear,' Perilla said.

'Marcus been good?' She grinned at me as she lay down on the third couch. 'The small one, I mean.'

'Good as gold. He's upstairs with Mysta, being changed. I think he's cutting his first tooth.'

'Yes, he is dribbling a lot.'

'So where did you go?'

'The Saepta.' Clarus settled down beside Marilla. 'Shopping.'

I winced; no wonder the guy was looking frayed round the edges. With two-and-a-half years of marriage under his belt, I'd've thought he would have developed shopping-avoidance strategies by now – after all, they're among the most essential survival skills for husbands – but evidently not. Still, living down in the Alban Hills he wouldn't't've had the practice.

'Marilla, you should have told me!' Perilla said. 'I'd've come with you.'

'It was only an afterthought.' Marilla looked round: Bathyllus had come up on her blind side, touting for orders. 'Oh. Some fruit juice, please, Bathyllus. And if dinner's going to be another hour, could you bring me a cheese roll? Or make it two. With a slice of ham and some pickles.'

'Certainly, madam.' He looked at Clarus. 'Sir?'

'Wine, Bathyllus. Just wine.'

I grinned. He was no great wine drinker, our Clarus; the shopping trip had obviously been Fraught.

'I'll have a top-up, too, little guy,' I said, draining my cup and handing it to him. 'Perilla?'

'No, not for me.'

Bathyllus went out.

'We'd actually intended to go up to Sallust Gardens, which we did,' Marilla said. 'But coming back we got a bit side-tracked. Still, it was only a sort of preliminary reconnaissance. I didn't buy much, and we can easily go again tomorrow.'

I didn't even *look* at Clarus.

'That'd be marvellous, dear,' Perilla said. 'We'll make a whole day of it. There are two new shops off Augustus Square you won't know about that are well worth a look.'

Marilla turned back to me.

'So how did it go, Corvinus?' she said.

'Ah . . . how did what go?'

'Your visit to what's-his-name. Your Palatine Watch Commander friend.' I hesitated. 'You *did* go over and talk to him this morning, didn't you?'

Hell; here we went. 'Decimus Lippillus,' I said. 'Yeah, more or less. First thing, as it happens. A complete coincidence, that. He's just been moved to Tuscan Street from Public Pond, and—'

'Did he agree to let you look into things?'

'In essence, but—'

'That's marvellous! So you'll be taking the case.'

'Um . . . no, not exactly.'

'*What?*'

'The fact is, Marilla, to tell you the truth, not to put too fine a point on it, I'm a bit busy with other things at present, so—'

'What sort of . . .?' She stopped. 'You toad! You lying toad! You're working on a case after all!'

'Come on, Princess! Give me a break, OK?' I glanced over at Perilla, but she was industriously picking a thread off her tunic. 'I can explain.'

'Are you or aren't you?'

'Uh . . . yeah, as it happens, I am, but—'

'You told me at breakfast yesterday that you weren't!'

'No. To be fair, what I actually *said* was—'

'All right. You fudged. Same difference. And you'd certainly told Clarus you weren't in so many words the morning before.'

'Hold on, Marilla! That was true enough at the time! Tullia sodding Gemella didn't tell me her sodding brother had been killed until that afternoon.'

'Marcus, dear, *please*,' Perilla murmured.

'Yeah, well.'

'I call it mean.' Marilla was glaring at me. 'Mean, despicable and toadlike.'

'She's right, Corvinus,' Clarus said.

Shit; what had happened to male solidarity? And I would've expected Perilla to have put in her pennyworth by now; she was as guilty as I was. I'd be having words with the lady later. Out of the corner of my eye, I saw Bathyllus come in with a loaded tray, do a sharp about-turn, and disappear again. Traitors, the lot of them.

'Very well,' Marilla said. 'One murder is as good as another, I suppose. You can tell us – Clarus and me – about it now, please, because I assume Perilla knows the full details already.' I saw the lady wince, and despite myself I grinned: she'd just have to grit her teeth, and frankly it served her damn well right. 'Tullia Gemella, you said.'

'Marilla, dear, I don't think—' Perilla began mildly.

The Princess just gave her a Look. I grinned again.

'OK, Bathyllus,' I said loudly. 'You can come in now. Serve away.' He did, like he was walking on eggs.

So while Marilla tucked into her cheese rolls, with pauses for mouth-full questions, I told them.

EIGHT

At least Marilla was committed to the extended shopping trip next day, and the more opportunities I had to establish clear lines of demarcation – i.e. it was my job to hike around Rome solving murders, and hers to keep off my back – the better.

Today was the Day of the Adulterous Wives. I started with Marcia.

The Capenan Gate, at the foot of the Caelian where Appian Road enters the south-east corner of the city, wasn't all that far, sure, but because I didn't have a name for the woman's mother finding the cookshop itself was tricky, and it took me until just short of mid-morning. The place seemed pretty popular, which was a good sign where the food on offer was concerned: there was a queue in front of me and two women and a girl of about nine or ten serving. I waited until the last of the punters had collected his flatbread-wrapped chickpea rissoles and left, then moved up to the counter.

'Yes, sir, what can I get you?' It was the younger of the two women, mid- to late twenties, so ten, maybe fifteen years younger than Festus; pretty enough, but with a pinched, drawn look to her face. Her eyes were red, too.

'Your name Marcia?' I said.

She frowned. 'Yes. Yes, it is.'

'You think we could talk somewhere in private?'

The frown deepened. 'What about?'

'The name's Corvinus. I'm looking into the death of a guy called Gaius Tullius. I understand you and he—'

Which was as far as I got before her eyes rolled up under the lids and she slipped down behind the counter, banging her head on the stonework. Shit.

The older woman and the girl were staring, frozen. Then the woman moved. She glared at me and crouched over the fallen body.

'Get a cup of water for me, dear,' she said sideways to the girl; from the facial resemblance, obviously her granddaughter and Marcia's daughter. Yeah: Festus had said she'd taken the children with her. 'Quickly, now.'

Without taking her eyes off Marcia, the kid edged over to the water pitcher, filled a cup, and handed it to her. The woman held it to Marcia's lips and looked up at me, still glaring.

'You!' she snapped. 'Outside!'

Yeah, well, in retrospect maybe I could've been a smidgeon more tactful, at that. Still, it was done now. I left without a word and stood by the door.

Marcia came out five minutes later, white as a ghost and with an angry-looking bruise on her forehead.

'I'm sorry,' she whispered.

'That's OK, lady. My fault.' There was a street fountain with a stone step next to us. 'You want to sit down?'

She did, and took several deep breaths.

'Gaius is dead?' she said at last.

'Yeah. Five days ago.'

'How?'

'He was stabbed in an alleyway off Trigemina Gate Street.'

She closed her eyes and said nothing. I waited.

'I'm sorry,' she said again. 'I didn't know. I've been here helping my mother with the shop, ever since—' She stopped.

'Ever since your husband found out about the affair and threw you out. Yeah. I know.'

Her eyes opened. 'Lucilius had nothing to do with it! He's a good man! He wouldn't hurt a fly!'

'OK.' I hesitated, then said, more gently: 'You like to tell me what happened that morning, exactly?'

'I had an anonymous letter pushed under the door, telling me Gaius wouldn't be seeing me any more, he'd taken up with Hermia, Titus Vecilius's wife. Lucilius was up already and he read it first. He was furious. He told me he was going round to Gaius's office, which he did. Luckily, nothing happened because Gaius was out.'

My mouth was open to ask the obvious question, but I decided to let it go at present. Instead, I said: 'So you went to Hermia's, right? To have it out with her?'

She nodded. 'I didn't think. I was just . . . so . . . *angry*! Gaius hadn't even had the courage to tell me himself, after we'd been . . .' She swallowed. 'I've known Hermia for years, I thought we were friends, and that made it worse. Anyway, we were screaming at each other when her husband walked in. He grabbed me and bundled me outside. Then I went back home, collected the children, and came straight here.'

Yeah, well; it all fitted with what Vecilius himself had told me. Not that it had anything specific to do with the actual murder, mind, but it was good to get independent confirmation. 'How long had the affair been going on?' I said.

'For just over a year. Gods, I was stupid! I told you, Lucilius is a good man, he loves me and he loves the children. I should never have allowed it to start.'

'So why did you?'

'Because I was bored and wanted a bit of excitement. Because Gaius was rich and good-looking, and a good talker. Eventually, because he was good in bed. Everything Lucilius isn't. And like I say, because I was stupid.'

I thought of Annia. Yeah, barring some aspects the same story. Tullius may have been a bastard, but clearly where women were concerned he was an attractive bastard. 'You knew he was married?'

'Yes. But I also knew he didn't get on with his wife, and that she wouldn't care what he got up to because she'd a lover of her own.'

'Oh?' I said. 'And who would that be?'

'Gaius's partner. Publius Poetelius.'

Shit. My spine went cold. 'He told you that? Tullius himself?'

'Yes. Right at the start. It was a loveless marriage on both sides, he said, but a divorce wasn't possible because his wife controlled the purse strings, and in any case they had their separate lives. That suited me. I wouldn't've wanted anything permanent anyway. All I wanted was a bit of excitement.' She sounded bitter as hell. 'Stupid, you see?'

I didn't comment. 'So who do you think sent the letter?'

She shrugged. 'I don't know.'

'OK. One more thing. You said that when your husband

went round to Tullius's office he didn't actually see him. How do you know that? I mean, if the last time you saw him was when he walked out the door on his way there—'

Her face clouded. 'But it wasn't. Of course it wasn't. You've talked to Lucilius, you must've done or you wouldn't've known where to find me.'

'You've seen him since?'

'Of course I have. He came round here the next day. In the afternoon.'

'He did *what*?'

'He wanted to make sure that I was all right. Me and the kids.' There were tears in her eyes. 'Just that. I thought he might ask me to come back, but he didn't. I wanted to, but he said it was too soon, he needed time to think things over. Didn't he tell you that?'

So Festus had an alibi for the whole day of the murder after all. Or on the face of it he did anyway, because the Capenan Gate and Trigemina Gate Street were on opposite sides of the city, and if he'd come all the way across here, he wouldn't've had time in a couple of hours to have done the murder as well. 'No,' I said. 'He didn't tell me. He said he'd gone to pay his respects at the Temple of Mercury. Now why the hell would he lie about that?'

She looked away. 'Because he's a proud man whose wife's been unfaithful to him for no reason at all,' she said. 'What cuckolded husband would admit going all the way across Rome just to make sure his wife was safely with her mother the day after he's told her to get out of the house and not come back? Of course he lied to you. He'd've lied to anyone.'

Yeah, well; I supposed it made sense, or some sort of sense, anyway. And at least, barring Vecilius as being responsible, I could draw a line through Festus as the killer.

'Fine, lady,' I said. 'Thanks for your help. It's been very useful.'

I turned to go.

'Corvinus?'

I turned back. 'Yeah?'

'If you see Lucilius, tell him I'm sorry. Just that.'

'I'll tell him,' I said, and left.

Gods! There'd been a couple of eye-openers there, and no mistake. Particularly the business about Annia and Poetelius. That opened a whole new can of worms, and it needed thinking about.

I set off towards Trigemina Gate Street and a possible interview with Hermia.

When I knocked on the door of the house next to the glass workshop I was keeping a leery eye out: judging by what had happened the last time our paths had crossed, Vecilius wouldn't exactly be overjoyed if he found me paying a visit to his wife, and I valued my teeth too much to take any risks. Eventually, the door was opened by a woman about Marcia's age. The gossipy owner of the wineshop hadn't been exaggerating, because she was a honey: small, plump, curvy, with jet-black hair and a heart-shaped face, currently disfigured by a beaut of a shiner the colour of an overripe plum.

'Yes?' she said.

I was staring at her eye. 'Uh . . . my name's Corvinus,' I said. 'Could I have a word with you, do you think? It's about Gaius Tullius.'

'Tullius is dead.' She made to shut the door.

I put out my hand to stop it closing. 'Yeah, I know. That's the point. I'm representing his widow, and I need to ask you a few questions. No hassle. It won't take long.'

For an instant, she looked frightened. She glanced past me towards the door of the workshop, hesitated, then shrugged and stepped back.

'Please yourself,' she murmured. 'Come in.'

I followed her inside: another two-up, two-down property with the public rooms either side of a central corridor. She opened one of the doors.

'In here. Make yourself comfortable.'

There were a couple of couches, two or three stools, and a dresser with crockery on it, plus a scattering of ornaments and a small family altar in the corner. Not exactly tidy, in fact the dresser and the altar showed distinct traces of dust. Clearly not the house-proud type, sweet little Hermia. I pulled up one of the stools and sat down, while she sat on one of the couches.

'All right,' she said. 'Let's have the questions.'

Cool enough, but her hands were clasped tightly together in her lap. I noticed they were trembling.

'You were having an affair with him, right?' I said.

'"Affair" is the wrong word. We were seeing each other, yes, but it hadn't gone beyond that.'

'OK. So when did things start?'

'Just under a month ago.' Black eye aside, she looked and sounded like a schoolgirl reciting a lesson to the teacher. 'Gaius had been at the workshop on business. When he came out, I was unlocking the house door. I was carrying some vegetables from the market, and I dropped a cabbage on the doorstep. He picked it up and brought it inside for me, so I asked him if he'd like a cup of wine before he went back to his office. Just politeness, you know?'

I nodded, but said nothing.

'Anyway, we chatted for about an hour, and the next day he came round again. To see me, not Titus, he made that clear at the start. The third time, a few days later, he was back, this time with a present – nothing big, just a trinket – and . . . well . . . he kissed me when he left. The fourth time—' she hesitated and lowered her eyes demurely – 'the fourth time he suggested we go to bed together. I refused point blank, of course, he apologized, and that was that. At least, I thought it was.' She raised her eyes again and gave me a straight look. 'In any case, that's all that ever happened between us as far as I was concerned. I swear it.'

'Fine.' Yeah, well, whatever the truth of it – and, oath or not, I wouldn't've trusted this little lady to give me the right time of day – the modus operandi fitted: bored young house-wife left on her own, good-looking admirer from a couple of notches above her in the social scale with a smooth line in chat that left the husband nowhere. Tullius had had it all worked out. 'The day before he died. You had a spat with his actual mistress, Marcia, right?'

She nodded. 'It was horrible. I've known Marcia for years, practically since she moved here, but I didn't know she was involved with Gaius. She came round to the house that morning and accused me of stealing him off her. Then Titus walked in.

We had a blazing row after she left.' She lowered her eyes. 'I managed to convince him there was nothing to it, that Gaius had only been trying it on, but I couldn't stop him going to the office to have things out. In the event he never saw him, because Gaius was away on business, so he came straight back.'

'So what happened the next day? The day of the murder?' I waited, but there was no answer. 'Come on, lady,' I said finally. 'If you don't tell me I'll just get it eventually from elsewhere. And playing coy might not be too hot an idea at this stage.'

She took a deep breath. 'We'd . . . Titus hadn't spoken a word to me since he got back from Gaius's office. When I woke up the next morning he'd already gone out. I had breakfast, then did the shopping. Titus usually comes home for lunch at midday, but that day he didn't, so I thought I'd make a special effort for dinner. Stuffed vegetables in a wine and onion sauce. They're his favourite. Anyway, I'd done the vegetables and I was just putting the pot on the stove when Gaius walked into the kitchen.'

I blinked, but said nothing.

'I never thought he'd come back. I wasn't expecting him, I swear it. The front door was open as usual, and he'd just let himself in. Before I could say or do anything, he grabbed me and started . . . pulling at my tunic, trying to kiss me. I was fighting him off when Titus came in, reeling drunk. He pulled Gaius away, and Gaius ran for the door. Titus started after him, but he tripped over a stool. I went to help him up and he hit me.' She touched her eye. 'Then he ran out after Gaius. That was the last I saw of him until two of his wineshop cronies carried him in drunk just before sunset.'

'And this was when, exactly?'

'Mid-afternoon, or thereabouts.'

Yeah, well, the timing and circumstantial details matched what the wineshop owner had told me. Sure, as far as the faithful housewife stuff and the accident with the stool were concerned the jury was still out and liable to stay that way, but in the main it all rang true. And it wasn't too difficult to reconstruct probable subsequent events, either. Still, whether

Tullius had come back by invitation or off his own bat the
guy had been a complete fool to take the risk. Personally, I
reckoned he'd deserved all he got.

Not that that let Vecilius off the hook, mind: murder's
murder, however you slice it.

'Your husband tell you anything about what had happened
in the interim? When he sobered up, I mean?' I said.

'He claimed that Gaius had given him the slip. He looked
for him but he couldn't find him, so he went back to the
wineshop.'

'"Claimed"? You don't believe him?'

'I don't *know*! You've no idea what life's been like these
past few days. We haven't exchanged more than a few words.
It's like living with a stranger.' She lowered her eyes again,
then said in a quiet, demure voice: 'If there was somewhere
I could go for a while, away from Titus, someone I could stay
with, who'd look after me—'

I stood up. 'Yeah. Right,' I said. 'Me, I wouldn't be too
worried. No doubt it'll all blow over in time. Anyway, thanks
for your help, lady.'

She gave me a glare. But I was already heading for the
door.

Well, I reckoned that just about put the lid on it. As far as
the attempted seduction itself was concerned, whether Hermia
had told the complete truth or given me the expurgated version
wasn't important, and no business of mine; the odds were
we'd got our killer.

Or at least we probably had. Or, there again, possibly not . . .

I frowned. Shit; Perilla had been right, it was all too pat.
There was still too much that needed thinking about, too many
loose ends. I glanced up at the sun. Well into its third quarter;
just time to drop in at my gabby wineshop owner's for a cup
of wine before I set off for the long walk back to the Caelian
and dinner.

I wasn't the only punter in evidence this time; there were a
couple of tunics propping up the bar, obviously locals. They
gave me an incurious stare and a nod and went back to their
wine-cups.

'Afternoon, sir. Nice to see you again.' The wineshop owner reached for an empty jug. 'Graviscan, wasn't it?'

'Yeah. Well remembered,' I said. 'Just a cup this time, though, pal.'

He replaced the jug, set a cup on the counter, and filled it from one of the jars on the shelf. 'You'll be having more business with Vecilius, then?' he said.

'Yeah, as it happens.' I reached for my purse and took out a silver piece.

'Only no offence but I was just wondering a bit more after you left yesterday whether it mightn't have to do with something other than glass. Seeing you were so interested in the man himself and all. I said so at the time, if you remember?' He gave me my change and pursed his lips. 'Terrible thing, that murder in Melobosis Alley, wasn't it?'

Subtle as a brick, and the casual tone wouldn't've fooled a mentally slow six-year-old. The two punters at the other end of the bar pricked up their ears and turned round. I sighed. Ah, well, it didn't make any odds, cosmically speaking. And I didn't owe Vecilius any favours.

'The name's Valerius Corvinus,' I said. 'I'm looking into Tullius's death.'

'There, now! That's just what I thought!' The owner slapped the counter and beamed at the two other customers. 'Didn't I tell you, lads?' He turned back to me. 'So Vecilius caught him messing around with his wife and knifed him, did he, sir? Well, I'm not surprised. Not that I blame him, poor devil, he probably had enough encouragement. She's always been a fast little piece, that one, and his temper being what it is—'

'Look, pal,' I said quickly, 'that's just one possibility. There're plenty of others.'

'Oh, you can't fool me, sir! He's your man, all right, no doubt at all about that. Although I don't blame you for being cautious about saying so outright to strangers, very laudable, that is. Prejudicial to the conduct of the investigation, that the legal phrase?'

'More or less,' I said. 'It'll do.'

'He'll get the chop, more than likely,' one of the punters said. 'Bound to, for killing a nob, whatever excuse he had.'

'Good news for somebody, anyhow,' the other punter said meditatively. 'That's a nice little business he's got there, a real money-spinner, and it'll all go to his widow.' He grinned and winked. 'Not that I'd mind a bit of Hermia myself, come to that, even without the money.'

Jupiter! Tried, convicted and buried inside two minutes! There spoke the vox pop. Still, I'd done my best, and like I said they were probably right about him having done it because it was the obvious answer. I took a swig of the Graviscan.

'Incidentally, what would those other possibilities you mentioned be, now, sir?' That was my muck-raking pal behind the bar, of course, angling predictably for extra scandal. 'If you don't mind me asking. Just idle curiosity, you understand. Between you and us and the doorpost, naturally. It won't go any further.'

I shrugged and took another sip of the wine.

''Course, in situations like these it's often the wife,' said the more ruminative of the two barflies. 'Hell hath no fury and so on. Little woman finds out that her hubby's getting a bit on the side, picks up a kitchen knife, and stiffs the bugger.'

His friend gave him a sideways look. 'Nah,' he said. 'This Tullius was a nob. Nobs' wives don't do that sort of thing. And she's probably never been inside of a kitchen.'

'No, not personally, sure; I don't mean *personally*. Nobs' wives would have somebody do it for them, wouldn't they? Stands to reason. Some man or other. Having it done for them's a different thing entirely. More respectable, like. That's how nobs work.' He turned to me. 'You keep the wife in mind, sir. If it wasn't Vecilius did it after all then I reckon the wife's your best bet, myself.'

'Thanks, pal,' I said. 'I'll do that.' I meant it, too. The guy had a valid point, and I was remembering what Marcia had told me about Annia being involved with Poetelius. Apropos of which . . . 'Uh, incidentally. Tullius had a partner. A man called Publius Poetelius. Ring any bells?' Blank faces all round; well, fair enough, the name on its own wasn't likely to mean anything. 'Tullius was the usual go-between where business was concerned, sure, so you might know him by sight, at least, but there's a chance his partner subbed for him

on occasion, when he was out of town. Youngish, mid-thirties.'
I described him. 'You happen to've seen him around here at
all recently?'

'Could have,' the wineshop owner said cautiously. He sucked
on a tooth. 'Might have done. Looks like a bit of a pen-pusher,
right? Lost out of reach of an abacus?'

'Yeah.' Jupiter! 'Yeah, that's him.'

'Ah.' He nodded, reached for an empty cup, filled it, and
took a slow, contemplative sip. He was enjoying this, I could
tell. 'Then I've seen him right enough, sir, in this very bar,
standing just where you are now. Day of the murder, it was,
too. About the middle of the afternoon. Yes, it must've been,
because I'd just got shot of that bastard Vecilius.'

Hey! 'You get talking at all?'

'Nah, he wasn't the talkative type.' He grinned. 'Well, well!
So that was the dead man's partner, was it? Interesting! Now
why would he—?'

'Thanks, pal.' I swigged the rest of my wine and set the
empty cup down on the counter. 'I'll see you around.'

Interesting was right, and in spades, to boot, because taken
together with Marcia's claim that Poetelius and Annia were
an item it put the guy squarely in a frame of his own as far
as motive and opportunity were concerned. Clearly, Vecilius
wasn't the only game in town after all.

I left them goggling and headed back to the Caelian.

NINE

Bathyllus opened the front door for me as I mounted the steps.

'Hi, pal,' I said. 'Not late for dinner, am I?' I'd cut it fine, I knew: the sun was just on the point of setting, and where Meton was concerned that practically constituted a dinner gong.

He handed me the obligatory cup of wine. 'Not at all, sir. In fact, dinner will be slightly later this evening.'

'Oh? Why's that?' I took my first restorative swallow.

He cleared his throat. 'We had a little fracas, sir, which has somewhat disrupted the domestic arrangements.'

Oh, shit. 'Don't tell me,' I said. 'Involving next door, right?'

'Indeed, sir. The mistress will explain. She's in the atrium.'

I went through. Perilla was lying on her couch with an open book-roll. She looked up, and I gave her the usual back-home kiss.

'OK, lady,' I said. 'Tell me the worst.'

'Nothing very drastic, dear.' She set the book aside. 'Just a small contretemps at the fruit market.' Jupiter! First a fracas, now a contretemps! 'There was no actual blood spilled, and Paullus will be perfectly all right when the concussion wears off.'

'Concussion? And who the hell is Paullus?'

'Next door's chef. Meton hit him with a melon. Quite a large one, I understand.'

'He did *what*?'

'Of course, next door aren't too happy about it, but from what Meton says it was largely the man's own fault.'

Gods! I put the wine-cup down on the table and yelled: '*Bathyllus!*'

He soft-sandalled in. 'Yes, sir?'

'Tell Meton I want to see him! *Now!*'

'Yes, sir.' He soft-sandalled out.

I turned back to Perilla. 'How much *not happy* would this be, then?' I said. 'On a scale, say, of one to ten?'

'That would be ten. At least.'

'Ah.' Bugger! This we could do without!

'I did go round to apologize to Tyndaris personally as soon as Marilla and I got back. She said it was bad enough living next door to cat-killers without having their staff launch murderous attacks on her own domestics. Also that Appropriate Steps would be Taken; the emphasis is hers. Then she threw me out. Very politely, of course.'

Fuck. Double fuck. 'Did she say—?'

'You wanted to see me?'

I turned to find Meton doing his usual looming act and wearing his customary put-upon expression.

'Only I've got a delicate sauce on the simmer, so it'll have to be quick.'

'Just tell me what happened, sunshine.'

'I was unduly provoked.'

I sighed: in Meton's book, undue provocation might be a raised eyebrow or a cough out of turn. Or even minor eyeballing. 'In what way, exactly?'

'I was at Mama Silvia's stall in the market, like, buyin' pears, an' he, that's that bastard Paullus, was standin' behind me in the queue. I says to Mama, "I'll take some of them Dolabellians for a compote, love," an' Paullus says, "Nah, you want Laterans for that, pal," then I turns round and says, "Rubbish, Laterans're too moist for a compote," then he says, "Moist? The way you cook, your lot wouldn't notice if you used bloody Falernians." So I picked up a melon and belted him with it.'

I winced. 'Ah . . . right. Right.'

'The bastard had it coming.'

'No doubt. But still—'

'I mean – *Falernians*! For a sodding *compote*? Give me a fucking break! An' he claims to be a chef!'

'Yeah, well, I can see why you'd find that shocking, pal, but perhaps your response was just a smidgeon—'

'Anicians, OK, they're on the tart side, sure, particularly if they're picked too early, but I could've taken Anicians in my stride. Falernians, now, that is just fucking *insulting*!'

I closed my eyes for a moment. 'Thank you, Meton. Very concisely and graphically explained. You can go.'

He went. I picked up my wine-cup, took a long swallow, and lay down on the second couch. 'Gods!'

'It *was* deliberate provocation, Marcus,' Perilla said.

'Yeah. Yeah, I know that.' Pushing Meton's button was simplicity itself, and these feuds tend to spread to the bought help pretty quickly. 'Even so—'

'Well, what's done is done.'

True. 'Where're the kids?' I said. 'Out gallivanting again? I thought you were all going shopping together?'

'Marilla and I did. Clarus said he had a doctor friend of his father's to see, over in Transtiber. He isn't back yet, and Marilla is upstairs playing with little Marcus.' A friend of his father's, eh? Maybe the boy was learning after all. I grinned. 'How was your day? Profitable?'

I gave her the rundown. 'So it looks like Festus is out of it,' I said. 'Vecilius is still the front runner, easy, but I'd risk a hefty side-bet on Poetelius.'

'The partner?' Her eyes widened in surprise. 'Is he the murdering type?'

'No. Or not especially. But the guy in the wineshop was right. Given a connection with Annia, he's got motivation in spades.'

'Namely?'

I ticked the points off. 'Tullius wouldn't agree to a divorce. If the affair's serious – and I'd guess that it is – getting rid of the husband's the only way forward.'

'You think it's *that* serious? After all, why should Poetelius bother? Tullius had no real interest in his wife, he had his own affairs which he took no great pains to keep secret, and he knew about the relationship already.'

'Poetelius told me he and Annia had been friends since they were kids. The impression I got when I talked to him was that he'd carried a candle for her from the start but that Tullius had sweet-talked her into marrying him instead. Which sounds like Tullius all over. And I'd've put Poetelius down as pretty conventional.'

'Not conventional enough to draw the line at adultery.'

'Come on, Perilla! The marriage was a sham, and he wasn't breaking up any happy households. Unlike his partner.'

'Hmm.' She was twisting a lock of her hair.

'Besides – second point – there's the financial aspect. Tullius was running the firm into the ground, making policy decisions for personal rather than business reasons. On the other side, Annia was providing the money that kept things going and Poetelius had the expertise. In the business sense, Tullius was nothing but dead weight. Worse, he was a liability. All in all, like a lot of people seem to be saying, the guy was a complete waste of space. Poetelius – and Annia – will be far better off without him.'

'It's still not necessarily a good enough reason for killing him.'

'Jupiter, lady, how much more do you want?' I took an exasperated swallow of the wine. 'OK, it's all provisional, I grant you. But it's a valid theory. And Poetelius sure as hell lied about being in the neighbourhood of Trigemina Gate Street the day of the murder.'

'No, he didn't. He simply didn't tell you that he was.'

'Yeah, well, that amounts to the same thing, doesn't it? Besides, what excuse did he have? He wasn't there on business seeing Vecilius or Festus, because liaising with the suppliers was Tullius's job, and if for some reason he had been they would've mentioned it. Plus it was a public holiday. And that part of town's on the way to nowhere except the Emporium and Pottery Mountain.'

'So what do you do now?'

I shrugged. 'Face him with it. See what he says. And have another talk with Annia. That lady has beans to spill.' The front door banged. 'That sounds like Clarus back.'

It was.

'Hi, Corvinus. Perilla,' he said when he came in. 'Sorry, I got held up. Old Theo got to reminiscing. Not late, am I?'

'No, no, you're fine, pal,' I said. 'Meton and next door's chef had a contretemps involving a melon, so things are a bit behind.'

He frowned. 'What?'

'Perilla'll explain.'

Bathyllus shimmied in. 'The chef says to inform you that dinner is ready whenever you are, sir. Finally.'

'I'll go and tell Marilla, Marcus,' Perilla said. 'You and Clarus go straight through.'

She went upstairs.

'"Theo"?' I said to Clarus.

He was looking shifty. 'Aemilius Theodorus,' he said. 'A friend of Dad's. I thought I'd look him up while we were here. While the women were off shopping.'

'Yeah. Right.' I waited. 'So, uh, where were you really?'

He grinned. 'I went back to the Pollio. I said: they've got a lot of stuff by Erasistratus there, and I didn't have time to see all of it I wanted.'

'Nothing to do with the guy who was stabbed? Marcus Correllius?'

He gave me a look of genuine puzzlement. 'No, of course not! Why the hell should it be?'

Right; right: we moved in different worlds, Clarus and me, except when they overlapped occasionally. And I knew it wouldn't've been a wineshop.

I turned to Bathyllus, who was still hovering.

'The dessert isn't pear compote, is it, sunshine?' I said.

'No.' He sniffed. 'Pear compote will not be featuring this evening, sir.'

'How about slightly damaged melon?'

Not a flicker: Bathyllus moved in a different world as well, and humour played a very small part in it.

'Not that either,' he said. 'I understand Meton has decided on a preserved fruit and honey pudding.'

Well, no doubt things would get back to normal when our socially disadvantaged chef had repaired his bridges with the local suppliers. Or just found one who didn't mind him using their produce as an offensive weapon.

'Fine,' I said.

We went through.

TEN

I called in at Poetelius's office first thing the next morning.
'Corvinus!' The guy was sitting behind his desk slaving over a hot abacus and a pile of wax tablets. 'How's the investigation going? Any progress?'

'Yeah,' I said. 'We're getting there.'

'Good.' He smiled. 'So what can I do for you?'

I pulled up the stool and sat down. 'For a start, pal, you can tell me what you were doing in Trigemina Gate Street the day your partner was murdered. And why you didn't feel obliged to mention being there the last time we talked.'

The smile faded. 'Ah.'

'"Ah" is right.'

His fingers drummed on the desk. 'Titus Vibius told you, presumably?'

'Vibius? Why Vibius?'

'Because it was him I went to see, of course.'

'There's no "of course" about it. Maybe you'd better give me the whys and wherefores from the beginning.'

'All right.' He took a deep breath. 'I told you: Vibius supplied most of our pottery prior to Festus, and he was much better all round. Not renewing his contract was Gaius's idea, not mine, quite the contrary. When Festus came here the day before threatening to punch Gaius's lights out I naturally assumed the business association was at an end, and that therefore we would be looking for a new supplier. Going back to Vibius – if he was willing, after the shabby way Gaius treated him – was the obvious solution, and I decided to sound him out. Coincidentally, the next day was a holiday, the office would be closed, and so I wouldn't have to explain my unaccustomed absence to Gaius.' He smiled. 'Or rather to invent a story explaining it, because as you can imagine I didn't want it to appear that I was going over his head.'

'So why didn't you tell me this in the first place?'

'Would you have, if you'd been me?' he said simply. 'When I knew where Gaius's body had been found?'

'It would've been more sensible.'

'Perhaps so, and I apologize. Anyway, now you can check with Vibius. He'll confirm matters.'

Yeah, well, he probably would. Although that didn't let the guy off the hook altogether, not by a long chalk. 'And you didn't bump into Tullius at all while you were there?'

'No. I didn't know it might be a possibility. In fact, if I had known I wouldn't't've gone there in the first place.'

'OK,' I said. 'One more thing. You're having an affair with Annia, right?'

He sat back. 'Who told you that?'

There was no reason not to tell him. 'Festus's wife, Marcia. She said Tullius had told her himself.'

'Then he was lying. Or she was. We're good friends, Annia and me, we have been most of our lives, but that's as far as it goes.' He stood up. 'And now I think you should go too, Corvinus. I've a lot to do this morning, and I've helped you all I can in this matter. Good day to you.'

Short and sweet. Yeah, well, if Poetelius was our man – and nothing he'd said went very far towards proving he wasn't – then I'd rattled his cage pretty thoroughly. I got up and replaced the stool.

'Fine,' I said. 'I'll be seeing you around, pal.'

He didn't answer. As I left, I could feel his eyes boring into my back.

OK, now for the lady. I retraced my steps down Head of Africa Road and through the Caelian to the junction with Ardeatina Gate Street at the Metrovian Gate, by which time the morning was mostly spent. Perfect timing, counting a stopover for a quick cup of wine, for a social call.

This time, she was sitting in the garden. Otherwise, history had repeated itself in the shape of the visitor in the other wickerwork chair opposite her.

'Valerius Corvinus,' Quintus Annius said, getting up. 'We were just talking about you.'

'Is that so, now?' I said.

His sister smiled. 'Nothing you couldn't have heard.' Then, to the slave who'd brought me out: 'Timon, another chair. And perhaps a cup of wine?' She looked at me.

'Thanks. That'd be great.'

'For you, Quintus?'

'No, I'm fine.' The slave left. 'Sit here, Corvinus, please. Timon won't be a moment. So. How are things going?'

I sat down. 'Pretty well, considering,' I said cautiously. Like the last time, I had the feeling that I'd walked in on something. Oh, the two of them were behaving naturally enough, and when you came down to it there was no reason why the guy shouldn't be seeing a lot of his sister at present, things being as they were. But the coincidence didn't sit easy all the same.

'Well,' he said, 'I won't press you for details. Particularly since as I said the last time we met I've no compelling desire to see my brother-in-law's killer caught.'

Jupiter, he was a cold bastard, this one! Me, under normal circumstances I'm all in favour of candour, but a brutal comment like that, especially delivered in the bloodless way Annius chose to do it, sent a chill down my spine.

'That's good of you,' I said. 'Much appreciated.'

The slave came out with the chair, set it down, then returned for the wine-cup. I sipped. Graviscan again, and pretty good stuff, streets ahead of what my nosey pal in the wineshop served. Whatever faults Tullius had had, he'd kept a good cellar.

'So,' Annia said. 'How can I help you this time?'

'Ah . . . it's a bit sensitive, lady,' I said, glancing at Annius.

'In that case' – Annius had just sat down; now he stood up again – 'I'll go. If you'll excuse me?'

'Don't be silly, Quintus!' Annia pulled him down and looked at me. 'Sensitive in what way? If you've learned something more about Gaius's philanderings then it probably won't come as news, let alone shock me. And I certainly won't mind if my brother hears it.'

'It's not about your husband.'

'Really?' Then, when I still hesitated: 'Oh, go on, Corvinus, please! I don't have any secrets from Quintus. Definitely none I would be ashamed of if he knew them.'

'OK, lady. The fact is I was told you were having an affair with Publius Poetelius.'

She stared at me. Then she laughed. 'Who on earth said that, for goodness' sake?'

'It isn't true?'

'Of course it's not true! We're friends. *Just* friends, and always have been. Again: who told you?'

'Lucilius Festus's wife, Marcia. She got it from your husband.'

'But that's ridiculous! Gaius would never have thought that!'

I shrugged. 'I'm only repeating what she said. And why should she make it up?'

Now it was Annia's turn to hesitate. She glanced at her brother, then looked back at me. 'Actually, she might have had a reason,' she said. 'A good one. To her mind, at least.'

'What would that be, now?'

'I said I didn't have any embarrassing secrets. That wasn't quite true, although the secret isn't a major one. The anonymous letter Marcia got, about Gaius taking up with a new girlfriend.'

'You wrote it?'

She nodded. 'I sent Timon over to deliver it late the previous evening. After she and her husband had gone to bed.'

Well, it came as no surprise; the chances were the letter had to have come from her or Poetelius. What was surprising was that she'd come straight out and admitted it.

'You care to tell me why?' I said.

'I thought it might stir things up a bit. Precipitate matters. Perhaps push Gaius into agreeing to a divorce. A silly thing to do, I know that now in retrospect, but there you are. All I can say is that it seemed a good idea at the time.'

Stir things up a bit. Certainly it'd done that, with a vengeance. And knowing for sure that Annia was responsible opened up a whole new line of possibilities. 'So what you're saying is that Marcia guessed who was responsible and was getting back at you?'

'It would seem reasonable, wouldn't it? In any event, it's the only explanation.'

I wouldn't go quite that far myself. And I could think of at least one other purpose to the letter that was a lot less innocent. 'Yeah. Yeah, fair enough,' I said. I swallowed the rest of my wine and stood up. 'Thanks, lady. I won't take up any more of your time.'

'But you haven't told us how the investigation's going! Surely you must've learned something concrete by now.'

There wasn't any reason not to tell her, quite the contrary, because if there was something screwy somewhere – and the feeling in my bones told me there was – starting up a decoy hare wouldn't go amiss. 'The chances are that Titus Vecilius did it,' I said. 'Hermia's husband. Certainly he had the best motive and opportunity.' I was watching her face for a telltale sign of relief. Not a flicker. But there again she'd taken the accusation of an affair with Poetelius in her stride, so that might mean nothing.

'There you are,' Annius said. 'I told you, dear. An open-and-shut case.'

'Uh-uh.' I shook my head. 'There's the little matter of proof. Not to mention a few loose ends flapping around.'

'Such as what?' Annius again, and it was snapped.

Such as the possibility that he, or his sister, or Poetelius was responsible, or any combination thereof. Not that I could say that out loud, of course. I went for safer ground. 'The business in Ostia, for a start. Oh, sure, the chances are that it was a straightforward accident, but—'

Annius was giving me a blank look. 'What business in Ostia?' he said.

'I didn't tell you, Quintus,' Annia said. 'It happened on the quayside three days before Gaius died. A crane dropped its load when he was practically underneath it.'

Her brother grunted. 'It doesn't sound too suspicious to me,' he said. 'Accidents like that do happen occasionally at the docks, and it's not always the stevedore who's at fault. Gaius was probably just not looking where he was going.'

'Yeah. Yeah, right,' I said. 'Still, as I say, it's a loose end to be checked.'

'Surely that's not necessary now,' Annia said. 'After all, if you're practically certain that Gaius's mistress's husband killed him then—'

I shrugged. 'Maybe not. But me, I like to tick all the boxes.' I
set the empty wine-cup on the chair. 'Thanks again, lady.
I'll keep in touch.'

My brain was buzzing as I left. I'd planned to take the long
hike to the Emporium straight away to check Poetelius's story
with Titus Vibius, but first a stopoff at a convenient wineshop
for a leisurely think seemed in order. I found a new one I
hadn't tried before near the Temple of Honour and Virtue –
trendy, with a suspiciously pricey wine list and a chichi snack
menu, but there you went – ordered a cup of Massic, and
settled down at one of the outside tables.

OK. Annia. As a suspect, the cool, calm, and collected
widow was definitely showing form. If she and Poetelius were
an item, which despite the lady's protestations and his was
still a possibility, then they had motive in spades, plus – now
that I knew that Poetelius had been in the neighbourhood the
day of the murder – opportunity as well. The big problem was
if, because possibility or not they'd both struck me as pretty
much on the level: both had seemed genuinely surprised at
the suggestion and denied the relationship flat, Poetelius had
been inches away from handing me my teeth in a bag, and
Annia had just laughed it off. Sure, it could've been an act
– when a husband gets stiffed, the obvious first suspects are
the wife and a lover, and they'd know that – but if so it was
a damn good one. On the other hand, conditions for an affair
developing were ideal. On Poetelius's side, as far as I knew
he was unattached, he'd obviously been in the running as a
possible fiancé, and the chances were that his feelings for
Annia still went way past friendship. Added to which, he
clearly had no liking or respect for his partner either on a
personal or a business level. On her side, she was locked in
a loveless marriage with no exit clause and an unfaithful
husband who wouldn't care what the hell she got up to so
long as she paid the bills at the end of the month.

The other tick in the credit column for an affair existing
– despite Annia's claim to the contrary – was Marcia. Like
I'd said, she'd no reason to make the story up; she'd told me
– and I believed her – that she didn't know who'd sent the

anonymous letter, and I'd got the impression that she didn't care, either. Certainly, she'd no spiteful feelings against Tullius's wife; the only person she blamed was herself for getting involved with the guy in the first place. And Annia's confession was just too slick. The letter might've prompted Marcia to invent a non-existent affair, sure, but more importantly what it'd certainly done was let the cat out of the bag where the two cuckolded husbands were concerned. If Annia had wanted Tullius killed by proxy, like my friend the barfly had suggested, or to set up a fall guy to take the rap for a crime she and her lover were planning to commit, she couldn't've staged things better.

Yeah, I could go for that pair, myself. I never did trust squeaky-clean, and Annia and Poetelius were certainly that.

The brother, now. Quintus Annius . . .

Annius was puzzling: I just didn't get Quintus Annius at all. On the one hand, barring an altruistic collusion with his sister to rid her of an unwanted husband, the guy had no motive for killing Tullius whatsoever. Or not one I knew about or could guess at, anyway. And brotherly devotion doesn't usually extend to helping out with a murder. In terms of pure common sense, Quintus Annius was a complete non-runner. There again, my gut feeling was that he was a wrong 'un somewhere along the line. Perilla would've slagged me off for even suggesting he was involved, sure, and she'd probably be right. But still—

I'd been ignoring the wine. Now I took a long swallow. Not bad after all; it might even be worth its inflated price. Trendy or not, I'd have to remember this place. If it lasted much more than five minutes, mind. That's the trouble with these designer wineshops: they spring up like mushrooms and when the fashion they cater for has gone they fold just as quickly. The edge of Circus Valley isn't exactly Young Upwardly Mobile country, either, so I'd be surprised if they had a regular clientele.

Ostia. That'd been odd, if you like. I'd only mentioned it for something to say and to get myself out of an embarrassing hole; the case had moved on since Annia had told me about the incident at the docks, and to tell you the truth I'd considered ignoring it, or at least putting the trip off indefinitely. Purely for selfish reasons: I'm no horseman, and a journey to Rome's port is almost thirty miles, there and back, probably with an overnight stay involved if the business took more than a couple of hours. Which, to be fair, with luck it might not, under the circumstances. I was glad that Lippillus hadn't pushed me re Marilla's Ostian businessman; interesting though the circumstances of Marcus Correllius's death – stabbing, whatever – had been, I just didn't need the complication at present. And if Marilla had got even a whiff of the notion that her pet personal murder case hadn't quite been shelved after all, she'd've pestered me to death to follow it up. Oh, sure, going down to Ostia would give me an excuse to shoot the breeze over a jug with my pal Agron, which didn't happen all that often, and no doubt he and his wife, Cass, would've arranged a bed for me, but thirty miles on the back of a horse isn't my idea of fun. Plus, like Annius had said, the business with the falling amphoras would probably turn out to be a run-of-the-mill, straightforward accident with no sinister connotations . . .

Only now, thinking back on the interview, if I was honest with myself I wasn't at all sure about that. Again, it was a gut feeling, with nothing particularly concrete to back it up: the mention of Ostia had touched a nerve somewhere, I'd swear to that. Which was strange, because again unless he was a damn good actor Gaius Tullius's nearly getting flattened had come as news to Annius, while if his sister didn't want me sticking my nose into the business's whys and wherefores then why the hell had she mentioned it in the first place?

It didn't make sense. But what it did mean was that I was going to make a trip to Ostia a priority after all.

I finished the wine and pressed on to Trigemina Gate Street. Well, if nothing else I was getting plenty of exercise this time around.

Vibius was at the pottery, talking to the guy who'd given me his address two days before. His eyes widened when he saw me.

'Corvinus, wasn't it?' he said. 'I'm sorry, as far as Gaius Tullius goes I've told you all I know.'

'It's not about him,' I said. 'Or not directly, anyway. I just wanted to check something. It won't take long.'

He turned back to the older guy. 'That's fine, Sextus. Tell Nomentanus delivery by the end of the month should be no problem.' The foreman left. 'Now, Corvinus, we'll go into the office. It'll be quieter in there.'

'Sure.' I followed him through the workshop to a small room at the back, with the usual desk and cubbyholes for the paperwork. He closed the door behind him.

'So how can I help you this time?'

'Publius Poetelius came to see you the day of the murder, is that right?'

He frowned. 'When would that be again, exactly?'

'Six days ago. On the Ides.'

'Then yes, he did.'

'You care to tell me why?'

'To ask if I'd be willing to act as the firm's supplier again. Seemingly his partner had had a major argument with Titus Vecilius and the contract wasn't likely to be fulfilled.'

'You agreed?'

'Of course I did. I'd no time for Tullius, as you know, but business is business, and like I said, it was a big order, and a regular one. So long as the man himself didn't put his face round my door in future – which was the first and only condition I made – I was happy to take it on. And I owed Poetelius a great deal, so it wasn't as difficult a decision to make as it might've been otherwise.' He gave me a straight look. 'What's this all about? You surely don't think that he'd anything to do with Tullius's death, do you? Because if so you're completely wrong.'

'No,' I said easily. 'No, I'm just checking, like I said. Uh . . . "owed"? Owed in what way?'

'I told you. When I lost the contract I'd my back squarely to the wall. Poetelius lent me some money, interest-free; not a lot, because he hasn't got it to spare, only a thousand or two, but it made servicing the debt to the money-lender and paying back the principal over time just the right side of possible. Without it, I'd've gone under in three months.'

'His own money? Not the firm's?'

'Oh, yes. He was very clear about that. Tullius knew nothing about it, and he wouldn't know, either. I paid Poetelius back as soon as I could, which was just about a month ago, but debts can be more than money, can't they?'

'Yeah,' I said. 'Yeah, they can.' I put my hand on the door knob. 'Well, thanks again, pal. And don't worry: you've probably seen the last of me this time.'

I was half out of the door when he called me back.

'Corvinus?'

I turned round. 'Yeah?'

'Wait. I can't let you go without telling you how much of a bastard Tullius was. Just so as you're clear about it.'

I went back in and closed the door behind me. 'Oh, I think I've got that pretty clear in my mind already,' I said.

He shook his head. 'No, you haven't. Or not clear enough. I told you my wife was dead; I didn't say how or why she died. She killed herself, just over a year ago. Two days before the contract was due for renewal.'

I said nothing, but I had a fair idea of what was coming. Score one for Perilla.

Vibius had turned his face away. 'Paullina was a good bit younger than me,' he said, 'and she was a looker. Or at least I thought so. Before she died she left a note on my chair, where I'd be sure to see it, saying that Gaius Tullius had been trying to seduce her for months. Finally, he'd offered her a trade: a new contract in exchange for a single . . . Well, you have the idea. She knew how important not losing the order was to me, so she agreed. Afterwards, Tullius told her that wasn't enough, she'd have to throw in our daughter as well, as a sweetener to the deal. He said to go away and think about it. She hanged herself that night.' He turned round again to face me and smiled. 'So you see, Corvinus, I've every reason to hope the bastard is burning in hell. And that you'll never catch the person who killed him.'

I got back home well in time for dinner, to find, when I walked into the atrium with my usual wine-cup, that from the look on Marilla's face I'd been seriously Waited For. As far as she was concerned, anyway. Not that there was anything at all wrong with that, in my view, quite the reverse: me, I'd've said that the Princess's interest in working out the whys and where-fores of a murder and fingering the perp was a pretty healthy sign in a young woman.

Perilla, now . . . well, for some strange, unaccountable reason she can be funny about these things. Sometimes I don't understand the way that lady's mind works at all.

Apropos of which, I wondered from the current vibes whether there hadn't just been a slight clash of personalities here. Clarus was toying with a cup of something probably non-alcoholic – like I say, he's no wine-drinker, Clarus – and looking a tad embarrassed as if he'd rather be somewhere else, while Perilla's attention seemed to be fixed on young Marcus Junior, currently lying face-up on the floor between her couch and Marilla's and Clarus's and trying his determined best to roll over onto his front.

'Hi, Corvinus.' Marilla was grinning at me. 'Have a good day?'

'Not bad.' I bent over to give Perilla the usual welcome-home kiss: frosty, distinctly frosty. 'How was yours, Princess?'

'OK. So. How's the investigation going? Did you talk to the two wives?'

I took my wine over to my usual couch and lay down. Opposite, the lady cleared her throat slightly, her eyes still on the Sprog. Her lips were pursed, but she didn't say anything. I grinned to myself: yeah, well, if there had been a personality clash it was clear who'd come out on top here. She's no pushover, young Marilla.

'Yeah. Among other things,' I said. I gave her the rundown of the day's activities, glancing at Perilla now and again. Frost or not, her ears were twitching. I grinned again: sometimes the lady is her own worst enemy, if she'd only realize it.

'So it's still an open field,' I finished. 'Leaving Vecilius aside, it's looking promising for Annia and A. N. Other, prob-ably Poetelius, but I'd take side bets on Quintus Annius, the gods know why. Vibius is in there too, now. That last bit about his wife sounded pretty close to self-justification, because he'd no cause to tell me how she died off his own bat. At the very least, he couldn't've made it plainer that he was glad to see Tullius dead and that all his sympathies were with the killer.'

Perilla was still watching the Sprog doing his rolling-about act.

'Do you think that's good for him, Clarus?' she said. 'Or should I give him a hand?'

'No, he's fine,' Clarus said. 'Leave him to it; he needs the exercise. And they all do that at his age.'

'If you're sure, dear.' She looked doubtful.

Uh-huh. Well, at least she was talking, if not to me or Marilla. And I noticed that Clarus was still keeping his head diplomatically below the parapet. I sympathized: neither lady was one to cross, and he'd probably been getting it from both sides recently. When that happens, you lie low and say nothing. Clarus was certainly learning fast.

'So how would it work, Corvinus?' Marilla said. 'In practical terms, I mean.'

'You want the odds?' I said.

'Yes, please. Just to be clear.'

'OK. Like I said, Annius is the least likely. Until we get a sniff of a genuine motive, at any rate. He and his sister are obviously very close, so if she did confide in anyone that she wanted rid of her husband he'd be first in the queue.'

'Assuming there's nothing between her and Poetelius.'

'Right. Unfortunately, that's as far as it goes. Otherwise, at present he's a non-starter. He may be a cold-hearted bastard' ('Marcus, *please!*' from Perilla; I ignored her) 'who wouldn't fight shy of murder – at least, I don't think he would – but he didn't have any connection with Tullius, either socially or business-wise, so—'

'Hang on! You don't know that for certain.'

'Yeah, I do. Poetelius confirmed it, and if Poetelius isn't A. N. Other, then what he says has weight.'

'Fair enough. But he is in business himself, and Tullius was his brother-in-law. And as far as "socially" is concerned, if he and Annia were in it together then it'd be easy to cover up any compromising details.' Marilla grinned. 'I'm just playing devil's advocate here, you understand.'

'OK. All that's true enough. But the bottom line is we've got nothing concrete on the guy. Poetelius, now, he's a lot more likely. He's got a motive, both personal – given the existence of the affair with Annia – and financial, and he's also got opportunity, because he was definitely in the area when the murder happened.'

'Oh, come on! He'd a good reason for being there!'

'I'm not so sure about that. At least, not of the reason he gave.'

'But Vibius confirmed it. He was there on business.'

'Look, Marilla, Vibius owes Poetelius for the fact that he's not short one pottery and signing on for the corn dole, OK? Plus the fact that he hated Tullius's guts for seducing his wife and driving her to suicide. Given the choice between confirming the guy's story and sending him up the creek without a paddle, which way do you think he'd jump?'

'Yes, well, if you put it like that, I suppose . . .' Marilla frowned.

'It still wouldn't explain how he engineered the opportunity, though, would it, Marcus?' Perilla said.

Hey! I turned towards her. 'How do you mean, lady?' I said.

'Poetelius couldn't have known that his partner would be in Trigemina Gate Street that day. It was a holiday, the office was closed. Oh, yes, as he said he had his reasons for going there himself. But Tullius didn't, or not as far as he was aware.'

Yeah; fair point. That had been bugging me, too. Sure, Tullius had called in on Hermia, that was certain. But it just didn't square that any erstwhile lover with a grain of common sense would deliberately plan a visit the day after the lady's husband had gone looking for him with a meat cleaver, nor that said lady would suggest it to him. A seized opportunity – straight in and straight out – while he was already in the neighbourhood for compelling and unrelated reasons, now, that might be another thing again. At least for a guy like Tullius. Which left the problem of the compelling reasons. If not to try it on with Hermia, then why the hell *had* he been there?

'It could've been coincidence,' I said. 'They could just have bumped into each other.'

'Marcus, do you honestly—?' There was a howl from the Sprog, who'd suddenly and spectacularly managed to flip

himself over and found he was face down on the mosaic tiling.
'Oh, my!'

Marilla got off her couch. 'Don't worry,' she said. 'It happens
every time. He's perfectly all right.'

She scooped him up and calmed him down, cradling him
against her shoulder and walking him around the room until
comparative peace was restored.

Well, the kid had a good pair of lungs, anyway.

'Sorry, lady, you were saying,' I said.

'Do you really believe that they could've met by accident,
dear?' Perilla said. 'Personally I would have thought that unless
the killer is Vecilius after all, everything points to the murder
having been planned.'

Hell. She was right; I didn't believe it, and it had been.
Planned right down to the last detail. Forget Vecilius, it was
far more complicated than that. Tullius had been suckered into
a meeting, he'd called in first at Hermia's and then gone on
to Melobosis's shrine, where whoever the killer was had knifed
him.

Maybe.

'All right,' I said. 'Then Poetelius could've arranged the
meeting himself.'

'Why should he?' Perilla said. 'They saw each other in the
office every day. Tullius would scarcely be persona grata in
any negotiations involving Vibius, and he'd have to be a
complete fool to think otherwise. Besides, as I said, it was
supposed to be a holiday. Poetelius couldn't possibly have
invented an excuse that Tullius would believe for one second.'

I sighed. True, all of it. Unless there was something I was
missing, which was perfectly possible. I took a morose slug
of wine.

'So what's the next step, Corvinus?' Marilla had settled
down on the couch again with the still-grizzling young Marcus.
'What're you going to do now?'

I hesitated. Bugger. Well, it had to be done. 'Actually,
Princess, I thought I might go down to Ostia tomorrow,' I said.
'Check out the—'

'*Ostia?* Great! While you're there you can—'

'No I can't,' I said firmly. 'Definitely not. Forget it, right?

The only reason I'm going to Ostia – the *only* reason, read my lips here – is to check out this business of the falling amphoras. Straight in, straight out, or as close to it as I can manage. Understand?'

'But surely if you're going there in any case—'

'No. That's final. As it is, the whole thing's probably a wild-goose chase. All it has going for it is that when I mentioned the place in front of Annia and her brother the idea of me going there went down like finding a slug in a salad. Like I say, it shouldn't take long because I've got the number of the quay where the accident happened.'

'Poetelius told you that, didn't he, Marcus?' Perilla was looking pensive.

I turned to her. 'Yeah. So?'

'It's just that surely it militates against him being the killer, doesn't it?'

I frowned. Bugger, she was right again: the fact that it'd been Poetelius who'd told me was relevant. In fact, it was crucial. If there was something screwy about the business with the amphoras and Poetelius was our man, then he'd be a fool to put me in the way of finding out what it was. Unless he was playing the innocent deliberately, of course, because I would've found out eventually and then he'd be in deep trouble. But then it'd been Annia who'd mentioned the accident unprompted in the first place, and if the two of them were in this together . . .

Ah, hell, it was just complication on complication, and nothing made sense anyway.

I'd just have to play it by ear. Leave it. We'd just have to wait and see what tomorrow brought.

ELEVEN

I left for Ostia at first light, and got there just after mid-morning, dropping in at Agron's cart-building yard first to say I was there, arrange to meet him in a wineshop I knew by the docks later on, and cadge a bed for the night if it proved necessary. Not that I hoped it would: Agron and Cass's first-floor tenement flat is pretty spacious as these things go, but with five hyperactive and very loud kids in the family however they fixed it it wasn't something I was looking forward to. I left the mare in the stables next door to rest up for what would hopefully be a one-day round trip and set off on foot for the main harbour and dockland area, just outside of town beyond the Tiber Gate.

OK. So first port of call, as it were, the harbour master's office, to check that Poetelius hadn't been spinning me a line on the basic whys and wherefores. They'd keep detailed records; certainly, they'd be able to point me in the right direction. I found it, went inside, explained what I wanted and was referred to a sharp-looking freedman at a desk in the far corner.

'Yes, sir,' he said. 'What can I do for you?'

'Just some information, pal,' I said. 'First off, about a ship called the *Circe* that was berthed at Quay Twenty-five A ten days ago.'

He smiled. 'That shouldn't be a problem, sir. If you'll just excuse me for a moment, I'll go and check.' He went off. I kicked my heels for two or three minutes until he came back with a hinged set of beechwood flimsies. 'Here you are, sir, the *Circe*. Thousand-amphora size, mixed cargo, largely domestic ware, pottery and glass, bound for Syracuse. Leaving the same day.'

'Yeah. Yeah, that's the one.' OK; so far so good. At least that checked. 'I understand there was an accident on the quay-side. A crane slipping its load.'

He frowned and consulted the flimsies again. 'No record of that, I'm afraid.'

'Would there be?'

'Of course. We're very careful about recording accidents, particularly where the loading and unloading of cargo's involved. The ship's captain would've lodged a claim with the quay-master, and he would've submitted a report. He hasn't, in this instance, so unless it was very minor and no damage or injury was involved no such accident occurred. Certainly a dropped load would've merited one.'

'You're sure?' He just looked at me. 'OK. So maybe it was elsewhere on the quay, connected with a ship at another berth. That possible?'

'It might be.' He turned over a leaf of the flimsies. 'There was one other ship, the *Porpoise*, at Twenty-five B. Cargo of wine and olive oil, bound for Aleria.'

'Wine and oil, right? That'd fit. The accident involved some dropped amphoras.'

'Perhaps so, sir, but there's no accident report attached.'

'Nothing else was berthed at that quay?'

'No. Not on the day in question, at least. You're sure you have the correct date?'

'Yeah. Absolutely certain.' Shit. This didn't make sense. 'You mentioned a quay-master. Could I talk to him myself, do you think?'

'Of course, if you like.' His tone implied that it'd be a waste of everyone's time. 'His name's Arrius. He's in charge of quays twenty to twenty-five, so you'll find him at one of them, no doubt. But really, I don't think he'll be able to tell you any more than I have.'

'Thanks,' I said, and left.

I found him chatting to a couple of stevedores on Quay Twenty-three.

'Your name Arrius, pal?' I said. 'The quay-master?'

'Right on both counts, sir.' He nodded to the stevedores, who drifted off. 'How can I help you?'

'I was told there was an accident ten days back on Quay Twenty-five.'

He shook his head. 'Nah. You've been misinformed. What kind of accident?'

'Involving a netful of amphoras dropped from a crane.'

'Nothing like that, no. Absolutely not.'

'You're sure?'

'Certain sure.' I must've looked doubtful, because he said patiently: 'See here, sir. My lads are responsible for the cargos until they're safely on board, right? Unless the shipper decides to use his own men, in which case the responsibility's his. If one of my lot had dropped so much as a wine flask on the quayside, five minutes later the ship's master or the owner or whoever was supervising the transfer would've been round at me screaming blue murder and demanding compensation, and quite rightly so. A whole netful of amphoras, now, well, I'd remember that no bother, wouldn't I? And it wouldn't matter who did the loading, the accident report would go in all the same.'

Hell. 'Fine, pal. Uh . . . just out of interest, who would've been the crane operator that day? You got a name for him?'

'Let's see, now.' He frowned, thinking. 'Quay Twenty-five, ten days ago, you say? You're sure that's right?'

'Uh-huh.'

'Then that'd be the *Circe* and the *Porpoise*. No, I tell a lie; the *Circe* had already been loaded the day before. She was just waiting to sail. The *Porpoise*, now, she used her own loaders. But the crane operator himself was one of ours, sure enough. More's the pity.' He chuckled. 'Name of Gaius Siddius. I'll grant you this much, sir, if anyone was likely to mess up on the loading – which, take my word for it, no one did – it'd be that dozy bugger.'

'Great! You think I could talk to him?'

'Nah. He doesn't work here any more.'

'Since when?'

'Since the following day, as a matter of fact. He turned up for work pissed as a newt – this at first light, mind! – so I sacked him on the spot. It wasn't the first time, either, so he couldn't complain.'

'You know where he lives?'

'Haven't the foggiest.'

'It's not possible that he could've covered things up, is it? I mean, if he somehow managed to square it with the captain?'

The quay-master laughed. 'Look, sir,' he said. 'Your average ship's captain isn't too forgiving when some dozy bastard of a crane-man writes off part of their cargo. And if Siddius had dropped a load of amphoras on the quayside, the damage would've amounted to more than he earned in a month. They'd be filled with wine or oil, right?'

'One or the other, yeah. So the clerk in the harbour office said, anyway.'

'There you go, then. And if it was the *Porpoise*, Siddius's chances of getting himself off the hook'd be zilch. Captain's a man by the name of Nigrinus, and he's the meanest-minded bugger in the trade. Plus if we're talking spilled oil or wine the quay would be swimming with the stuff. Me, I'm round there three or four times a day, just to check everything's as it should be, and believe me something like that I'd've spotted straight off, even if he'd tried to clean it up. So your answer, sir, is no. There was no accident that day, I'd stake my reputation on it.'

I thanked him, and left.

Shit!

The wineshop where I'd arranged to meet Agron was right by the Tiber Gate. Nothing special from the outside, nor on the inside, either, to tell the truth – with that location it catered almost exclusively for dockhands and the like, and those guys don't go much for the frills – but it sold a very decent Massic and the owner was a cheese-lover like Agron, so it suited both of us.

I was early, but not early enough to put off ordering. Besides, if I'd waited Agron would've insisted on picking up the bill. So I went up to the counter and asked for a jug of Massic and two cups.

'What's your best cheese today, pal?' I said while the landlord was filling the jug.

'I've just got a very nice sheep's one in, sir,' he said. 'Fidenan. Not one of your classy names, but none the worse for that.'

'Fine. Give us a double portion.' I thought for a moment. 'No, make that a triple. And some olives, bread, and sausage. Two lots of those'll be enough.' The olives and sausage were mainly for me; Agron would account for most of the cheese, which was fair because he wouldn't make too much of a dent in the Massic.

The wineshop door opened, but it wasn't Agron, just a guy with the look of a stevedore. The build and muscles, too. I turned back to the counter, laid some coins down, and picked up the jug and the two cups to take them to one of the side tables.

The big guy moved towards the bar. There was plenty of room to pass, but as we drew level he deliberately lurched sideways. His shoulder caught mine. It was like colliding with a bullock, and I spun round, spilling half the wine.

'Jupiter, pal, watch where you're going, right?' I said to his back.

He stopped and turned. He gave me a long stare. Then he grinned.

'Is there a problem, friend?' he said.

Uh-oh. Without taking my eyes off him, I set the wine jug and cups down slowly on the nearest table and straightened.

'Because if so,' he went on, 'then you know what you can fucking do about it.'

He took a step towards me and raised his fist, just as the door opened a second time. I steadied myself.

'Having trouble, Corvinus?'

I risked a quick glance over my shoulder. Agron was standing there, frowning. He's a big lad, Agron, and he filled most of the doorway. Then I looked back at chummie. He lowered his fist, and I relaxed.

'Just a little accident,' I said. 'No harm done.'

Agron's eyes never left the stevedore's. 'So long as you're sure,' he said evenly. 'That's OK.'

Chummie pushed past me, heading for the door. After the barest hesitation, Agron stepped aside to let him through.

Yeah, well, we'd certainly caught the attention of the rest of the punters. You could've heard a pin drop as I picked up the cups and half-empty wine jug and went back to the bar.

'Fill it up again, would you?' I said to the landlord. He took the jug without a word, filled it, and handed it back.

'On the house,' he said.

I nodded. 'Thanks.'

'So.' Agron was standing beside me. 'What was that all about?'

'Search me.' I filled one of the cups and drank. 'I'd never set eyes on the guy until two minutes ago. Who was he?' I asked the owner.

'Name of Nigrinus.' The landlord set the plate of cheese, sausage, and olives on the counter and added a hunk of bread. 'Sextus Nigrinus. He and his brother've been in here a few times, but I don't encourage either of them. They're both bad lots.'

'Nigrinus?' I said sharply. 'Connected with the *Porpoise*?'

'Yeah. The brother is, anyway. Titus. He's the captain. You know him?'

'No, we've never met. I've just heard the name.'

'Sextus is no sailor. The two of them used to work the *Porpoise* together, but he throws up in a flat calm. Now he takes what jobs he can at the docks. I'm sorry about that, sir. We don't have trouble like that in here, usually.'

'Forget it, pal,' I said. 'Not your fault.' I picked up the jug and my own wine-cup and carried them to the table I'd originally been heading for. Agron followed with the rest of the stuff.

'OK, Marcus,' he said when we'd got settled. 'So what *is* going on?'

'Just a case,' I said. 'It's complicated.' Jupiter! If there was no accident with the amphoras – and the quay-master had been pretty certain that there hadn't been – then how did the *Porpoise* fit into this? Not to mention why and how I'd been so conveniently and rapidly targeted. Because that was what had just happened. It couldn't be a coincidence; no way could it be a coincidence. 'And it's getting more complicated by the minute. Don't ask. Just don't.'

'Fine.' Agron filled his cup and took a bit of the cheese. 'Even so, if you need any help—'

'Actually, pal, there is something you can do, if you will.'

I took a swallow of wine. 'I need to talk to a guy named Siddius. Gaius Siddius. Up to nine days ago, he worked as a dockside crane-man, but he was sacked for being drunk and the quay-master didn't have an address. You think you can trace him for me?'

Agron shrugged. 'I can try, sure. That's all you have to go on?'

'That's it.'

'Then it won't be easy. But I can put the word out. If he lives locally – which he probably does if he's a dockhand – one of my dockyard mates might know him. There again, if he's a crane-man, not just your usual unskilled labourer, and he's taken another job, the possibilities are limited.'

'He's not particularly skilled. Not from what the quay-master told me.'

'In that case, he could be anywhere.' He took another slice of cheese. 'Never mind, leave it with me and I'll do my best. It'll take time, sure, but if I can find him I'll get in touch.'

'Great. Now just forget it for now, OK, pal? The case can wait, and I reckon my brain deserves a break.' I refilled the wine-cups. 'How are Cass and the kids?'

We batted it around for a bit, until the wine and nibbles gave out; like I say, I don't see much of Agron usually, except when Cass bullies him into a shopping trip to the big city and we put them up. Finally . . .

'You want the other half?' I said, holding up the empty jug.

He shook his head. 'Some of us have work to do. You staying over?'

I grinned: like I say, although Agron and Cass had a pretty big flat, as those things go, and I'd be made very welcome, overnighting with five young and very voluble kids in close proximity isn't my idea of fun.

'No, that's OK, thanks,' I said. 'I'll be getting back.'

'Fair enough.' He stood up. 'We'll call it a day, then. You left your horse in the stables next to my yard, right?'

'Yeah. But I've got another bit of business to see to first. You go ahead.'

'Regards to Perilla and the youngsters. And I won't forget about this Gaius Siddius.'

'Sure. Thanks, Agron.'

He left.

OK; so back to the harbour office. If that run-in with Sextus Nigrinus had been no accident – which it hadn't – then his brother and the *Porpoise* figured somewhere along the line. Whereabouts and how, let alone why, I'd no idea, but six got you ten there was some connection. Certainly I couldn't leave Ostia without following the thing up as far as I could.

'Good afternoon, sir.' The freedman clerk I'd talked to earlier smiled at me. 'Did you find Arrius?'

'Yeah, no problem, pal,' I said.

'And he confirmed what I told you about no accident being reported?'

'Yeah.'

'So. How can I help you this time?'

'That other ship you mentioned berthed at Quay Twenty-five. The *Porpoise*.'

'Yes, sir.'

'The captain's name is Titus Nigrinus, right?'

'Just a moment and I'll fetch the appropriate record. Ten days ago, wasn't it?'

'That's right.' I waited until he came back with the flimsy. 'Whose was the cargo?'

'Captain Titus Nigrinus, yes.' He ran his finger down the page. 'A single-owner shipment. Eight hundred amphoras, which would be the ship's full capacity. Five hundred of oil, three of wine. Belonging to a Marcus Correllius.'

'*What?*' I stared at him.

Shit!

TWELVE

I t was late when I got home, and Perilla had gone to bed. Bathyllus was still padding around, though, buffing up the brasses, and since I'd told him to have the furnace lit just in case I managed the trip in a oner, I was able to have a long, luxurious steam in the bath while he sweet-talked a tray-load of cold cuts out of Meton. The accompanying half jug of wine went in with me; after fourteen miles in the saddle on top of the previous fourteen, that was a priority.

Not that I was going to do much thinking while I sweated; I'd had plenty of time for that on the ride back, and it'd got me absolutely nowhere. However you sliced it, the business with the amphoras just didn't make sense. On the one hand, if it hadn't happened, like the quay-master was convinced it hadn't, then why had Tullius gone to the trouble of inventing it? Or, since the only evidence for it had come from Annia, why had she? And most important of all if it hadn't happened, then why – leaving aside the interesting question of how he'd known I was shoving my nose into things in the first place – should my wineshop pal Nigrinus tail me and try to beat my brains out?

So it must've happened. Only it couldn't have . . .

Then, of course, there was the matter of Correllius. That had been a facer, and no mistake, and it had come completely out of the blue. Like it or not – and Marilla would be crowing when she heard, I knew – the stabbing at the Pollio had become relevant with a vengeance. I'd have to look into the Correllius business after all.

Bugger!

Clearly, I wasn't just missing a few pieces of the puzzle; I'd hardly touched the surface. Worse, I couldn't even make out the overall picture any more. Ah, hell. We'd just have to see whether Agron came up with an address for this Siddius guy. Meanwhile, I reckoned another talk with Annia was in order. Plus, of course, a visit to Decimus Lippillus in Tuscan Street for an update on the Correllius case. If he had anything new at all, that was.

Bathyllus had laid the cold cuts and sundries out on the dining-room table for me, but after the bath and the wine I was too knackered to eat them. I dragged my still-stiff-and-saddle-sore carcase up to bed and crashed out.

The bath must've done some good, mind, because although I was late up the next morning – even later than Perilla, let alone the kids, who were long gone on their day's junketing by the time I surfaced – I wasn't suffering too many ill effects. I had a good breakfast, brought the lady up to date with things as far as that was possible, particularly re the Correllius business, and set out for Ardeatina Gate Street . . .

Or at least I started to.

I was just in time to see the sign-painter who'd been working on next door's garden wall pack up his paint pot, brushes, and ladder. He gave me a friendly nod and went off whistling down the street.

Odd. It wasn't election time, nor were we on the main drag where graffiti artists use your property as a billboard to tell the world about their current loves and hates. Besides, these bastards usually work unsocial hours. There hadn't been anything clandestine about this guy; quite the reverse.

Just out of curiosity, I went over to see what he'd been writing. In letters two feet high, the inscription read:

MY NEXT-DOOR NEIGHBOUR IS A CAT-KILLER

Oh, shit. I went back inside and through to the dining room, where Perilla was just spreading her third roll with honey.

'I'm afraid the, uh, feud with the Petillius household seems to have racked up another notch, lady,' I said.

She looked up, startled.

'What?'

I told her.

'But that's ridiculous! Can he do that?'

I shrugged. 'It's his wall.'

'It's also defamation.'

'Sure it is. On the other hand, if I go down to the city judge's office and bring an action, I'm going to look pretty silly, aren't I? Leaving aside the fact that to take the bugger to court would be a declaration of out-and-out war.'

'So what do we do?'

'What can we do? Send Bathyllus out under cover of darkness with a brush and a bucket of whitewash? That'd be almost as bad, especially if he got caught.'

'The whole thing's just silly!'

I sighed. 'Yeah. No arguments there. But you know Petillius and Tyndaris; they aren't rational. Me, I'd be inclined just to ignore it, let things blow over.' I kissed her. 'Anyway, I've got other fish to fry at present. I'll see you later.'

It was raining slightly when I came back out: May in Rome can be a pretty unsettled month, and although we'd been lucky so far there'd been some wet days earlier on. Still, it wasn't too bad, and although Ardeatina Gate Street was a fair hike I reckoned I'd do well enough with my ordinary cloak. As it was, by the time I'd reached the edge of the Caelian ridge and was on the downhill slope towards the Metrovian Gate the sky had cleared and the sun was out again. Good walking weather.

I knocked on Annia's door and the door-slave took me through to where the lady was sitting in the atrium. She was alone: no brother this time, which made a pleasant change.

'Back again, Corvinus?' she said. 'I understood you were going down to Ostia.'

I pulled up a stool and sat down. 'Yeah. Yeah, I was. I did, yesterday.'

'And?'

'Funny thing, that. According to the quay-master in charge of the wharf where your husband was supervising that shipment that day there was no accident at all.'

She frowned. 'That's nonsense! There must've been!'

I'd deliberately hit her with it point-blank, and the puzzled look on her face seemed genuine enough. Even so—

'He's absolutely certain,' I said. 'And, believe me, lady, if there had been then he'd've known. These things all get reported, seemingly.'

'But Gaius told me distinctly! He wouldn't've made something like that up. I mean, why should he?'

'Right,' I said. 'It's an oddity. You care to go over again just what your husband said? Exactly, word for word, if you can.'

'If you want me to.' She took a moment to think. 'He said he was walking along the quay towards the bit at the end where the ship carrying his cargo was berthed. While he was about to pass another ship that was being loaded the crane that was doing it dropped a netful of amphoras right in front of him. I said something fatuous like, "Good heavens, you might've been killed!" and he laughed and said, "No, I was just lucky, that's all." And then he changed the subject and asked me how my day had been.'

I played the words back in my head, but they still didn't make sense.

'Hang on, lady,' I said. 'He said, "No". You're sure about that? "No", not "Yes"?'

'That's right. "No, I was just lucky". I remember thinking was a bit strange at the time, but it was clear what he meant.'

Strange was right, and the more you thought about it the stranger it got. I filed the problem for later reference. 'The chances are that the other ship was called the *Porpoise*. Ring any bells?'

'No.'

'How about the name Nigrinus?'

'No, I've never heard of him. Who's Nigrinus?'

'The *Porpoise*'s captain. It doesn't matter. How about Correllius? Marcus Correllius?' She shook her head. Again, there hadn't been the slightest twitch of an eyelid. 'Fair enough. Leave it. Another strange thing. Your husband's partner, Poetelius. He told me he didn't know anything about the incident.'

'Did he?' Annia didn't sound too surprised, or indeed interested. 'Well, that's no great wonder. Gaius and Publius didn't have very much to say to each other outside actual business, from what I understood.' She got up. 'But I'm being inhospitable, Corvinus. I'll have Timon bring you a cup of wine.'

'No, that's OK, lady.' I got up too. 'I only dropped in. I have to be getting on.'

I needed to think.

I might as well go over to Tuscan Street, while I was at it, see if Lippillus was around. That meant going back up Ardeatina, cutting left onto the Appian Road, then along the Palatine side of the Racetrack. Which was what I started to do.

There'd been another change in the weather, very much for the worse; black clouds were moving in from the west, and the first drops of rain were falling. Big ones, too. Bugger. The detour was possibly a mistake after all: the centre was a long way off, and this wasn't good wineshop country. I wrapped myself in my cloak and headed as fast as I could towards the Appian junction.

Five minutes later, the heavens opened good and proper and the rain came battering down as if Jupiter had opened the celestial stopcock as far as it would go. What pedestrians there were – and there weren't many of them – were running for cover. The downpour wouldn't last, sure, but in the meantime I was getting soaked. There was a stonemason's yard just up ahead, with a roofed-over section for the carts. I put up the hood of my cloak and made a dash for it.

I wasn't alone. A punter behind me had obviously had the same idea, and we both reached it together. Once inside, I took off my waterlogged cloak to shake it out.

'Lucky this place was here, pal, right?' I said to the guy. 'Another couple of minutes and—'

Which was as far as I got before he went for me. I just managed to bring my cloak round before the knife he was holding drove at my stomach and the hood fell back from his face.

Nigrinus.

There was no time for niceties. It was a heavy cloak, made heavier by a couple of gallons of rainwater. When the knife went through it I threw myself to one side and let it fall over his arm, tangling round it in a sodden bundle, then piled in hard with my full weight while he was off-balance. We went over together, with me on top, and things got pretty busy for a while, mostly where I was concerned involving a desperate effort to keep the bastard's knife-arm immobile with my left hand while I tried to force his windpipe through the back of his neck with my right.

Not that I was having much success either way. The guy had muscles like rocks held together with steel cables, and he plainly wanted me dead. It was only a matter of time . . .

'Hey! What's going on there?'

I glanced up and round. A couple of seriously beefy guys – obviously the proprietor himself and one of his slaves – were coming towards us from further in in the yard. They were carrying hammers, and they didn't look happy. With a sudden effort, Nigrinus heaved me off and stood up. I thought he'd try to knife me again – I could see him thinking of it – but his hand and arm were still tangled with the cloak, and the guys with the hammers had broken into a run. He took to his heels.

'You all right, mate?' the proprietor said to me as I picked myself up.

'Sure. No permanent damage.' I looked towards the road, but Nigrinus was long gone. 'Thanks, pal. Things were getting pretty bad there for a minute.'

'What the hell happened?'

'Robber. After my purse. I caught him at it and he turned nasty.'

'A robber? In broad daylight?'

'Yeah, well. Maybe they work shifts.'

He gave me a nervous look. 'Uh . . . right. Right. Well, so long as you're OK that's all that matters. We'll be getting back to work.'

'Thanks again,' I said.

'Don't mention it,' the stonemason said.

They left, quickly.

Lippillus was at his desk, writing what was presumably a report. There was a stack of note tablets at his elbow. Yeah, well, he'd said he was snowed under at present. The joys of being a Watch Commander in the modern Watch.

'Oh, hello, Marcus,' he said absently. 'Be with you in a minute. How do you spell "concupiscent"?'

'I don't.'

'Fair enough. Pull up a stool.' He wrote on for another couple of minutes, then looked up.

His eyes widened.

'What the hell happened to you?' he said.

'A brush with a guy by the name of Sextus Nigrinus. Long story.'

'Part of the current case?'

'Yeah. Very much so, although how he fits in I don't know yet. He's an Ostian. At least, that's where he's based.'

'Is he, now?' Lippillus put the pen down. 'Interesting.'

'More interesting than you know, pal. It turns out that your Marcus Correllius was the person shipping the amphoras that nearly fell on top of my victim at the Ostia docks, three days before he was actually murdered.'

'*What?*'

I told him the story; at least, the relevant bits. 'You got any more information from your side?'

'Yeah, actually. I was going to send you it,' he said, 'but I thought there wasn't any real hurry. We've a witness to the stabbing after all, at least we probably have; a lady's maid by the name of Picentina. Mistress was occupied in the Danaid Porch, seemingly, and she'd sent the girl out into the garden while she got on with things.' Right; no prizes for guessing what the 'things' would entail: the Danaid Porch next to the Pollio is one of Rome's principal pick-up points, where your better class of would-be adulterers and adulteresses troll for prospective soul-mates. 'We got her through a complete fluke. The mistress had lost an earring in the Porch and she'd sent the girl to ask at the library desk if it'd been handed in. The freedman on duty was smart enough to check with her on our behalf whether she'd seen anything, and that was that. Not that I've had time to interview the girl properly yet.' He indicated the pile of note tablets. 'As you can see.'

'That's OK. I can do it for you, if you like. You got an address?'

'The mistress's name is Publilia Clementa. Married to a Turius Gratus, with a house not all that far from your place. On the edge of the Carinae, just past the Head of Africa junction with the Sacred Way.'

'Perfect,' I said. 'How about Correllius's address in Ostia?'

'You're going back over there?'

'Seems I'll have to now, doesn't it?' And for much longer, this time. Which meant bunking down for the duration on Agron's floor. Bugger!

'Fine. Like I said, the family property's on the Hinge, about halfway between the Market Square and the Laurentian Gate.'

'Got you,' I said. 'Family, you say?'

'According to Mercurius – that's the slave Correllius had with him, if you remember – he has a wife called Mamilia. That's all I've got, I'm afraid.'

'No problem. It'll do to be going on with, anyway.' I stood up. 'In the meantime, anything else and you know where to find me.'

'Sure,' Lippillus said. 'Good luck, Marcus.'

At least when I went back outside the weather had improved. Not that it mattered much: what with one thing and another, both my cloak and my tunic were pretty well sodden, and caked with mud into the bargain. Before I did anything else a complete change of clothes was called for.

I set off back to the Caelian.

THIRTEEN

'But how did he know?' Perilla asked when I told her about Nigrinus and we'd gone through the usual Oh-Marcus-you-could've-been-killed routine. Me, so long as I come out the other end of things with all my bits still in working order, I'm pretty good about being attacked. It shows I'm doing something right somewhere. Not that it's too pleasant at the time, mind. 'How to find you, I mean,' she added.

I'd changed out of the soaking, mud-stained tunic and was stretched out on the couch with a restorative cup of the Special. When he'd seen the condition my cloak was in – Nigrinus had dropped it when he ran, and it'd been lying in the gutter further up the street – Bathyllus had sniffed and consigned it to the rag-bag. A pity: I'd liked that cloak.

'Yeah, good question,' I said. I'd wondered about that myself. Seriously wondered. 'Oh, sure, the Ostia side of things could've been accidental. The guy works at the docks there, so it's just possible that he could've got wind of a nosey purple-striper from Rome asking awkward questions and trailed me to the wineshop. The business in Ardeatina Gate Street, though, that's a different thing altogether. He couldn't've tracked me there from Ostia off his own bat, no way.'

'You mean he was acting on instructions from someone in Rome.'

'And on information received. Yeah. It's the only logical explanation. It'd still be tricky, mind, and it'd involve some fancy footwork, but it's feasible. X in Rome – could be Annia, could be the brother, could be Poetelius, or a combination – knows I'm going to Ostia, and that the chances are I'll stumble across the connection with the *Porpoise*, which for reasons unknown they really, *really* don't want me to do. So they—'

'Hold on, Marcus! I'll allow you Annia and her brother, yes, but not Poetelius. He didn't know you intended going to Ostia at all.'

'Sure he did. Maybe not when, but he knew I knew about the accident, and he knew I'd be looking into it. That'd be enough. So X sends to Nigrinus, warning him that I'm coming, telling him to look out for me and to take appropriate action.'

'It still doesn't explain how this Nigrinus knew you'd be over at Ardeatina Gate Street this morning.'

I shrugged. 'I gave Annia my address right at the start, and either of the other two could've got it from her easily enough, even if she isn't involved herself. Given that X's instructions to Nigrinus were to follow things through at the Rome end if need be – which they must've been – that'd be all he'd need to be able to tail me. Then it'd just be a case of jumping me and finishing the job the first chance he got.'

'Do you think Annia *is* involved?'

Yeah, that was the question I'd been asking myself, and I still didn't have a definite answer.

'Lady, I don't know,' I said. 'On the one hand, for things to make any kind of sense she's got to be. There's certainly steel there, and a brain, and where the cui bono's concerned she has motive in spades. If anyone could plan a murder, I reckon she could.'

'And the execution?'

'No,' I said slowly. 'No, I don't think she'd be quite up for that. But it doesn't matter, she wouldn't be in it alone, and she'd provide the necessary link.'

'How so?'

'The only other two front runners are Poetelius and Brother Annius, right?'

Perilla sniffed. 'If you say so.'

I grinned. 'OK. *Possibly* them. The problem is, neither fits the frame on his own. Sure, in Poetelius's case he's got the motive that his business partner's a liability, and it's turned out he had the opportunity as well, so in a way he's by far the more likely. The guy's no natural killer, not on relatively slim grounds like that, I'd take my oath there, but if he and Annia were having a serious affair – serious on both sides

– then that'd be a completely different story. Tullius might not've cared about the hole-in-corner stuff, but I'd bet Poetelius did. He's a pretty conventional guy, he'd want marriage, and without a divorce he couldn't have it. Added to which, under the status quo Annia's stuck with a philandering husband who only keeps her for her money and has no intentions of giving her up. Get rid of Tullius and all their problems are solved at a stroke. It'd be just too convenient a solution to ignore, especially with Annia behind him, maybe doing the pushing.'

'If the affair existed in the first place. It all hinges on that.'

'Sure. Granted. But then why would Tullius tell Marcia it did when it didn't?'

'Marcus, you really are naive sometimes. Marcia may have been bored and looking for some excitement, but she was a respectable married woman. There's a big difference between starting a relationship with a man who has a faithful wife at home and one whose wife already has a lover of her own. If Tullius wanted to seduce Marcia, then presenting himself as a husband in a loveless marriage would be a natural ploy for him to use.'

I frowned. 'Yeah. Yeah, I suppose that's possible. Even so—'

'How about your second possibility? The brother?'

'That's just pure gut feeling. Annius is a cold bastard, and as far as temperament goes I'd back him as a killer over Poetelius any time. If Annius is our man, though, then his sister really has to be mixed up in this, because the only motive he's got is sheer altruism. Not that that's a barrier necessarily, because they're obviously pretty close.'

'Would that be enough?'

'Maybe not in itself. But remember, lady, we're dealing with business families here, and they take the financial side of things very seriously. Annia's already bankrolling her husband's company on a month-to-month basis and watching him in effect throw the money away to finance his tomcatting. I'm guessing, sure, but let's say things have got worse recently – as, from what Poetelius told me, they probably have –and he's pressing her to release some of the capital. Her brother's a businessman himself, he'd be a natural for her to go to for advice. And being the guy he is, unlike in Poetelius's case, I reckon where Annius is concerned that might be enough to swing it. Opportunity – well, we don't know anything about his movements at all, do we? The day of the murder, he could've been anywhere.'

'Hmm.' She was quiet for a long time. Then she said: 'Marcus, you do realize that none of this explains the Ostia connection, don't you? Quite the contrary. And there's no room for Correllius at all. Where does he fit in? If indeed he does.'

I took a swig of wine, and made a face. 'Yeah. That's the stumbling block, and it's a biggie. Correllius must fit in somewhere, that's for sure. And the fact that he and Tullius were both stabbed – taking Correllius's stabbing as murder, which to all intents and purposes it was as far as the perp was concerned – we're almost certainly looking for a single killer. Ostia's starting to look like a major lead, but for it to work then Annia must be on the level. Or the chances are that she is, at any rate, because if she was responsible at least in part for her husband's death then why the hell put me on to it in the first place? Plus, when I talked to her today I'd swear she genuinely didn't know any more about it than she told me.' I set the wine-cup down. 'Ah, hell. Leave it. Maybe Agron'll come up with something on the Siddius front. And then I've got this lady's maid to see. If we're really, *really* lucky, she'll be able to give us a good description of the guy at the Pollio, in which case we might be home and clear.'

Perilla was twisting her hair. 'You're absolutely sure that Annia, her brother and Poetelius are the only likely suspects?'

I stared at her. 'Yeah, more or less. If you discount Vecilius, but I thought we'd agreed that solution was too simple.'

'I don't mean Vecilius.'

'Jupiter, lady! Who else is there?'

'Marcia. Or rather, Marcia and her husband.'

'Perilla, that's crazy! Marcia was long gone, helping her mother in the cookshop by the Capenan Gate. And the day of the murder Festus was either at the pottery or over there with her.'

'So she told you, certainly. You don't have any definite proof of that, though, do you? They both had a motive, after all.

And setting it up would be easy. Marcia could've persuaded Tullius into a meeting at the shrine, say by suggesting she might be willing to discuss sharing him with his new girlfriend. And then Festus would've done the actual killing.'

Oh, shit. It was possible, sure it was. The lady was right. All the information I had for Marcia's and Festus's movements and actions on the two days in question came from the pair themselves. And even then there'd been a discrepancy, with Festus telling me he'd filled in the missing few hours on the day of the murder with a visit to the Temple of Mercury.

'What about the Ostia side of things?' I said. 'Neither Marcia nor Festus has anything to do with—' I stopped.

'Marcus? *Marcus!*'

'When I talked to the local Watch Commander – Memmius – he said that when Festus had married her Marcia had been a widow from out of town. If "out of town" was Ostia, as well it might be, then she'd still have connections there.' Gods! 'Oh, it could be coincidence, and the accident on the quayside happened two days before Annia sent her the letter, but all it'd take for that not to matter would be that Marcia already knew she'd been ditched and made her own arrangements. There'd still be the problem of how she worked things, sure, but it's at least feasible.'

'And the Correllius side of things?'

'Lady, I told you: I don't *know* yet. So get off my back, OK? Correllius was Ostian, we're talking Ostia, that's as far as it goes at this stage.'

'Very well. Then how about the spat with Hermia? Surely if Marcia knew that Tullius was being unfaithful already, before the letter arrived, then she'd already have confronted her.'

'Look, Perilla, this was your theory originally, not mine, so cut it out, right? I know there are problems. But we've got problems all down the line in this case, so what's different?'

She smiled. 'I'm simply raising reasonable objections, dear. Actually, if it did arise from a deliberate decision on her part as opposed to being a spur-of-the-moment reaction like she told you then it would make perfect sense. After all,

now Festus knew about the affair there was nothing lost, and
the result of the spat was that Vecilius was out for Tullius's
blood too.'

'Vecilius walked in on them. She couldn't've known he'd
turn up.'

'Even so.' She stretched. 'You said yourself it's only a
theory. And yes, I'm sure there're lots of problems with it we
haven't even considered yet.'

Yeah, there were. Still, it ticked a lot of the boxes. Too many,
certainly, to dismiss it out of hand. And Memmius had also
said that where Marcia was concerned, her husband couldn't
look past her. Love and the desire for revenge are powerful
motives in anyone's book. Add contrition on the wife's part
– and whatever lies she'd told me, I was sure Marcia's contrition was genuine – and you've got a pretty strong incentive
for murder. The hows and whys would come, no doubt, if they
were there. Or, of course, the whole thing might be a load of
horse feathers. You pays your money and you takes your choice.
We'd just have to see what transpired.

'So we'll be going through to Ostia shortly, will we?' Perilla
said. 'And for quite a while, probably, things being as they are.'

'Hmm?' I looked up from my wine-cup. 'I will, lady, sure.
Why the hell would you want to tag along? A straw mattress
on Agron and Cass's floor isn't exactly much of an inducement.'

'Oh, I've been thinking about that, dear, since you mentioned
the Correllius connection this morning and it became a likely
possibility. You know Caesia Fulvina?'

'One of your poetry-klatsch pals. Yeah, you've mentioned
her. Why?'

'She and her husband have a villa on the coast half a mile
from the town. They only use it in the summer, so it's empty
at present, apart from the caretaker staff.'

'Hey!' I brightened. 'You think she'd lend it to us?' I had
to admit that the prospect of dossing down at Agron's hadn't
exactly had me rubbing my hands.

'She already has, if and when we want it. I went round to
see her this morning, just after you left.'

'Brilliant!' I got up, went over, and kissed her. 'Lady, that
is *brilliant*!' A sudden thought struck me. 'What about the

kids? Clarus and Marilla? Would they be coming too, or would they be staying here?' Probably the former: I couldn't envisage Marilla passing up the opportunity to be cheek-by-jowl with a developing case, particularly one she had, now, a vested interest in. Probably a hands-on opportunity, too; certainly that was an aspect of things I'd have to fight her over. Bugger.

'Ah.' Perilla smiled. 'Actually that was another thing I was going to mention. There was a message waiting when I got back, from Lupercus.' Lupercus was Clarus and Marilla's major-domo in Castrimoenium. 'The locum that Clarus arranged to cover his practice has come down with mumps, so I'm afraid they'll have to cut the holiday short. Not that it matters all that much: they were only staying for a few days in any case, and Castrimoenium is only a few hours' drive away. They can come back another time, or of course we can go down to them.'

'Mumps,' I said. 'Really. How many adults come down with mumps?'

'Quite fortuitous, isn't it?'

'Yeah, it is. Very. Uh . . . you're not a witch, are you, lady, by any chance?'

'No, dear. Of course not. You'd've noticed.'

'Yeah. Yeah, I suppose I would.' I went back over to my couch and drained my wine-cup. 'The Princess is going to throw a fit.'

'She won't be happy, no. But it might be good for her in the end to know that she can't get her own way all the time. And Clarus won't mind. I suspect he might even be rather relieved to get back to normal.'

That I would believe. Still, when they rolled in later Marilla was definitely not going to be a happy bunny. Speaking of which—

'Meton vouchsafe anything about the timing for dinner today?' I said.

'Actually, it'll be later than usual. Marilla and Clarus wanted to take little Marcus over to Caesar's Gardens on the other side of the river.' She sniffed. 'I *told* Marilla that the weather was too unsettled today for a long trip, and of course I was right, but you know her, she insisted. In any case, she persuaded Meton to delay dinner until an hour after sunset, so that they didn't have to hurry back. I was sure you wouldn't mind.'

Jupiter! Me, if I'd suggested to our touchy chef that he postpone a meal without a cast-iron reason and at least three days' notice in writing I'd be taking my life in my hands. But then Meton, as I say, like Bathyllus, had always had a soft spot for the Princess. And, although the Sprog wasn't quite up to roasted pheasant with a saffron nut sauce as yet, he got positively gooey over young Marcus. As gooey as Meton ever got over anything but a top-grade sturgeon, that is, but even so . . .

'Uh-uh. I don't mind at all,' I said. 'In fact it'll give me time to go round and see this lady's maid. There's a fair chunk of the afternoon left yet, and she's just up by the Carinae.'

'Very well, dear.' Perilla got up too. 'Meanwhile I'll start making the preparations for the Ostia trip. You'll want to go quite soon, won't you?'

'Yeah. Within the next couple of days, if that's possible.'

'Oh, yes. As I said, Fulvina told me we could have the villa at any time we liked. It'll just be a case of sending a messenger ahead to warn the staff that we're coming. And I'd imagine that Clarus will want to get back to Castrimoenium straight away.'

Smug as hell. Still, she had a right to be this time round, I supposed.

'Fair enough, then,' I said. 'I'll see you later.'

I went to see Picentina.

The house was tucked away in a side alley off the main drag. I knocked at the door and it was opened by a young slave in a natty lime-green tunic.

'The name's Valerius Corvinus,' I said. 'You have a lady's maid here called Picentina?'

His eyes widened, which was more than the gap in the doorway did. Well, the guy couldn't get many purple-stripers turning up on his doorstep asking for one of the bought help, could he, now?

'Yes, sir,' he said. 'As a matter of fact we do.'

'Could I talk to her, do you think?'

He hesitated. 'That would be up to the mistress, sir. Could I ask your business, please?'

'It's about a stabbing she witnessed – possibly witnessed – two or three days ago at the Pollio Library.'

'Oh, *that*!' A barely concealed sniff. 'If you'd like to wait in the lobby, I'll tell the mistress you're here.'

'Fair enough,' I said. I went in and he closed the door behind me, then trotted off to do that small thing.

I looked around. Pretty poky, as lobbies went, but decorated to kill, with an outsize fresco on the wall showing the tradesmen's god Mercury hob-nobbing with a bald-headed guy in a plain mantle standing in the middle of what was clearly a shoemaking workshop: various slaves round about him were doing cobblery things involving bits of leather, lasts, hammers, and bradawls. No prizes for guessing what business the master of the house was in anyway, and he clearly wanted his visitors to know he was doing pretty well out of it.

The slave in the lime-green tunic came back.

'The mistress will see you,' he said. 'Follow me.'

We went through to the atrium. The lady herself was sitting with her back to me in a chair by the ornamental pool, completely swathed from the neck down in a sheet, while a young girl – Picentina, presumably – applied make-up to the face under the elaborately coiffeured wig.

'Ah . . . Publilia Clementa?' I said.

'Yes. That's right.' The head never moved. I went round the front where we could see each other properly. Mistake. Me, if I'd been Picentina, I'd've used a trowel; not the most prepossessing of females, Publilia Clementa, with a face like one of her husband's less successful productions and in need of all the artificial help it could get. 'Who are you?'

'Valerius Corvinus.'

'Yes, I know your name, but who exactly *are* you?'

'Uh . . .'

'You're very well-turned-out for a Watchman. Quite spruce. And are you *entitled* to that purple stripe?'

'Yeah. Yeah, I am.' Jupiter! 'And I'm not part of the Watch, as it happens. I'm just doing a favour for the Palatine District Commander. He's a friend of mine.'

'Indeed. Well, keep it short. As you can see, I'm extremely

busy. My husband and I are attending a very important official dinner this evening. A guild dinner. He is the current guild president.'

'Actually, I wanted to talk to your maid if that's convenient.' The girl looked up, cosmetics pad poised. 'It shouldn't take long.'

'About this silly stabbing business at the Pollio. Yes, my door-slave told me that too. Very well.' Then, to the girl: 'Get on with it, spit-spot. Tell the man what you saw.'

'Ah . . . maybe we could go somewhere private?' I said.

'Certainly not! Your reason for calling may be as innocent as you say, but I will take no chances. You will conduct the interview in my presence, please.'

Gods! Still, if that was the way she wanted it, it was no skin off my nose. I turned to the girl.

'You like to tell the story in your own way, Picentina?' I said. 'Just as it happened, OK? Right from the start. You were in the Pollio gardens, yes?'

The girl put the make-up stuff down on the ledge beside the pool.

''S right,' she said. 'The mistress sent me there while she was, like, chatting to her young man.'

'We'll leave the incidental details aside if you don't mind, Picentina,' Publilia snapped. 'She means Quintus Rubrius, Corvinus. A charming boy, one of my husband's clerks. Very cultured. He happens to have a great interest in art, as I do myself, and we met in the Porch quite by chance. Now just get on with it, girl!'

'Yeah, so anyway,' the maid went on. 'I was coming down the path from the Porch, like, and I sees this man standing behind another man, a fat old gentleman, sitting on one of the benches, like, sort of slumped against one end. Very close, they were, practically touching, like. He looks up and sees me, the first man does, I mean, and then he like walks away quickly. That's it, really, I didn't pay no more attention to the fat old gentleman 'cos he was asleep, or at least I thought he was at the time, like. When I went back there next day to ask about the mistress's missing earring and heard he'd like actually been murdered you could of knocked me down with a feather. And the thought that I'd, like, seen the monster what done it fair made my skin crawl.'

'Can you describe him at all?' I said. 'The, uh, monster?'

'Oh, he was ever so rough-looking. And I'll never forget the look he gave me when he, like, saw me coming towards him.' She shuddered, delicately. 'He had, like, these sort of mad, staring eyes, proper sink-holes of depravity, they were, that like bored straight through you. You could tell at once he was a ruthless killer.'

Yeah. Right. Gods! 'Age?'

'Oh, oldish. Not nearly as old as the other man, like, but too old for me, I noticed that straight off. But he was like fit, you know? Well-built, like. Sort of rugged and solid. He'd a lot of, like, muscle under his tunic. And he kept himself in shape, you could tell that by how he moved. Sort of *rippled*, like. Lithe as a cat stalking what it might devour. It brought me out all over in goosebumps.' She paused. 'Lovely crinkly hair he had, though. Bit like yours, sir, matter of fact.'

'Tall? Short?'

'Like, sort of medium. Tallish rather than shortish. I prefer them tall, me. Especially the crinkly haired ones.'

She gave me a dazzling smile. I ignored it.

'Clothes?'

'Just the tunic, like. Nothing special, plain grey wool incarnadined with the blood from the, like, dastardly deed he'd just perpetrated.'

'Anything else about him you can remember?'

'No.' She sighed. 'That was it, really. It was all over in a minute, like.'

Yeah, well, I was lucky to have got what I had, if you, like, made allowances for the verbal tic and discounted the Alexandrian bodice-ripper bits. Still, a lady's maid's job couldn't have much excitement in it, so if she'd been milking it for all it was worth I couldn't blame her. And the description fitted Nigrinus, that was certainly true; the only false note was that 'oldish', but to someone like Picentina anyone older than, say, thirty would qualify for an over-the-hill tag. Particularly where her obvious area of interest lay.

'There, now. If you have all the information you want,

Valerius Corvinus,' Clementa said frostily, 'perhaps you'll allow the girl to return to her proper duties and get back to yours. Good luck with your investigations. So nice to have met you.'

I let myself out.

FOURTEEN

First thing just before dawn two days later we took the carriage over to Ostia, together with Perilla's maid Phryne, Bathyllus up front next to driver Lysias, and Meton perched on the roof clutching his set of kitchen knives and best omelette pan: there'd be caretaker staff at the villa, sure, but they wouldn't run to either a ranking major-domo or a proper chef, and if we weren't going to be dossing down on Agron and Cass's living-room floor after all then I'd no intention whatsoever of slumming it. Perilla had got clear directions from her poetry pal before we left – fortunately, as it turned out, because the villa was one of several along the coast south of the town itself – and we arrived just a whisker shy of noon.

Caesia Fulvina had sent a skivvy through the previous day to say we'd be coming, so at least we were expected. While Bathyllus organized the local bought help to transfer the luggage from the coach and Meton went off to inspect the kitchen facilities, Perilla and I did the tour of the premises.

Fulvina and her husband – he was something big in Aqueducts and Sewers, I remembered – weren't short of a silver piece or two, that was certain; they might only use the villa as a holiday home, but it was absolute top-of-the-range. Building space in Rome is at a premium, of course, even on the hills, and unless your last name is Caesar, or close to it, or your annual income's well over the six-figure mark so you can afford a little property over on the Janiculan with its four dining rooms, covered riding exercise yard, and small private zoo, you can't be too ambitious. Ostia's different. Oh, yeah, sure, a seaside villa on the Bay of Naples'll set you back an arm and a leg, but property prices along the Laurentian coast are still pretty reasonable, and for what you'd pay for a house on one of the better-class hills in Rome there you could buy – or build – a villa three times the size and still have some loose change left in your pouch.

Certainly the place's owners hadn't spared any expense, either where scale or decoration were concerned. The driveway up from the gate passed through carefully landscaped grounds planted with trees and bushes that screened the house itself from the coastal road and the shoreline beyond it. The rooms were twice as big as the ones we had at home, and there were more of them. Most of the ones downstairs had mosaic-inlaid floors – there was a lovely one in the atrium with its centre-piece Neptune's chariot drawn by seahorses, surrounded by conch-blowing Tritons – and at least one wall with a full-scale fresco on it; while the bedrooms upstairs were big enough to swing several cats, were floored with cedar, and had windows looking out to sea or down onto the porticoed garden studded with statues to the rear. There was even, off to one side, a small cistern-fed bath suite.

'But this is lovely!' Perilla said as we made our way back downstairs. 'Absolutely perfect!'

Yeah, I had to agree. I'd been through to Ostia quite a few times over the years, but by the nature of things they'd been flying visits, and they'd been restricted to the town itself with, when I couldn't manage the thing in a oner, a shakedown on the couch at Agron's place. Getting the use of Fulvina's villa had been a real stroke of genius on the lady's part. Once Meton had sussed out the local market – which, knowing Meton's scale of priorities, would be as soon as he'd laid out his chef's knives, made sure everything was hunky-dory where equipment and larder were concerned, and terrified the wollocks off Fulvina's kitchen skivvies – I reckoned we'd be as well-set-up here as we were at home. Better.

'Fine,' I said. 'I'll just leave you to settle in and get on with things.'

She stopped, and stared at me. 'Oh, Marcus! Be reasonable!' she said. 'You're not going to start straight away, surely?'

'Naturally I am. What did you expect?'

'Come on, dear! We are on holiday after all.'

I grinned. 'You may be, lady. Me, I've got a job to go to. And after six hours twiddling my thumbs in the coach I could do with the walk.' True: I'm no coach-traveller, me, and fourteen-plus miles with only a couple of cushions between

me and the Ostian Road cobbles, even if Lysias had stuck to
the unpaved verge whenever he could, had left me in sore
need of exercise. 'Sore' being the operative word. 'Enjoy. I'll
see you later.'

Like I said, the villa was on the coast road, and the town itself
was a bare half-mile away, at the Tiber's mouth. An easy
distance to walk, particularly given the weather we had at
present: it was distinctly cooler here than in Rome, and much
fresher-smelling, although that wouldn't've been difficult,
particularly at the height of summer in comparison to anywhere
in the city downwind of the river, with a pleasant, salt-tangy
breeze off the sea. Perfect weather for walking, in fact, especially after a six-hour carriage-drive. The countryside wasn't
bad, either: the Laurentian coast on the inland side of the road
grows a fair proportion of the town's fruit and vegetables, and
most of the space between the big villas is taken up with small
farms and market gardens, with the occasional vineyard or
orchard; while on the sea side you get the small family owned
boats that supply the town's fish market.

Yeah, well, maybe Perilla's point about being on holiday
wasn't too far off the mark after all; the case aside, I reckoned
we could spend a very pleasant few days here. The lady's pal
Fulvina and her husband certainly had the right idea. Perhaps
we should get out of the city more often.

I still had most of the afternoon to play with when I reached
the Laurentian Gate. Coming from the east along the main
road as I always did when I travelled through from Rome, I
wasn't too familiar with this part of town. The Tiber, with its
various wharves, landing stages, warehouses, and so on, not
to mention the main dockyard area just outside the walls at
Tiber Mouth itself and most of the public buildings – my usual
stamping ground – was on the northern side; the Laurentian
quarter to the south was almost exclusively upmarket residen-
tial. Even so, Ostia's not big; you can walk across it from end
to end practically inside of half an hour. And although the old
fort that was built originally to protect Rome's harbour is long
gone, for practical purposes it's given the place an overall
shape. The street leading up from Laurentian Gate – the Hinge

– takes you directly to the Market Square, the original fort's centre, where it crosses the main drag, Boundary Marker Street, which runs the length of the town to the Roman Gate.

Easy-peasy, right? Especially when you compare it with Rome, which is a town planner's nightmare. Mind you, off the main drag things got a bit more haphazard.

So; where to start? I'd have to call in on Agron, of course, to say we were here, check if he'd managed to trace the cack-handed crane operator Siddius for me, and maybe invite him and Cass round for dinner, but his yard was diagonally across town, by the river on the Roman Gate side. Lippillus had said that Correllius's house – or his widow's, now; what was her name? Mamilia, right – was one of the big properties south of Market Square on the Hinge itself. As a first port of call, then, that made sense; at the very least I could suss out where it was for later reference.

I carried on up the Hinge. Not altogether an easy matter: the street was pretty narrow, and there were quite a few pedestrians around, although not as many as there would've been in Rome at that time of day, plus – as wouldn't be the case in Rome – you had the occasional cart to contend with. The locals didn't seem to be in all that much of a hurry, either, as they would've been at home, which slowed things up further. Lippillus had been right, though: judging by the overall length and carefully maintained condition of their frontages the houses in this part of town were definitely well upmarket. I spotted a door-slave sunning himself outside one of them and asked for directions to the Correllius place, which turned out to be a scant twenty yards further up the street.

There was a door-slave there as well: a much bigger guy this time, bald as an egg but with arms as thick – and hairy – as an ape's. Definitely prime bouncer material, which in a laid-back place like Ostia was interesting.

I went up to him, getting a long, suspicious stare all the way.

'Afternoon, pal,' I said when I'd reached conversational distance. 'Would this be the Correllius house?'

He considered for a while, inserted a little finger into an ear the size and general shape of a cabbage leaf, wiggled it around, withdrew it, inspected the result, and wiped it off on his tunic.

'It might be,' he said finally.

I wondered for an instant whether that might be one of those weird philosophical paradoxes, like Achilles and the tortoise, but then Zeno the guy definitely wasn't. What we had here was obfuscation, which was interesting again. I sighed.

'Look,' I said. 'I know the master's dead, right, but I was wondering if I could have a word with your mistress. That possible at all?'

'Mistress is out.'

'OK. Make it someone else, then. You choose.'

'Business or social?'

'Business. I'm through from Rome. It's about your master's death, as it happens.'

That got me another long, suspicious stare. Then he grunted and stood up.

'Mister Doccius do?' he said.

'Perfect. Who's Mister Doccius?'

'The master's deputy.'

'Great. Mister Doccius it is.'

'OK. You wait here, right?' He paused, his hand on the door knob. 'Name?'

'Corvinus. Valerius Corvinus.'

Another grunt. He disappeared inside, closing the door behind him, and I kicked my heels for a good five minutes before he reappeared.

'Mister Doccius'll see you,' he said. 'Follow me.'

I did. Once through the front door I'd been expecting the usual standard arrangement of lobby plus atrium with rooms off to the sides and back, plus a peristyle garden to the rear, which was in effect what I got. But then chummie led me straight through the peristyle to a block of rooms on its far side whose doors opened onto a series of what, from their furnishings, were obviously offices. Most of them had clerks beavering away inside them, and the place had a definite busy feel about it that didn't square at all with the private house side of things.

Interesting yet again.

'In here,' chummie said, and without another word turned on his heel and disappeared back into the house proper, presumably to excavate the cabbage-leaf's partner in comfort.

It was the middle room of the line, and bigger than the rest, but without the office furnishings. There were a couple of chairs facing outwards and a small table with the makings of a meal on it. The guy sitting on one of the chairs working his way through a plateful of bread, cheese, and cold vegetables was mid-thirties with black curly hair. If he wasn't quite in the door-slave's class for size, he was big enough, and most of it was muscle. One good step up socially from the bouncer on the door, this Mister Doccius, but clearly out of the same mould. I was beginning to get some pretty definite signals here: your ordinary provincial merchant establishment, let alone laid-back Ostian private residence, this place clearly wasn't.

'Sorry, pal,' I said. 'Bad timing. I'm interrupting your lunch.'

He gave me a long, considering look. Then, finally, he grunted and speared a piece of cheese with his knife.

'That's OK,' he said. Grudging as hell; clearly not one for the pleasantries, Correllius's exec. 'Corvinus, wasn't it? Through from Rome about the boss's death.'

'That's right.'

'Sit down.' I did, and he chewed for a bit in silence, watching me. 'This official in some way?' he said finally, and then before I could answer: 'Only we were told the death was natural. No surprises there. Correllius was fat as a pig, sixty plus, and he got breathless just walking across a room. He could've gone any time these past five years, so his doctor said.'

Delivered deadpan, and without so much as a smidgeon of sympathy. In fact, if anything there was a trace of contempt in the tone.

'Yeah, it was natural,' I said. 'Matter of fact, the guy who found the body was my son-in-law. He's a doctor himself, and he made the diagnosis. Also by coincidence the Watchman the clerks at the Pollio notified is an old friend of mine.'

'Is that so, now? Bully for you.' Doccius picked up the wine-cup and took a swig. 'So. If the boss just up and died natural, then what's this all about?'

'He was stabbed. After he was already dead, sure, so there's no actual crime involved, or not much of one as far as the Watch is concerned, but still. You knew that, presumably?'

'Sure I did. I'm not blind, and I saw the body when they brought it back.'

I waited, but there was nothing more.

'And you don't think that's worth looking into,' I said at last, making it a clear statement, not a question, and loading it with as much sarcasm as I could.

His eyes never shifted from my face, and he carried on eating.

'Should I?' he said finally.

'Yeah, I'd say that'd be a reasonable assumption.' I was beginning to get angry now, and I was more than a little puzzled. 'You're his deputy, after all, or so the door-slave told me. The guy may've died naturally, but that's only a technicality. In effect he was murdered.'

He speared another piece of cheese, chewed deliberately and swallowed.

'"Murdered" is a strong word,' he said at last. 'And you admit yourself that it's the wrong one, because Correllius was already dead. Me, now, I'll settle for the technicality. If that's OK with you and the Roman Watch. It saves a lot of hassle that way, and hassle I can do without. We all can here.'

I just didn't believe this. 'Look,' I said. 'Seemingly he'd arranged to meet a guy that day, a business associate by the name of Pullius. Marcus Pullius.'

Doccius's hand, poised over the bowl of vegetables, stopped in mid-air.

'Who told you that?' he said sharply.

Hey! We'd got a reaction at last! 'The slave he had with him. Mercurius. Or at least that was the name he gave to my Watchman friend. You know anything about him?'

He picked up the bread and broke it.

'Not a thing,' he said. 'Pullius is no one I've ever heard of, that's for sure. And you don't want to believe anything that dozy bugger Mercurius said. He always did have his head up his backside.'

'You can ask him for yourself. He's on the premises, presumably.'

'Was.' He took another swig of the wine.

'How do you mean, "was"?'

'I told you: he was a dozy bugger without the sense he was born with. He had an accident twelve or fifteen days back. Fell off the roof while he was up replacing a cracked tile and broke his neck.' His eyes challenged me over the lifted wine-cup. 'So that's that. I'm sorry, but you've had a wasted journey.'

'OK. Fine.' I was having real trouble keeping my temper now, but if he wanted me to lose it I wasn't going to give the bastard the satisfaction. 'Just one more thing before I go, pal. Correllius was in the import-export business, right? Wine and oil, specifically?'

A blink, and the answer was too long in coming. 'Yeah. We deal in wine and oil, among other things. So forget your "specifically", because the company has various business interests covering a pretty wide range.'

Yeah; that, from what I was beginning to glean about the set-up here, was probably true. And I'd bet that not all of them would figure among the Ostian Honest Trader of the Year categories.

'Your boss had a consignment about half a month back bound for Aleria on a ship called the *Porpoise*, master Titus Nigrinus,' I said. 'That right?'

Again the hesitation, and his eyes definitely flickered. 'Possibly,' he said. 'I'd have to check the records to be sure, but I'll take your word for it. Again, so what?'

I gave him my best smile. 'Probably nothing. Certainly nothing to do with your boss's murder; sorry, *death*. Just a snippet of information I came across recently in connection with something else. Don't let it worry you.'

'Why should it worry me?' But he was rattled; obviously so. 'Now, Corvinus, that's my lunch break over and I've got more to do today than I've time for. You mind?'

'Not at all.' I got up. 'Thanks for your trouble.'

'A pleasure.' Not what his eyes said; not by a long chalk. 'I'll see you out.'

We walked through the peristyle garden and into the house proper. I was crossing the atrium when I came face-to-face

with a stylish middle-aged woman coming from the direction
of the lobby.

She stopped.

'And who might you be?' she said.

'This is Valerius Corvinus, madam,' Doccius said. 'From
Rome. He came to talk to me about the boss's death. He's
just leaving.'

A complete change of tone: he didn't exactly go the length
of tugging his forelock, but the impression I got was that he
wasn't all that far off it.

'You're Mamilia, yes?' I said. 'Marcus Correllius's wife?' I
was tactful enough to avoid the word 'widow'. Mind you – and
it was odd, to say the least – the lady was wearing everyday
dress, not a mourning mantle. Pretty expensive everyday dress
at that, and slap bang up to fashion, if I was any judge. Plus
for a woman who'd lost her husband under tragic circumstances
less than a month before she wasn't looking exactly prostrate
with grief. She was wearing full make-up, for a start, and I'd
bet that wherever she'd been it wasn't to sob at the late
Correllius's graveside.

Like I say, odd. And very, very interesting.

'I am indeed Mamilia,' she said. She was giving me a long,
considering look. 'Corvinus, your name was?'

'Yeah. Actually, it was you I came to see in the first place,
but your door-slave said you were out.'

'Which was quite true. I was, but as you can see I'm back.'
The eyes finally shifted, as if she'd been carefully weighing
up a range of options and finally come to a decision. 'So by
all means you can talk to me now, if you wish.' Doccius
opened his mouth to say something, but she held up a hand
and he closed it. 'That will do for now, Publius. Thank you
for taking care of Valerius Corvinus in my absence, but you
have work of your own, I'm sure.'

'Yes, madam.' He shot me a look that wouldn't've disgraced
a basilisk, turned on his heel and went back out through the
peristyle.

Mamilia watched him go, then turned back to me. 'Sit down,
Valerius Corvinus,' she said. 'You'll find that couch beside
you perfectly comfortable.' She sat down herself in the chair

beside the ornamental pool and tidied the folds of her mantle.
'Now. Marcus's death. First of all, if you don't mind my
asking, what precisely is your interest in the matter?'
I repeated more or less what I'd told Doccius. She frowned.
'Forgive me,' she said. 'But I need to have this clear. Your
friend the Watch Commander. He's of the opinion that no real
crime was committed since my husband was already dead,
yes?'
'Uh, yeah, more or less. Or rather not of the level that would
warrant a full-scale official investigation. But—'
'Don't you think, then, that we should simply leave things
as they are? I mean, if poor Marcus was dead already when
he was stabbed then what, really, is the point?' I just gaped
at her: Doccius was one thing, but this lady was Correllius's
widow, for the gods' sakes! 'Or don't you agree?'
Bland as hell. Jupiter! I counted, mentally, to ten. 'The man
was murdered, lady,' I said carefully. 'Or just as good as. All
that happened was that whoever stuck the knife in him thought
he was asleep. No, of course I don't f—' I stopped myself
just in time. 'Of course I don't agree.'
'Then that's unfortunate. But whether you do or not makes
no difference, does it? If the Roman authorities decline to
investigate the matter then the decision passes to the family,
in other words to myself. Marcus is dead. That is . . .' she
paused – 'regrettable, but the fact is that he died of natural
causes. Anything else is a needless complication, and at base
irrelevant. Certainly, and I have no wish to be rude, it is no
business whatsoever of yours.'
True. Technically, at least. Even so, I just didn't believe
this; *unnatural* didn't go far enough.
'He ever mention a man called Marcus Pullius?' I asked.
Not a flicker. 'No,' she said. 'Who might that be?'
'A business acquaintance, presumably. Only the strange
thing is that no one seems to have heard of him barring the
slave who was with your husband that day and who's now
dead himself.' I just stopped myself in time from glossing the
adjective with a 'conveniently'.
'Ah, yes. That would be Mercurius. A tragic accident.
Tragic.'

'Yeah.' I managed to keep the sarcasm out of my voice. 'Anyway, this Pullius seems to have vanished into thin air. According to Mercurius, he was supposed to meet Correllius outside the Pollio, but he never showed up. Or at least if he did then he was probably the killer.'

Mamilia frowned. 'Excuse me, Valerius Corvinus,' she said. 'I'm sorry to repeat myself, but "killer" is the wrong word here, and I do think we should keep that fact firmly in mind. And I'm afraid I know nothing about Marcus's business concerns. He didn't confide.' Interesting: she was lying there, I was sure of it. 'Certainly he never mentioned a Marcus Pullius to me, not in any context.'

'The thing is,' I said, 'if this Pullius was involved then we've got what amounts to a description of him.'

'Oh?' That came out sharply.

'Yeah. From a lady's maid who happened to come into the garden just as, presumably, your husband was being stabbed. Or immediately afterwards, anyway, because she caught sight of the man before he walked off.'

'Very interesting. But, as I said, not of much practical use to anyone.' She smoothed a non-existent crease from her mantle. 'Now I've no wish to be rude or inhospitable, but there really is no need to prolong this conversation. Marcus was not a well man, and had not been so for some years. He is now dead, his death was not unexpected, and it occurred, your doctor son-in-law says, from natural causes completely consistent with his illness. To me that is what is important and there's an end of the matter. From what you say, the authorities are in complete agreement with this opinion. Accordingly, I would be grateful if you minded your own business, whatever that is, and returned to Rome. Do I make myself clear?'

Gods!

'Yeah. Perfectly clear. Thank you, lady.' I was quietly fizzing. I stood up. So did she.

'I'm sorry you had a wasted journey.' She gave me a brittle smile: evidently now I'd had the firm brush-off there was scope for a return to the social graces. 'Were you staying locally or are you just through from Rome for the day?'

'Oh, I'm staying.' Damn right I would be! 'For the foreseeable future, anyway. A friend of my wife's is letting us use her villa.'

'How delightful. So your journey won't be a complete waste after all; I'm glad. That would be one of the villas on the coast, I suppose?' I said nothing. 'Yes, they are very nice, aren't they? I did try to persuade Marcus to build or buy us one – so much more pleasant than a house in town, particularly in the summer months – but he preferred to be in the centre of things. And, as you've seen, he virtually worked from home.' She held out her hand. 'I'm very pleased to have met you, Valerius Corvinus, and believe me I do appreciate your concern and the trouble you've gone to. I hope I haven't given any offence; certainly none was intended. But I really do think this is for the best.'

Yeah. Right. And I was Cleopatra's grandmother. I shook and turned to go . . .

A man was coming through from the lobby: late forties, fit-looking, grizzled hair well-barbered, and a snappy plain mantle. He stopped when he saw me.

'I'm sorry, Mamilia,' he said. 'Your door-slave sent me straight through. He didn't tell me you had company.'

'That's OK,' I said. 'I was just leaving.' I glanced at Mamilia. Her face was set.

'The gentleman's name is Valerius Corvinus,' she said. 'He came to enquire about Marcus's death.'

The man grunted. 'Publius Fundanius,' he said, putting out his hand.

I shook it. 'Friend of the family?'

He hesitated. 'Business associate.' He turned to Mamilia. 'I just called round to offer my condolences and ask if there was anything I could do.'

'Kind of you,' Mamilia said; you could've used her tone to ice wine.

'Well, I'll be going,' I said; then, to Mamilia: 'Thanks for taking the time to talk to me.'

'You're very welcome.'

This time, not so much as a blink. I left.

FIFTEEN

So; time for a cup of wine, and a think. A serious think: matters were getting complicated.

I carried on up the Hinge in the direction of Market Square, keeping an eye out for wineshops: like I say, this was a part of town I hardly knew at all, and my preferred ones all lay nearer the river. I spotted one down an alleyway just short of the back of the Temple of Rome and Augustus at the Square's southern end and went inside.

Pretty basic, hardly more than a counter, with only one punter in evidence, an oldish guy in a worker's tunic who was nursing a wine-cup and chatting with the middle-aged woman behind the bar. We nodded to each other and I saw his eyes widen at my purple stripe, but he turned back to his drink.

'Afternoon, sir,' the woman said. 'What can I get you?'

I looked up at the board: Veian, eh? Now there was a wine you didn't see all that often. Still, I'd be heading for Agron's yard later, and no doubt if he'd time to spare we'd be splitting half a jug in his local, so maybe just a cup would do.

'A cup of your Veian'd be good,' I said.

She poured it, and I took a sip: not bad, not bad at all. Excellent, in fact. Basic or not, I'd have to add this place to my list.

'You over here from the city?' the other punter said.

I turned towards him; obviously the chatty type, which was lucky. Me, I always have time for talkative local barflies, particularly when I'm on a case, and the thinking could wait for a bit.

'Yeah,' I said. 'Yeah, I am, as it happens.'

'Business?'

'Of a kind. Name's Corvinus. Marcus Corvinus.'

'Titus Rubrius. We don't see many purple-stripers in here, do we, Vinnia?' he said to the barwoman. 'Raises the tone of the place no end. You'll have to be hiring a set of musicians and a floor show soon, eh?' She didn't respond, and he turned back to me. 'I mean no offence, sir. You're very welcome.'

'No offence taken. And it's their loss. That's the best wineshop Veian I've tasted in a long time.'

I glanced at the barwoman, but she'd turned away and was replacing the flask in its cradle. It isn't very often that a wineshop owner'll let a compliment pass them by without some sort of response, or at least a smile, and I'd got neither, just the back view of her tunic. Not one of nature's born talkers, obviously, this Vinnia. Not the sunniest of dispositions, either, I suspected.

The old guy nodded. 'Aye, it's good stuff, the Veian,' he said. 'Vinnia here gets it from a cousin of one of the other regulars. He's got a farm up that way, not a big one but he's a dab hand with the vines. Most of it goes locally, but he sends her a few flasks every year. That right, lass?'

She turned and reached for the empty plate in front of him. Not a smile; not an anything, really.

'It's a nice enough wine,' she said, washing the plate in the sink by the counter and reaching for the drying cloth. 'I've had no complaints.'

I took another swallow, a larger one this time. For a wineshop owner – and I assumed, now, that the lady was the owner – she wasn't exactly showing all that much in the way of customer rapport. Maybe that was why the place was so empty; certainly it had nothing to do with the quality of the wine, and your usual wineshop punter expects a bit of chat with his lunchtime cup. Still, it took all sorts. Maybe Ostian punters were a more introspective bunch than their Roman counterparts.

I leaned my elbows on the counter and turned back to my more communicative fellow-drinker.

'You live around here yourself, pal?' I said.

'Nah. Not exactly. I'm up by Tiber Gate, me. But I've a butcher's shop in the market, so it's handy. I'm in here most days for an hour or so this time, after the morning rush is past, while my daughter looks after things.' He drank some of his own wine. 'What sort of business are you in yourself, sir? If you don't mind me asking.'

'It's, uh, a bit complicated.' Well, there was no harm in fishing; you never knew your luck, and I always say that if it's local information you want the best place to get it is in the nearest wineshop. 'You happen to know a man by the name of Correllius? Marcus Correllius? Lives near here. Big house on the Hinge.'

The woman set the dry plate down hard on the stone counter with a sharp *click*, and I wondered if it had broken. I gave her a curious glance, but she was already turning away and standing with her back to me.

'That who your business is with?' the old man said casually. Too casually, and I'd noticed his eyes flick to the woman's back and away again.

'Not exactly, no,' I said.

He grunted, raised the wine-cup to his lips, took a sip and set it down carefully, then cleared his throat.

'You know Correllius well yourself, do you?' he said.

Over-casual again. Something was screwy here; what it was, I didn't know, but we definitely had an Atmosphere.

'No, I've never even met the guy,' I said. 'It was an honest question, no strings.'

'Honest question, eh? In that case, and you'll forgive me for saying so, because it's kindly meant, if it was me doing the business I'd watch my step.'

Uh-huh. 'Yeah?' I said. 'In what way?'

He hesitated. 'Let's just say "honest" and "Correllius" aren't words that go together all that neatly.'

'You're telling me he was a crook?'

'"Was"?' He frowned. 'How do you mean, "was"?'

I cursed, mentally, but the damage was done. 'He's dead, as it happens. About half a month ago, over in Rome.'

Rubrius looked at Vinnia and I followed his eyes. She still had her back to us, but she was standing rigid, the dishcloth clutched in her hand, obviously listening hard.

'Well now,' he said slowly and softly; his eyes didn't waver. 'There's a thing.' He turned back to me. 'And that'd be why you're here, would it, sir? The "business" you mentioned?'

'Yeah, more or less. Like I said, it's complicated.'

'Now there's good news, eh, Vinnia?' Rubrius said to the

woman. There was no answer, but she turned round. Her face was as grey as the dishrag she was holding, and she was staring at me like I'd just grown an extra head. 'Come on, girl! What's wrong with you?'

Yeah; me, I'd've liked to know the answer to that as well. I'd definitely touched a nerve here, that was for sure, but what it was I hadn't a clue.

'You have some sort of connection with the guy, lady?' I said to her.

'No.' That came out in a whisper. She still hadn't taken her eyes off me.

Rubrius chuckled. 'Come on, lass!' he said again. 'You've told me a dozen times that—'

'You hold your tongue, Titus!' she snapped at him.

He frowned, opened his mouth to say something, then shrugged, picked up his wine-cup, drained it, and set it down on the counter.

'Fair enough, girl,' he said. 'As you like. Have it your own way.' He stood up. 'I'd best be getting back in any case. A pleasure to meet you, sir.'

'Yeah. Likewise.' Gods! What was going on here?

He went out, closing the door behind him. The woman set the dishcloth down, picked up the plate she'd been drying – it couldn't't've broken after all – and turned her back on me again as she laid the plate with the others on the shelf above the wine flasks.

There was a long pause.

Finally: 'No hassle, sister,' I said gently. 'None in the world. All I wanted to know was—'

'Look.' She turned round. 'You asked and I answered, right? There's an end to it. Now I'm sorry, sir, but I'd be grateful if you'd just finish your wine and go. You understand?'

'Sure. No problem.' I took a last swallow, put the empty cup down on the counter, paid, and left.

Interesting. And, to say the least, puzzling.

The market area wasn't far off, in the triangular space formed by the junction of Ditch Street and Sea Gate Road. This late in the afternoon there weren't many shoppers around – like

Rubrius had said, the main rush, where foodstuffs are concerned, certainly, is in the morning when the punters are putting together the wherewithal for dinner, and most of the shops and stalls were closed. I found the butchers' section easily enough, opposite the west gate of the old fort; just in time, because Rubrius and a middle-aged woman I assumed was his daughter were hauling down the shutters.

'Hi again, pal,' I said. 'Can you spare a minute?'

He was bent down fixing the padlock to its hasp. He straightened and turned, and there was no surprise in his face.

'Oh, it's you, sir,' he said. 'I thought it wouldn't be long before you looked me up.' Then, to the woman: 'You get yourself off home, girl. I'll follow you directly.' She gave me a quick, curious look – the purple stripe again – nodded and left. 'By the horse trough do you? I could do with a sit-down.'

'Sure,' I said. 'Wherever you like.'

We went over to the horse trough and sat side by side on the stone lip.

'How did he die?' Rubrius said.

'I told you, it's complicated. But basically he was stabbed from behind, on a bench outside the Pollio Library in Rome.'

'Uh-huh.' He nodded. 'And the family want you to find out who did it, right?'

'Not exactly.'

I thought the answer would surprise him, but he just grunted.

'Vinnia's a widow,' he said. 'Has been for the past ten years. Her husband's name was Manutius, Gaius Manutius, and he worked for your Marcus Correllius.'

Uh-huh; it had to be something along those lines, because I couldn't really see the lady in the role of a jilted mistress. Mind you, it wasn't altogether beyond the bounds of possibility; there was no accounting for personal taste, and from what I'd heard of him so far Corellius hadn't exactly been an Adonis himself.

'Is that so, now?' I said. 'Doing what?'

He hesitated. 'Well, sir, that I can't rightly say, and Vinnia's never told me. That's if she knows herself, of course. It was nothing too grand, but it brought in the silver pieces hand over fist, and no mistake. Which was how she had the money to buy the wineshop after Manutius died.'

'You're telling me there was something shady going on, yes?'

Another hesitation. 'As to that, I wouldn't like to swear,' he said. 'But, well, it's more than likely, under the circumstances and given the gentleman in question. Not where Vinnia was concerned, mind, I'd not believe that for a moment. She's a good girl, is Vinnia, hard as nails, sure. She keeps herself to herself and no mistake, like you saw, and she has a tongue like a razor. But she's straight, straight as they come. Manutius, now, he was another thing altogether. A bit of a bad lot all round, by all accounts. She wouldn't thank me for saying so but she's better off without him.'

'So what exactly happened? How did he die?'

'There was an accident. Over at the docks.'

'An accident?'

'That's the story, at any rate, and me, I couldn't tell you no different. Vinnia, now . . . well, she's always been sure it was Correllius's doing.'

'She say why?'

'No. Like I said, she's close-mouthed at the best of times, and that goes double where Manutius is concerned. But she hates Correllius like poison, that I can say.'

'You have any details? About the accident, I mean.'

'Nah. I never knew the man myself. I only know Vinnia through the wineshop.'

'You know of anyone who did?'

He considered. 'She's talked about a Cispius once or twice. Him and Manutius worked together, and they were close mates, seemingly. The place was pretty run down when she bought it, and he did a few odd jobs for her as a favour when she was putting it to rights. Plastering and that.'

'Where would I find him?'

'Haven't a clue, sir. That was before my day, and he was no spring chicken even then. He's probably retired now, or maybe even dead himself.' Bugger. 'Except—' He frowned. 'Hold on, hold on! Let me think.' I waited, while he stared into space. 'There was a daughter that Vinnia mentioned once.

I can't recall her name, but she was married to a fuller with a shop up by the river near Guildsmen's Square.'

Yeah, well, it was better than nothing. And a fuller's shop in that part of town shouldn't be too difficult to trace; I could give it a shot, at any rate.

'Vinnia runs the wineshop on her own, right?' I said. 'No family?'

'Not in Ostia. Not even in Italy, for all I know; she's from Gaul originally, Narbo, I think, down in the south. Her first husband – there was one before Manutius, but I can't even tell you his name – emigrated to Ostia with her and died a year or two later. Then she took up with Manutius, the gods know why, and remarried. She has a brother, that I do know, but he's in the army. He signed up twenty-odd years back, so he's in Germany now, on the Rhine with the Second Augustan, and liable to stay there.'

'No kids?'

'Not by the first marriage, no. She and Manutius had two, but they died young.'

'And she didn't think of marrying again after his accident?' A fair question; it'd been ten years, after all, and for someone in Vinnia's position getting by as a woman on her own wouldn't be easy.

He shook his head. 'No,' he said. 'It hasn't been for want of asking, neither; it's eight years since my Atellia died, and I'd've taken the lass on myself like a shot, still would if she'd have me.'

Uh-huh. Well, I reckoned I'd got just about all that was going at present where our taciturn wineshop lady was concerned. Not that I was complaining, mind: at least I'd got another strand to follow up, and you never knew; something might come of it in the end.

I stood up. 'Thanks, pal. You've been really helpful.'

'You're welcome. Don't mention it. I mean, *really* don't mention it. If she found out I'd been blabbing she'd have the skin off me. And I've still hopes in that direction.'

I nodded. 'Fair enough,' I said. 'You've got it, friend; my lips are sealed. And good luck with the lady, OK?' I paused.

'Oh – one more thing, before I go. You happen to know a guy by the name of Fundanius?'

He frowned. 'I've heard of him.'

'Businessman, right?'

'Not the kind I'd care to do business with, or any of mine.'

'Crooked?'

Rubrius hesitated and tugged at his ear. 'Well, now, sir, that I wouldn't like to say, not in so many words, like. He's a big wheel locally, he has a finger in quite a few pies on the business side, and he's well in with the gentlemen that run the guilds. A past president himself, as it happens, a year or two back. But the word on the street is that he can sail pretty close to the wind, and he's not above cutting corners when he can get away with it. Him and Correllius are a pair, if you want the truth. I'd not trust either of them to tell me the time of day.' He glanced up at me. 'You have a reason for asking?'

'Not particularly. It's just when I was at Correllius's house earlier on talking to his widow the guy showed up to offer his condolences.'

Rubrius chuckled. 'Is that so, now?' he said. 'Well, there's a turn-up!'

'Yeah? How so?'

'From what I've heard the buggers couldn't stand each other. Famous for it. They've been at daggers drawn for years.'

'Really?'

'Sure. Personal and business both. Give either of them the chance to do the other down and they'd grab it with both hands any day of the month. I said they were a pair, but cat and dog's more like it. Or maybe two dogs after the same bone. "Condolences", right? Me, I'd've thought Fundanius was more likely to spit on Correllius's grave.'

Uh-huh. Interesting. And it might explain Mamilia's reaction, too, when the guy had walked in; there was no love lost there, from what I could tell. Mind you, if that was the case it didn't explain why Fundanius had called round in the first place. Quite the reverse, in fact . . .

'You happen to know where he lives?' I said.

'He has one of them fancy villas outside of town, on the coast between the two gates.'

So we were practically neighbours, currently. I logged the information for possible future use. 'Fine,' I said. 'Thanks again, pal. I'll let you get home. Apologize to your daughter for me, will you?'

'Bless you, Secunda won't mind. She'll be busy enough getting the dinner ready, and I'm always grateful for a chat. I'll see you again some time no doubt, if you're back in to Vinnia's place.'

'Yeah, that I can guarantee.' I could, as well: close-mouthed or not, the lady had serious beans to spill, that was for sure. 'And the wine's on me, right?'

'That's kind of you, sir, although there's no need. I look forward to it. You'll remember your promise, though?'

'Sure. No worries.'

I gave him a wave, and set off for Agron's yard. The afternoon was wearing on now, Agron's was on the other side of town and if I wanted to avoid putting Meton's nose out of joint over the dinner timing – always a bad idea – what with recent developments, it would have to be a quickie. Still, I'd plenty of time now the accommodation problem was sorted out: tracking down Vinnia's ex-husband's pal, although Guildsmen's Square was on my way, could wait for another day. As could the question of Fundanius. That looked like opening up a profitable avenue to explore as well. All in all, then, I was left with plenty of food for thought here, and no mistake. A talk with Perilla was definitely in order.

Things were progressing nicely.

SIXTEEN

I was lucky; Agron was still at his yard, helping one of his workmen to fit the wheels onto a new cart. He looked up when I came through the gate and did a double-take.

'Corvinus?' he said. 'What're you doing here?'

'Hi, pal.' I went over. 'How's it going?'

'Busy, as you see. We've got an urgent order in. Give me a moment, right?' He lifted the wheel he was holding onto the raised axle, gentled it into position, fitted the restraining bolt, and stepped back. 'So. What brings you back to Ostia?'

I shrugged. 'You know that case I mentioned?' I said. 'Well, there've been developments.'

'Just leave it at that, Sextus,' he said to the workman. 'We'll finish the job tomorrow.' Then, to me: 'Involving that Nigrinus bastard? The guy who was going to punch your lights out in the wineshop?'

'Possibly. Probably, in fact. But not directly, at least for the present. It's a long story. You got the time to split a jug?'

He grinned and wiped his forehead with a rag. 'Make it a cupful. Cass was expecting me back an hour ago. Unless you want to come straight round to the house, of course. You staying?'

'No, not this time. At least, I am, but we've made arrangements.' I told him about Fulvina's villa. 'And a quick cup is just fine with me, because I'll have to be getting back too.'

'Fair enough.' He took the gate key from his belt and laid it on the cart's tailgate. 'Lock up when you go, right, Sextus? I'll see you in the morning.' He turned back to me. 'Balbus's it is. But no more than a few minutes, mind, because Cass'll kill me. You too, when I tell her.'

Yeah, that I'd believe: Agron's wife, Cass, was a lady that you did not cross. 'Deal,' I said.

The wineshop wasn't far, opposite the theatre at the corner of Boundary Marker Street and on Agron's way home. We went in, I ordered two cups of Massic, and we took them to one of the side tables.

'So,' Agron said. 'What exactly is this case of yours?'

I took a sip of the wine. 'You know a guy by the name of Marcus Correllius? Local businessman. One of the town's Great and Not-so-Good, if I've got it right.'

Agron frowned. 'Yeah,' he said. 'I've heard of him, certainly. And from what I've heard, Not-so-Good's putting it mildly. He involved in this?'

'In a way. He's dead, murdered or as good as.' I gave him the details. 'Me, I'd like to know why, but it turns out I'm in a minority of one. Even his wife seems to be glad enough to be shot of him. When I called round she practically threw me out on my ear.'

Agron was still frowning; a serious-minded guy, Agron, at the best of times, but he was currently looking even more serious than usual.

'You want a piece of advice?' he said.

'Sure. Always in the market.'

'Then drop it. Just take this case of yours, at least the Correllius part, to the deepest hole you can find, drop it in, and pile the dirt on the top. When that bastard was alive he wasn't a safe man to mess with. If someone killed him then it goes double where they're concerned.'

Ouch. Even so, I shook my head. 'I can't do that, pal. You know I can't.'

He grunted. 'Then be careful. Be very, very careful. You hear me?'

I took a swallow of my wine. 'So, ah, why would that be? If he was an out-and-out crook, surely the authorities—'

'Listen, Marcus.' Agron set his cup down on the table. 'I've just heard vague stories, right? Stories and rumours, third, fourth hand. I don't actually *know* anything. On the face of it, Marcus Correllius is – was, now, from what you're saying – one of the town's top businessmen. As far as the legal side of things goes, he's squeaky-clean respectable, and he was careful to keep it that way. But there've been . . . accidents. People who've run foul of him have got them-selves hurt, one way or another. Businesswise, financially, physically, you name it. Sometimes fatally hurt, OK?' I remembered the wineshop owner Vinnia's husband. 'Nothing anyone can prove, that's the point. Certainly nothing to implicate Correllius himself. So my advice, particularly if no one's twisting your arm over this, is just back off. It isn't worth the risk. Understand?'

'Yeah, I understand. Point taken.'

'But it won't make a blind bit of difference, yes?'

I grinned. 'How about a Publius Fundanius? You heard of him as well?'

He was staring at me. 'Gods alive, Corvinus! You certainly know how to pick them, don't you?'

'It'd seem so, yeah. He's crooked as well?'

'Fake as a wooden denarius. Everything I said about Correllius applies to him too. In spades.'

Uh-huh. I'd thought it might, at that. Bugger. 'OK. To change the subject. Or rather, not to, but you know what I mean. You manage to trace Siddius yet? The careless crane operator who dropped or didn't drop that load of amphoras over at the docks?'

'No. No luck so far. I'm still trying.'

A pity; Siddius was someone I really wanted to talk to. Even so, Agron and his contacts had jobs and lives of their own to see to. I couldn't expect a twelve-hours-a-day job, and I couldn't expect miracles.

'Look,' he said. 'You need any help here? Help in general, I mean. This isn't your town, and I know some pretty big lads who'd be glad to act as minders. Watch your back for you, that sort of thing.'

I shook my head again. 'Uh-uh. Thanks, Agron, but I'm OK. At least, I think I am.'

'Thinking isn't the same as being sure, and it can get you killed. I'll say it again: Ostia isn't Rome. We may be a small pond here, but our big fish have pretty large teeth, and it's those bastards' pond.'

'I won't forget.'

'Fair enough. But remember, the offer's always open if you change your mind.' He drained his cup and stood up. 'Right. I'd best be shifting. Keep in touch, OK?'

'Sure. We'll have you and Cass round to dinner at the villa once Meton gets his act together.'

'Look forward to it. Say hello to Perilla for me.' He turned to go, then turned back. 'And Corvinus. One last warning: no heroics, agreed? If you can't be smart then be sensible.'

'You've got it.'

He left. I finished my own wine, took the cups back to the counter, and set off for the villa.

SEVENTEEN

I got back in time for a quick steam in the bathhouse before the dinner gong went. Then, changed into a fresh tunic, I joined Perilla in the garden. Bathyllus had had the local minions carry out the requisite furniture, and he was currently supervising the ferrying of the starters.

'We eating al fresco then, little guy?' I asked him as I stretched out on the other couch.

'That was my idea, Marcus,' Perilla said. 'It's a lovely evening, and it'd be a shame to eat inside. Besides, it's part of the holiday.'

'Fair enough.' I held up my wine-cup for Bathyllus to pour. 'So what are we having tonight, Bathyllus?'

'Braised chicken with a pungent ginger dressing, puréed greens with a lovage-savory sauce, and a chickpea and fennel casserole, sir. Meton brought the ingredients in the coach with us from Rome.'

Yeah; that made sense: Meton likes to do his market shopping first thing, as soon as the stalls open for the day. And he would've as soon sent out for a takeaway from the nearest cookshop as trust the local staff to order in before we arrived. He might be a surly bugger when he liked, which was most of the time, but where food was concerned he was a professional to his grubby fingernails.

'Great.' I reached out for a quail's egg and dipped it in fish sauce.

'So.' Perilla did the same. 'How did your afternoon go?'

I gave her the rundown. 'The Correllius ménage is a weird set-up. And my informants – Agron and my butcher pal – were pretty much agreed that the guy was crooked as they come, or the next thing to it.'

'It's odd that his wife wasn't interested in finding out who stabbed him, isn't it?'

'Yeah, well, there could be several reasons for that.

Barring the simplest one that she's just a cold-hearted bitch.'
I leaned over for the wine jug and topped up my cup. 'Which
she is, no question. Mind you, from what I know of Correllius
they weren't exactly a well-matched couple. He had a good
twenty years on her for a start, and he was a real barrel of
lard, while she wouldn't've been out of place at a Top Five
Hundred get-together. *Soignée*. That the Greek word?'

'It'll do.'

'Right. That lady was *soignée* in spades.'

Perilla selected a fried broad-bean rissole. 'Do you think
she might've been behind the stabbing herself?' she said.

'It's the most obvious explanation, sure.' I took a swallow
of the wine: if Meton had brought along a stock of culinary
supplies with us, I'd had Bathyllus do the same on the liquid
side, and we were well-fixed. Oh, the villa would have a pretty
good cellar, no question, and Fulvina's husband would keep
it stocked, but you can take cadging too far. Besides, I wouldn't
altogether trust a guy whose métier was Aqueducts and Sewers
to have a good nose for wine. 'The fact that he hadn't actually
been murdered and the authorities weren't interested in an
investigation would be a godsend to her. And we wouldn't
have to look far for the actual perp. His exec, Doccius, fits
the maid's description perfectly, Mamilia clearly has him eating
out of her hand, and equally clearly he's not too cut up about
his boss's death either.'

Perilla set the remaining half of the rissole down on her plate.

'You're saying that Doccius and the missing businessman,
Marcus Pullius, are the same person?' she said.

'Yeah. Why not?'

'But, Marcus, dear, that's impossible!'

'Oh? How so?'

'Well, obviously it is! Correllius saw Doccius every day.
He was hardly likely to get away with arranging a meeting
with him under another name, now, was he?'

'Hang on, lady. We don't know that Correllius set the meeting
up with this Pullius guy personally, or even that he'd ever
clapped eyes on him. He might've done it at second hand. In
which case as his deputy Doccius could well have made the
arrangements himself.'

'That's hardly likely. Not if whatever deal Pullius wanted, or claimed he wanted, to discuss was important enough to warrant a sick old man travelling all the way to Rome in person. Either he'd have been personally involved at the start or sent Doccius in his stead.' Perilla dipped the second half of the rissole into the fish sauce. 'Besides, Doccius couldn't have known that Correllius would fall asleep – call it that – on the Pollio bench. The chances were that he'd be in full possession of his faculties when they met face-to-face, as they'd have to do, and he'd certainly know him then.' She popped the rissole into her mouth and chewed. 'No, it's just silly.'

The lady was absolutely right, of course; put like that it was silly. Still—

'OK,' I said. 'Maybe Pullius wasn't Doccius himself. But the principle holds good. Doccius – with or without Mamilia's collusion – could've arranged the phoney meeting to manoeuvre Correllius into a position where he was on his own and they could take him out in relative safety, using a hitman. The phantom Pullius. After all, why Rome anyway, if it wasn't to get the guy off his usual patch?'

'But why should Doccius – or Mamilia, for that matter – *want* Correllius dead?'

I sighed. 'Come on, Perilla! Doccius was Correllius's right-hand man, from the looks of things he's the one actually running the business on a day-to-day basis, and he's a good-looking devil in himself. Mamilia's not all that much older than he is, she may not be a stunner, exactly, but she's well set-up all the same and knows it, and she was married to a fat sixty-odd-year-old slob. Probably a seriously rich fat sixty-odd-year-old slob, at that. Do the maths yourself.'

'Correllius was also not a well man.'

'According to Doccius, sure, but—'

'Marcus, he died a natural death, and Clarus was of the opinion that that wasn't surprising in the case of a man of his age and in his physical condition.'

'OK,' I said grudgingly. 'So?'

'So if it were a case of dead man's shoes, sexual attraction, whatever, then why go to the trouble of murdering him? After

all, the situation would resolve itself before very long. It just
wouldn't be worth the risk. I think we can give Doccius the
benefit of the doubt here, don't you?'

True. At least on present showing. Bugger.

We'd finished with the nibbles, and Bathyllus was wheeling
in the main course. I helped myself to some of the braised
chicken and the puréed greens.

'Yeah, well,' I said. 'The Mamilia–Doccius pairing's too
good just to let slide. And we're only at the start of things
here.' I passed her the chicken, and she spooned some onto
her plate with a helping of the chickpea casserole. Not a great
one for greens, Perilla.

'Fair enough,' she said. 'Leave that aspect of it for the
moment. What else have you got?'

'The most interesting thing is a guy by the name of Fundanius.
Publius Fundanius. Turns out he's a crook as well and that he
and Correllius had been at daggers drawn for years.'

'Hmm.' She held up her cup for Bathyllus to pour in some
of the fruit juice and mint concoction she was currently
favouring. 'Same objection, surely. If the man hadn't gone the
length of murder before, then why do it now?'

'I don't know, lady. Like I say, it's early days to be theorizing.
Maybe the situation had changed somehow recently, or
Correllius had done something that really got up his nose.
Maybe he'd just got out of the wrong side of bed one morning
and decided he might as well stiff the guy and be done with
him. In any case, Fundanius is a front runner, and from what I
saw he might well be up for it.'

'You've met him?'

'Briefly. At Correllius's house. He dropped by to give
Mamilia his condolences. Or at least that's what he said.' I
frowned. 'That was odd, if you like.'

'In what way?'

'Come on, Perilla! Why should he? Like I say, he was no
friend of the family, and according to my butcher pal Rubrius
he was more likely to spit in Correllius's urn than shed a tear
over it. And there was no love lost between him and the
widow, that was for sure.'

'Perhaps it was just good manners on his part. It does

happen between business rivals. Correllius was dead, and so presumably was the feud, whatever it was about. Perhaps he was simply making overtures.'

'Yeah.' I was still frowning. 'Even so, it smells. And putting together a case – a hypothetical one, anyway – wouldn't be too difficult.'

'Namely?'

I laid down my spoon. 'OK. Say for some reason Fundanius was responsible for knifing the guy. There's no mileage in rousing Mamilia's suspicions, is there? Quite the opposite. Oh, sure, at present he's not exactly persona grata in the Correllius household, but with the boss dead the family business is bound to be drifting a bit. Say that "making overtures" was exactly his intention, that he was angling for some sort of merger, or at least a spheres-of-activity deal. Oh, not right away, that'd be asking too much. But softening things up might be another matter. Like I said, we don't know the exact circumstances – or not as yet, anyway – but something along those lines might well give him a viable motive.'

'Of course,' Perilla moved the chickpeas on her plate around with her spoon, 'there is another possibility. Extension, rather. Not that I'm advocating it, mind, but it's worth considering.'

'Yeah? And what's that?'

'That your Fundanius and Mamilia were in it together from the start.'

I'd picked up my spoon again and had a piece of Meton's chicken stew halfway to my mouth. I laid it down.

'What?'

'It's as good a theory as any, dear. You've already suggested that Mamilia might be involved sexually with Doccius. Why not with Fundanius instead? In fact, he's a lot more probable. At least he's from the same social level.'

'Lady, you weren't there! When the guy came in you could've cut the atmosphere with a knife!'

'But of course you could. I'm sure the last thing she would have expected or wanted was for her lover and partner-in-crime to drop by when a stranger whose declared intention was to investigate her husband's death was present. All that

would be needed is that she would have the nous and acting
ability to carry the thing off. Or do you think she'd be incap-
able of that?'

Shit; it made sense. All kinds of sense. And it would explain
a lot of the oddness: the fact that Fundanius, persona non
grata or not, had been able just to walk in past the door-slaves,
the fact that Mamilia was obviously completely un-cut-up
about her husband's death, and not least the fact that, to put
it mildly, she wasn't too keen on the circumstances being dug
into. And if I'd ever met a lady who had the coolness and
sheer brass neck to become mistress of the situation at the
drop of a hat, then Mamilia was the one.

'It's possible,' I said carefully: if I've learned anything these
twenty-odd years it's not to let Perilla see she's slipped one
past me.

'I mean, how did Fundanius strike you in himself? The sort
of man someone like Mamilia would go for, all being equal?'

'He was OK, yeah.' Better than OK, particularly when you
compared him with the dead husband: near the lady's age,
good-looking, fit as a flea, and with an urbane polish about
him that matched hers. Successful, too; that, I was sure, would
weigh with a hard-nosed woman like Mamilia.

'There you are, then. And the sexual element isn't particularly necessary. You say that, as a businessman or whatever
you like to call it, Correllius wasn't held in very high regard?
By his chief assistant Doccius, at least?'

'Yeah, well, that was the impression I got. But then it may've
been wrong.'

'Assume that it wasn't, which is a fair assumption under
the circumstances: in his delicate physical condition Correllius
couldn't have been totally on top of things. If Mamilia was
ambitious in her own right – and from your description of her
I'd say that was extremely likely – then she may well have
decided to cut her losses and make a more profitable alliance.'

I thought of Doccius's changed manner when he was talking
to the lady. Yeah, that would fit, too. Despite Mamilia's claim to
me that she'd no connection with the business side of her
husband's affairs I'd lay a pretty hefty bet she was involved
up to her carefully plucked eyebrows. And not as a silent

partner, either. I suspected that, however things had started out, latterly there'd been only one real boss of Correllius's outfit, and that boss hadn't been Correllius. Or even, given his behaviour vis-à-vis Mamilia, Doccius.

The theory was beginning to make sense in spades. Certainly, I'd be looking into Publius Fundanius before we were much older.

'Well?' Perilla finally spooned up some of the chickpeas she'd been shoving around on her plate. 'What do you think? Viable or not?'

'Sure it's viable,' I said. 'Whether it's right is another matter. Mind you, for it to work it'd need Doccius to be in on things off his own bat.'

'How so?'

'Because Correllius might be slipping his cogs where the business was concerned, but I'll bet you anything you like his deputy was well up to speed. Mamilia might be the brains of the outfit, but she's still a woman.'

'Marcus, that is pure sexism!'

I grinned. 'Agreed. But like it or not, whatever dealings the company was involved in – legit or crooked, it doesn't matter – business is a man's world. She'd need someone to front for her at the top level with clients and customers, and Doccius'd be too much in place already to bypass. Too smart and full of himself to con, too. Besides, it would've made things much easier where the Pullius angle was concerned.'

'You think that there was an actual Pullius, then?' Perilla took a sip of her fruit juice. 'I mean, that he existed as an individual in his own right?'

I shrugged. 'Not necessarily under that name. But sure, he must have done for the thing to work, because we need an actual perp who also had to be a stranger to Correllius, a complete outsider. And whatever they claim to the contrary I'd bet a flask of Caecuban against a used corn plaster that both Doccius and Mamilia know perfectly well who he was. If your conspiracy theory's right then my guess would be that the three of them – counting Fundanius – invented the sham business meeting to get Correllius over to Rome where their specially hired hitman Pullius could safely stick his knife in.

In the event, of course, that wasn't necessary, but they weren't to know that at the time. And it would certainly explain the cover-up now.'

'You don't think Doccius would have any issues with working for Fundanius? After all, he'd been the number one rival for years. There must've been at least a bit of bad blood, or at least distrust.'

I shook my head. 'Uh-uh. I didn't see much of the guy, sure, but I'd put him down as a professional to his finger-ends. Not a leader himself, but the sort who has to know that his boss is a professional too. Whatever Correllius had been in the past, he'd lost it, and he'd lost Doccius's respect. Mamilia, on the other hand – well, Doccius clearly has a lot of respect for Mamilia, which is significant in itself. And if she decided to join forces with someone like Publius Fundanius, then I can't see him kicking up too much of a fuss.'

'Hmm.' Perilla helped herself to more of the chicken; she has a good appetite, the lady, bigger than mine, and no doubt the drive from Rome and the change of air would've helped. 'So. What about this wineshop business?'

I pushed my own plate away. 'Right. That was interesting enough, but whether or not it's relevant, and if so how it fits in, I haven't the faintest idea. The owner – Vinnia – had a five-star grudge against Correllius, that was for sure, but just having a grudge against someone isn't enough when you're planning a murder. Besides, he died in Rome, not Ostia, and to most Ostians at her level and of her profession the big city's a million miles away. How would she set things up?'

'Marcus, you don't know for a fact that she had no connections with Rome. Ostia is only fourteen miles away, it's a small town, and by no means everyone who was born here stays here. She may have relatives there and gone through regularly.'

'Uh-uh. No relatives. The lady's from Gaul originally, and Rubrius told me categorically that she'd no family in Italy at all. In any case, the theory's too complicated. Why the hell should she make things difficult for herself when the guy only lives round the corner? Plus the fact she's a woman, and our perp was definitely male.'

'You know the answer to your first objection yourself, dear,' Perilla said. 'Security. Correllius was a powerful man in Ostia, with a large organization. Creating an opportunity to murder him here would have been difficult, to say the least; Rome would be much easier. As for your second point, yes, I agree that she can't have stabbed the man herself, but there's no reason why she couldn't have had someone else do the job for her, is there?'

'Such as who?'

'I don't know. How could I? Your butcher friend, perhaps. You said he was quite smitten with her.'

I laughed. '*Rubrius?* You're joking!'

She ducked her head and smiled. 'Actually, Marcus, yes, I am. He wouldn't fit the maid's description, for one thing, or I'm assuming he wouldn't. But the principle holds good: she could have had a male accomplice.'

'Yeah, well, whoever he was he'd have to be willing to risk putting his head into the strangler's noose for her. Finding someone like that wouldn't've come easy.' I took a swallow of wine. 'No, like I say it's far too complicated. Leave it out. We've better fish to fry than Vinnia.'

'Mm.' She set the spoon down on her empty plate. 'The way her husband died is a bit of a coincidence, though, isn't it? I mean, as the result of an accident at the docks, assuming she's right and that it was no accident at all. If the business with the falling amphoras in Gaius Tullius's case wasn't an accident either but his killer's first attempt at murder, then—'

'Too many ifs, Perilla.' I refilled my cup. 'Oh, I'll grant you the coincidence, although on the surface both accidents could well have been just that. Ostia docks are no kids' sandpit. There's a lot going on there, a lot of heavy stuff being shifted around on a daily basis, and with the best will in the world accidents – even fatal ones – are bound to happen now and again. We can't factor either of those into a proper theory until I've had a chance to talk to our cack-handed crane operator Siddius and Vinnia's dead husband's pal Cispius. If he's still around, that is.'

'Do you know where he lives?' Perilla had finished off the chicken and chickpeas.

'Uh-uh. Or not exactly. According to Rubrius he had a daughter whose husband has a fuller's shop near Guildsmen's Square. I might as well hunt her down tomorrow, for what it's worth. I'll pay a call on Fundanius, too. According to Rubrius, he's practically a neighbour of ours, so I can use that as an excuse.' I looked round; Bathyllus was hovering. 'Yeah, little guy, we're just about done. You can clear away. What's for dessert?'

'The chef has made a dried-fruit compote, sir.' Bathyllus snapped his fingers for the skivvies with the trays. 'He apologizes and promises that normal service will be resumed tomorrow when he can investigate the local fruit market.'

'Compote's great,' I said. 'And just top up the wine flask while you're at it, OK?'

I stretched out on the couch. Eating al fresco had been a good idea: it'd settled in for a very pleasant evening. A bit on the cool side with the breeze from the sea, but from our raised terrace we had a fantastic view of the coast and the sunset; taken altogether, Ostia – or this stretch of coastline, rather – was not too bad. Not too bad at all. Certainly I couldn't complain that this time round the case hadn't had its incidental perks.

I glanced over at Perilla. The lady was watching me and smiling.

'It is nice here, isn't it, Marcus?' she said quietly.

'Yeah, it's OK,' I said. Perilla, it was clear, was really enjoying the break. Maybe we should hock some of the family silver and invest in a small out-of-town place of our own, and the advantage of Ostia over most of the places we'd been outside of Rome was that it didn't offer much in the way of sightseeing. A definite plus, in my book: me, I'd go for the quiet life any time.

The case could wait for tomorrow. I took another swallow of wine, settled back, and closed my eyes.

EIGHTEEN

I was out and about at a reasonable hour the next morning. Not too early, because the plan was to kick off with a visit to Publius Fundanius. Neighbour was right: according to Caesia Fulvina's bought help his villa was only two along from us, practically a stone's throw away on the road into town; in fact, I'd registered it on my walk the day before, a solid little property a bit bigger than Fulvina's but with no flash about it and obviously kept in pristine condition.

I'd thought carefully about how I was going to play this. From what Agron had said, taking the direct, in-your-face approach and rattling the guy's cage for him would be a bad, bad idea: Agron was no scaremonger, Ostia was his town, and if he'd warned me in no uncertain terms to be careful how I went, then I'd be a fool not to listen. So I'd keep this friendly, or as friendly as I could on my side, and if Mamilia had already warned Fundanius to be wary of me – which, if Perilla's collusion theory was right, the odds were she probably would've done – then, as the Greeks say, *tant pis*. The neighbour ploy was good enough, but I reckoned I could improve on it: there must be properties along the Laurentian coastline for sale or let, and as a local – and already a casual acquaintance – Fundanius would be the natural person to ask about them. Particularly if he was in business on his own account.

I came abreast of the villa. It was no different, from the outside, at least, to any of the other coastal ones I'd seen so far; clearly, we'd got a different set-up here to the one I'd met with at the Correllius place, much more laid-back and normal. On the face of it, anyway.

The gate-slave was an inoffensive old guy who looked like the slightest puff of wind would blow him away, and he was dozing on a stool in the morning sunshine with his back against the villa's wall. I woke him up.

'The master at home, pal?' I said. 'Publius Fundanius?'

'Yes, sir.' He got arthritically to his feet. 'I expect he's just finishing breakfast. You wanted to see him?'

'Yeah. If it's convenient.'

'Oh, that shouldn't be a problem. He doesn't usually leave for town before mid-morning. If you'd like to come inside and wait in the garden for a minute or so, I'll tell him you're here. What name should I say?'

'Corvinus. Valerius Corvinus. We met yesterday.'

'That should be perfectly in order, sir. Was it business, or a private visit?'

'A bit of both. I'm staying at Caesia Fulvina's place.' I couldn't for the moment remember the husband's name. 'Just up the road. I thought I'd call in on the off-chance since I was passing.'

'Oh, yes. I know the villa well, sir. And the Lady Caesia.' He opened the gate. 'Now, as I say, if you'd like to wait in the garden I'll see if the master is receiving. The bench over by the hedge there should be perfectly comfortable.'

He hobbled off up the drive, and I settled down on the bench and looked around me. Nice garden, and like the rest of the place, from what I could see of it now that I was inside the grounds, impeccably kept. The bits and bobs were impressive too – some nice statues, obviously copies of Greek originals, and not too many to clutter the place up. Whatever his questionable business interests, Fundanius had good taste, and if he had money then he knew how to spend it. I'd reckon that if he and Mamilia did have a thing going she'd be far more his type than her late husband's. And she'd said that she'd been trying to persuade Correllius into buying a seaside property, hadn't she? Maybe she'd get her wish. Second-hand, as it were.

Clearly kindred spirits, in essence anyway, whatever contrary circumstances there might be. Some sort of alliance between Mamilia and Fundanius, unlikely as it seemed, was beginning to look like a viable proposition.

The slave came back.

'The master will see you, sir,' he said. 'He's on the breakfast terrace. If you'd like to follow me?'

We went round the corner of the villa's nearside wing. That part of the garden – the east side – had a terrace sheltered by a trellised vine. Fundanius was sitting at a table with the remains of an al fresco breakfast on it.

He stood up.

'Corvinus,' he said. 'This is an unexpected pleasure. Have a seat. You've breakfasted?'

'Yeah. Yes, thanks.' I sat down on one of the Gallic wickerwork chairs. 'I'm sorry to disturb you so early, but like I told your gate-slave I'm staying just up the road and I thought I'd just drop in in passing on my way to town.'

'Oh, my dear chap! Don't give it another thought! You're very welcome at any time, as is any friend of Aelius Tubero's.' Yeah, that was the Sewers and Aqueducts husband's name. 'I don't see much of him, but he's an excellent neighbour when he and his wife do come through to Ostia. Very good company, both of them. You must give him my regards when next you see him.' He sat down again. 'Now. Partly business, my slave said. What would that be?' Straight to the point, and for all the bonhomie, there was more than a smidgeon of reserve and suspicion in the guy's voice; I'd have my work cut out here. 'Nothing to do with Marcus Correllius's death, I hope, because there I'm afraid I can't be of any help to you at all.'

'No.' I crossed my legs and went into my prepared spiel. 'Actually, we were thinking – my wife and I, that is – about renting or buying one of the villas along the coast. Nothing too grand, just somewhere to get away to now and again. I was wondering, if it's not too much trouble, as a local man – businessman – if you might be able to point us in the right direction.'

'Ah.' He smiled, and I could almost feel him relax. 'It is very pleasant here after Rome, isn't it? Especially in the summer months. Not too pricey, either, compared with some places. I hear that the Alban Hills are getting really expensive, and as for Baiae and the Bay of Naples prices are simply ridiculous. And you've come to the right man. I don't specialize in that area myself, but I do keep my ear to the ground. Coincidentally, there is a very nice little property just come onto the rental market not too far away. A bit further along the coast from where you're staying, so not quite as handy for town, but that's reflected in the price. The Rusticellius place. I know the person who's handling it, and I can give you the details, if you like.'

'That'd be marvellous,' I said. 'It's just an idea so far, but we thought that while we're in the area we'd check out the possibilities.'

'Very wise. Very wise. I'll see you get them before you leave.' He settled back in his chair. 'So. You're enjoying your time in Ostia?'

'Very much so. Like you say, it's a lot more pleasant here than in Rome this time of year.'

'A shame that the circumstances of your visit aren't . . . well, a little more conducive to enjoyment. Or so I'd assume from our brief meeting yesterday at poor Correllius's house.'

Uh-huh; well, he'd brought the subject up himself. Almost certainly deliberately: now that I'd shown, as far as he was concerned, my bona fides I was about to be squeezed dry. Which was absolutely fine with me, because it gave me the latitude to do a little gentle return squeezing on my own account.

'My wife was just saying the same,' I said.

'He was stabbed, I understand. After he had died a natural death, of course.'

I'd've very much liked to ask the guy how exactly he'd come by that little nugget of information, because the answer would've been interesting, but I was playing careful here. Careful, garrulous, and dumb. Besides, I could make an educated guess.

'That's right,' I said. 'My adopted daughter found the body. And my son-in-law examined it. He's the local doctor at Castrimoenium, up in the Alban Hills, and they were through on a visit. Not the sort of thing you'd expect to happen when you're on holiday, is it?'

'No, indeed. Strange business. Strange.' Fundanius was frowning. 'And you're investigating? Off your own bat, I mean, not at the request of the authorities or of Correllius's family?' I said nothing. 'Why would that be, now?'

I shrugged. 'Simple curiosity. Like I said, my daughter and son-in-law were there at the time.'

His interest sharpened. 'At the actual time of the stabbing? They witnessed it?'

'No. But they didn't miss it by much. At least, that's how it appears.'

'Have you any idea who the perpetrator was?'

'The chances are that it was a man by the name of Pullius.' Not a flicker, and I was watching for it. 'Certainly he'd arranged to meet Correllius in front of the Pollio Library. And he seems to have disappeared without a trace. We have a description, of course, but—'

'Really?'

'Oh, yes. A lady's maid saw the whole thing, although she didn't realize at the time there was something funny going on.'

'What were the man's reasons? Do you know?' Casual; too casual. I could hear the note of underlying interest in his voice.

'Not so far,' I said. Then, casually in my turn: 'Might you have any idea yourself? I mean, you knew Correllius, as a business associate at least. You may even have come across this Pullius, if the business angle was legitimate.'

He was shaking his head. 'No,' he said. 'I told you, I can't be of any assistance whatsoever in that area, unfortunately. And although Marcus Correllius and I did have some dealings together I'd call us friendly rivals rather than associates as such; I certainly wouldn't have any inside information as to his business affairs. As for your Pullius, I've never heard of the man. If he is involved in business of any kind, then I can assure you he transacts none of it here in Ostia.'

'That's what I thought.' I leaned back in my chair. 'My theory is that he's either from well out of town or more probably the name is false and the business meeting was just an excuse to set Correllius up. Who'd want to do a thing like that, do you imagine? Anyone spring to mind?'

'No one I can think of offhand, certainly.' His tone was bland. 'He had his enemies, business rivals, rather, as do I and all of us, yes, of course he did. None of them would go to that extreme. But where Pullius himself is concerned surely you've already asked Publius Doccius if he can shed any light? After all, he is – was, now, I suppose – poor Correllius's right-hand man. He would be the natural person to ask.'

'I did. Doccius had never heard of him. Nor had Mamilia, for that matter.' I paused, then added, casually again: 'She was closely involved with her husband's business, wasn't she? At least, that was the impression I got.'

'Did you, indeed? I can't imagine how. Naturally, as I say, I have only an outsider's knowledge of Correllius's affairs, but I think it's most unlikely.' He was frowning again, and his fingers – maybe unconsciously – were tapping the table in front of him. For all the smooth exterior, the guy was perceptibly rattled. 'Mamilia has many excellent qualities, but she is a woman, after all. I doubt that she has much of a head for business, or very much interest in it.'

'Yes, well, maybe you're right.' I'd got what I wanted, and there was no sense in pushing things past the point of safety. Time to back off; seriously back off. 'I was probably mistaken. My wife Perilla's the same. Lovely lady, but a head full of fluff.'

He laughed. 'Best arrangement, I always think,' he said. 'My own was no different.'

Uh-huh; *was*, eh? Interesting, in view of the Mamilia side of things. 'I'm sorry,' I said. 'You're a widower?'

'Divorced, thank goodness. As of eighteen months ago. It was very civilized, and quite amicable. If you're from Rome, you'll readily understand that these things happen.'

So; as far as the feasibility of the in-it-together theory went we could tick another box, couldn't we? 'Yes. Yes, I do,' I said. 'Best thing for all concerned, sometimes. I'm all in favour of a civilized parting of the ways myself.' I paused, to take the weight off the next question. 'So. If not property then what sort of business are you in? If you don't mind my asking?'

'This and that,' he said. Blandly, again. 'Like Correllius, a lot of my dealings involve the import and export trade. Which explains the friendly rivalry. And you?'

Evidently, that was all I was going to get. Which wasn't too unexpected.

'I've no head for business, I'm afraid,' I said. 'Hardly a better one than my wife, to be honest. I'm a bit of a dilettante, really. Some property here and there, in Rome and else-where, that I inherited from my grandfather. The income keeps the wolf from the door, so I'm not complaining.'

All perfectly true; he smiled slightly, and rather contemp-
tuously. Which was absolutely fine by me. If he'd marked
me down as a lightweight upper-class bubble-brain with more
money than sense then I'd created the impression I wanted
to create.

'So,' he said. 'How long are you planning on staying in
Ostia? On this occasion, at least.'

'Oh, we're quite open on that,' I said. 'Me, just as long as it
takes to do everything I want to do. Or maybe, which is more
likely, until I'm satisfied the investigation's going nowhere or
I get bored with it. On the other hand, Perilla's really enjoying
the break, and there's the villa-hunting aspect of things now to
think about. We're in no particular hurry, and it's just nice to
get out of Rome for a change. Any excuse, right?'

'Quite. Quite.' He was completely relaxed now, and his tone
of voice was just a polite smidgeon away from the outright
contemptuous. 'It's always best not to let these things take too
firm a grip and become obsessions. And if you're not acting
for a third party or have a genuine vested interest, then there
isn't really much point, is there? So what comes next?'

'In the investigation, you mean? Actually, I haven't really
thought about that. I'll probably just bumble around like I
usually do, asking stupid questions and not listening to the
answers.'

He nodded benignly: impression of bubble-headedness
confirmed. 'Then I wish you luck,' he said. 'It's a strange business, as I said, but ultimately perhaps under the circumstances
it's better to let sleeping dogs lie. After all, what does it
really matter? Poor Correllius is dead, and despite the curious
business of the stabbing, from natural causes. It's none of my
concern, of course, but I really do think it'd be best just to
draw a line.'

'Yes. His widow feels the same way. Quite understandable.
Still, I've got to go through the motions, if only for my own
satisfaction, haven't I?'

'Of course you do, my dear fellow. And it's highly commend-
able. Needless to say, should you find the explanation I'd be
very grateful – and interested – to know what it was. And it
goes without saying that if I can help in any way—'

'I'll be sure to ask.' I stood up. 'Well, thanks for your patience with me. I've disturbed you long enough.'

He stood up too. 'Not at all, Valerius Corvinus, it was a pleasure. In fact, if your wife doesn't mind a bachelor's establishment she and you must come to dinner one evening before you leave. Oh . . . but I was forgetting. I promised to give you the contact details for the agent handling the Rusticellius let. If you can wait just a moment—'

'No, that's OK,' I said. 'Like I told you, it's only an idea at present. We'll take a stroll over there within the next few days and have a look at the place from the outside, see what my wife thinks. Plenty of time to contact the agent when we decide we're interested.'

'Very well. Don't leave it too long, mind. It really is a first-class bargain, and it's bound to be snapped up quickly.' He held out his hand. 'Delighted to meet you properly. Enjoy your stay, and don't forget the dinner invitation. We'll leave it open. Any day suits me, just send one of your slaves over to say you're coming.'

We shook, and I left.

Yeah, that had gone OK, in the end. And there had been some interesting scraps of food for thought.

I was making my way round the corner of the villa towards the gate in the wall when I happened to glance in the direction of the other wing. There was a door in the side, and as I looked it opened and a man came out. He saw me, did a double-take, and ducked back quickly inside, shutting the door behind him, but not before I'd seen who it was.

Doccius.

Well, well, well.

NINETEEN

S o. Time to dot the i's and cross the t's before we sat down and had a really hard think about how to go about things from here, and if that meant fishing for red herrings, maybe landing one or two, then so be it. Starting with the Vinnia side of things.

Oh, sure, the coincidence of the two dockyard accidents – Tullius's and Vinnia's ex-husband, Manutius's – might just be that, a pure coincidence, especially since they were ten years apart; but the fact that the name Correllius figured in both of them lifted the thing just that necessary smidgeon clear of the bracket. If I was lucky, a talk with Manutius's old pal Cispius, who'd worked for Correllius himself, might throw up some useful information. I needed badly to talk to someone on the inside, and that wasn't likely to happen any other way, was it? The explanation of why Gaius Tullius had been stiffed lay here, at the Ostian end, I'd bet my last copper piece on that; the business with the *Porpoise* and its master's brother Sextus Nigrinus – that bastard I knew I hadn't seen the last of, unfortunately, but we'd cross that particular bridge when we came to it – made it a virtual certainty. How Correllius fitted in, mind, barring that his name was on the manifest as the cargo's owner and that he'd been crooked as a Suburan dice game, I hadn't the faintest idea as yet; but fit in he did, sure as eggs is eggs. It was just a question, as usual, of furkling around in the dark and seeing what I could turn up.

Cispius it was, then. Assuming, from what Rubrius had told me, that his daughter still had her fuller's place near Guildsmen's Square and the old guy himself was still above ground . . .

I'd just have to keep my fingers crossed.

Guildsmen's Square, where the Ostian trade guilds' offices are, is on the Roman Gate side of town, between the theatre and the river. There were quite a few side streets and alleyways in that part, but finding a fuller's shop is always easy: all you have to do is follow your nose. Literally. So that's what I did, and found the place no problem.

It was tucked away in a cul-de-sac just past the town baths, a single large room opening out directly onto the pavement and with a couple of mantles hanging from a clothes line stretched between the buildings either side. I edged carefully round them, trying not to breathe through my nose – fullers may be used to the smell of well-matured urine, but for those whose olfactory sense hasn't been already blunted it's a pleasure to be rationed – and went inside.

There were a couple of guys in loincloths knee-deep in a vat, treading the hell out of a bundle of dirty mantles, and a grey-haired man in a badly stained tunic ladling sulphur from a bag into a sulphur-burner. Obviously the boss: the first perk of seniority in the fulling trade is that you don't spend a large slice of your working day up to the knees in diluted piss.

'Good morning, sir.' He set the cracked wine-cup he was using as a ladle down on the bench. 'How can I help you?'

'Hi,' I said. 'I was looking for a man by the name of Cispius.'

'The Dad?' His eyes widened, and I saw them stray to the purple stripe on my tunic. 'Yeah, he's upstairs. What do you want with him?'

Hey! At least I'd got the right place. And, it seemed, old Cispius was still alive and breathing. If being upstairs from a fuller's establishment wasn't a mixed blessing where the latter was concerned.

'Just a word or two,' I said. 'It's about a pal of his who died about ten years back. A Gaius Manutius. I understand he kept up for a while with the widow.'

The man grinned. '"Kept up", is it? Well, the Dad's always been a bit of a dark horse, but I never heard of no widow, me. Not that sort, anyway. Still, you're more than welcome to go up and talk to him, whatever it's about. You'll be doing him a favour, stuck in that room on his own all day with only the wife for company. Stairs just outside and to the left there. I'd take you up myself but the wife would have a fit unless I'd had a good wash first.'

'Fair enough,' I said. 'Thanks, pal. Your wife's at home?'

'Nah, she won't be back for an hour or two yet. Out doing the shopping. But you'll have no trouble finding him.'

I went outside again and up the stairs. There was a wooden door at the top. I knocked and went in.

The room above the shop was empty, but the lady of the house was obviously the house-proud type: swept and dusted to an inch of its life, and what little furniture there was had been carefully polished with wax. There was even a bowl of fresh flowers on the table. Not a single sniff of urine.

'That you back already, Cispilla, girl?'

An old man's voice, from the room adjoining. I went through.

It was a bedroom, smaller than the living room, mostly taken up with a big bed, carefully made with a chequered cover. Next to it was a single unmade truckle bed propped sideways against the wall, and a high-backed chair next to a window overlooking the main street, with the old man sitting in it. His legs were swathed in a rug.

'Who are you?' he said.

'My name's Corvinus. Marcus Corvinus. Your son-in-law said it'd be OK to come up.'

'That's as may be. What do you want?'

'Just a chat, if it's OK with you,' I said equably. 'You mind if I sit down?'

'Suit yourself.' His eyes, like his son-in-law's, were on the purple stripe. 'What's your business here?'

I sat down on the edge of the bed next to him. 'I was hoping you could help me out with something. It's about a friend of yours. A colleague, really. Guy by the name of Gaius Manutius?'

The suspicion hadn't left the old man's voice. 'I knew a Gaius Manutius, sure. But he's long dead, ten years back.'

'Yeah, I know. That's the point. I was hoping you could tell me about how he died.'

'Why do you want to know that?'

'It's . . . well, it's a bit complicated. But it has to do with a man by the name of Marcus Correllius. You both used to work for him, I understand?'

'Correllius, eh?' The thin mouth twisted into a smile with

no humour in it. 'That bastard! What's your connection with him?'

'He's dead as well. Murdered, in fact.' Best to keep things simple. 'I'm looking into the whys and wherefores.'

'You were a friend of his?'

This, I suspected, would weigh. 'Uh-uh.' I shook my head decisively. 'Definitely not. In fact, I never even met him. I told you: it's complicated. But I need to find out more about him.'

'He was a crook. I'll tell you that straight. And if he's dead – murdered – the bastard had it coming. You won't find me shedding tears for Marcus Correllius.'

'So if he was a crook, what sort of crook was he, exactly?'

'Every kind. You name it, he was into it. So long as it turned a profit, that was fine with him.'

'Can you give me some examples?'

Cispius frowned. 'Look,' he said. 'I used to work for him, right? Nothing fancy, just the heavy stuff. Loading, unloading, carts or ships mostly, sometimes on the regular quayside, sometimes up or down the coast at a time and place when there wasn't no one around to notice. Doing what I was told and no more. I kept my eyes shut and my mouth closed, and I didn't ask no questions. Never, ever. And if I did see something I shouldn't've seen, or something happening that didn't quite square with the law, then I put it out of my mind straight off. The pay was good, compared with what I'd've got breaking my back heaving wine jars and so on over at the docks, so I wasn't complaining. I even put by enough to give Cispilla and her man a hand paying to set up the business. So no, purple-striper, I can't give you no examples, because I was fucking careful not to think about what I was doing. Clear?'

'Yeah, it's clear. Clear and understood.' I waited until the frown had left his face. 'So. What about Gaius Manutius?' I prompted gently.

Cispius grunted. 'Manutius was different,' he said. 'He was a proper bad one, was Gaius Manutius. Cocky on top of it, thought he was smart, the sharpest knife in the box. Oh, don't get me wrong; he was a good mate, best I ever had although he was young enough to be a son, and I'd've trusted him with my last copper coin. But he was too smart for his own good. That's what did for him in the end, the poor bugger.'

'Yeah? So what happened?'

Cispius frowned again. 'If you want details, you'll have to whistle for them,' he said. 'I told you: I didn't ask, and if he'd offered to tell me, I'd've shut him up as soon as he started. All I know is he'd got hold somehow of some information he should never've had and tried to make something out of it on his own account. Next thing, we were down at the docks doing a bit of loading and the crane slips its load right above where he was standing. Smashed the poor bugger's head to pulp like a ripe melon. And that was that.'

'It could've been an accident.'

'Sure it could. And pigs can fly.'

'What makes you so sure it wasn't?'

'Look. We all worked as a team, right? Same lads, every time. Each of us had a job to do, and it was a man by the name of Geminus who worked the crane. Only that day Geminus had been transferred to another job at one of the other quays and there was someone else at the levers. Youngish guy, name of Doccius. You come across him in your travels?'

'Yeah,' I said. 'I know Doccius.'

'He's gone up in the world since, I've heard. Not that I'm surprised, the bastard. Anyway, that was him on the crane. He swore blind the cog had slipped its ratchet, but these things are checked regular, and if it had slipped then it'd been fixed to slip. The report went in to the dock authorities, sure, but whatever they may tell you all they care about is their harbour dues, and if one of their own men isn't working the crane and being paid through the nose by the shipper for doing it, then if someone gets hurt or a load gets dropped and smashed then it's just hard cheese. No, what happened to Manutius was no accident. You take my word for it.'

I said nothing.

'So that was me. Last job I ever did for that bastard Correllius, good money or not, and if he didn't like it he could lump it. I walked away from the quay and I didn't look back. First thing I did was go round to Manutius's house to break

the news to his widow. Vinnia, her name was. You met her?'
I nodded. 'I told her the whole story, just like I've told it to
you. Like I say, Manutius was no saint, and he had his faults,
but doing badly by his wife wasn't one of them. He'd a bit
put by, like I had, and I helped her get set up in a little wineshop by the Square and get the business running.' He chuckled.
'There wasn't no more to it than that, mind. She was a fine-
looking girl in sore need of another husband, but she was no
older at the time than Cispilla, and besides my Sosta was still
alive, and if I'd even looked at another woman she'd've had
my head. Then a few months before she died this started to
come on' – he patted his legs – 'and by the time I buried her
I was past walking through the front door, let alone marrying
again. There now. That's all about it. Get what you came for?'

'Yeah,' I said. 'Yeah, thanks. Uh . . . this Vinnia. There was
no one else to look after her? Family, that sort of thing?'

'No one local. She wasn't from around here, originally;
from somewhere in Gaul, I think. She'd a brother; has, if
they're both still alive. Gaius, his name was. Went for a soldier
early on, must be a good twenty-odd years back, with one of
the legions on the Rhine. Last I heard, which is a few years
ago now, he was doing pretty well for himself. Made it up
to optio and was set fair for his centurion's stick. Manutius,
now, his two brothers both died young. The parents were both
dead, too, like Vinnia's were, and she'd no other kin that I
ever knew of.'

Hmm. I stood up. 'Thanks, pal,' I said. 'You've been really
helpful.'

'How did he die? Correllius?'

'Stabbed in the back, over in Rome.'

Cispius nodded slowly and with satisfaction. 'Good. Good,'
he said. 'Well, I thank you for coming. Corvinus, was it?'

'Yeah. Marcus Corvinus.'

'Corvinus, then. I'll sleep better tonight for the visit,
Corvinus. And Manutius would've been pleased, too. If I'd
had the guts and the opportunity, I'd've knifed the murdering
bastard myself. Doccius, too.'

I left.

*   *   *

It hadn't been much of a day's work – the sun was barely past the midday point – but I reckoned we'd done pretty well here. Seeing Doccius at Fundanius's place more or less confirmed that we were on the right track about some sort of collusion between Fundanius and Mamilia, which meant that barring the details we could regard the Correllius side of things – or his stabbing, at least – as being pretty well sewn up. Of course, there might always be a more innocent explanation: I'd left Correllius's house practically at the moment that Fundanius had arrived, and so whatever had passed between him and the lady I knew nothing at all about it. Perilla's first point, that the guy had come round with the specific intention of burying the feud now that Correllius himself was out of things, could well be true; in which case, comings and goings between the two households might've eased off a tad.

There again, to quote Cispius, 'and pigs can fly'.

If Mamilia hadn't been putting on an act for my benefit, then I'd guess the meeting would've been pretty short and stormy, and ended with Fundanius being escorted from the premises with a flea in his ear: long-standing feuds don't get buried that quickly, and if I was any judge of character, Mamilia would've been as easy to get round as an elephant in an alleyway. Added to the fact was that, if everything had been above board, when he caught sight of me Doccius wouldn't have shot back in the door he was coming out of fast as a High Priest of Jupiter spotted sticking his nose out of the entrance to a brothel.

So scrub that idea.

Anyway, there wasn't much point in faffing around town with no particular end in view as opposed to going back to talk things over with Perilla and relaxing before dinner with a cup of wine or three. We might, in fact, if the lady felt like it, do what I'd told Fundanius we'd do and take a walk further down the coast road to have a look at the villa for rent that he'd mentioned: ploy it might have been, but I hadn't been totally unserious about looking around for a cheapish property in the area, and this Rusticellius place had sounded promising. Taking it would mean, for a start, that on the occasions when I did go through to Ostia I didn't have to spend the night kipping out in Agron's living room with the jolly prospect of being woken first thing by a gang of screaming kids.

So when I'd left the fuller's shop I started off for the Laurentian Gate and home.

I'd just got through the city wall and was walking along the coast road when I realized I had company. Oh, there'd been other pedestrians and carts on the road, sure, although not as many as there would've been earlier: the coast road's only used for local traffic, Ostia's much more laid-back than Rome, most of the locals – the agricultural element, anyway – take their main meal in the middle of the day, and in the summer over the next couple of hours or so, when the sun's at its hottest, they tend to get their heads down for a snooze. Still, despite the fact that the rest of the road as far as I could see was empty at present there were these two guys behind me, one a good bit in front of the other. The nearer of the two had on a cloak with the hood up; strange enough, on a warm day without a rain cloud in sight, but if he wanted to broil that was his own affair. Thing was, the first time I'd glanced back, he'd been keeping pace; the second time, he'd speeded up and the gap between us was closing.

Yeah, well; maybe I was just being over-suspicious here: the guy was probably just a local farmer late for dinner, with a wife who took that sort of thing seriously. I turned round and carried on walking . . .

I'd only got a few more yards when a sixth sense made me turn round again. Which was lucky, because another few steps and the bastard would've had me cold. As it was, I barely had the time to spot the knife he was carrying hidden under his cloak when he was on me. I grabbed at his wrist, but this time I'd misjudged things, and I felt the blade slice across the outside edge of my hand. My knee came up into his groin, but he stepped back in time, swore and lunged at me again . . .

Which was when somebody grabbed him from behind, pulling him off balance like he weighed nothing at all, then followed up with a swinging punch that would've felled a bull. The guy went down, catching the side of his head with a sickening crunch against a boulder by the side of the road, and lay still.

Shit.

'You all right, Corvinus?' the other guy, the one who'd punched him, said.

I knew him now: one of Agron's lads, the biggest of the bunch.

'Yeah,' I said. 'More or less.' I looked at my hand. He'd cut me, sure, and there was a lot of blood, but the wound was shallow, no more than a long thin gash from knuckle to wrist. It could've been worse. Easily worse. 'I'll live. Thanks, pal.'

He grinned. 'Agron thought you'd need a babysitter after all,' he said.

'Just as well.' I held the wound closed against my tunic. Bathyllus was going to have a fit: bloodstains were hell to get out, and the tunic was practically new. Not to mention Perilla, when she saw it. The lady gets quite upset when I'm beaten up or similar during a case. 'My mistake.'

Maybe I hadn't been as disingenuous with Fundanius as I thought I'd been. Unless, of course, he was one of Mamilia's boys. I looked down at him.

The hood had slipped back early in the struggle. He wasn't Fundanius's, or Mamilia's, as far as I knew, or not as such, anyway. He was Sextus Nigrinus. Had been, rather: from the looks of the damage to his head, and the way he was lying, he was definitely an ex.

Fuck.

The big guy didn't look too concerned. He lifted what was left of Nigrinus, hefted him across his shoulder, carried him into the bushes at the side of the road, and dumped him.

'You should be OK now,' he said. 'Don't worry, I'll bring a cart along after dark and get rid of him properly.'

'Right. Right.' I was feeling just a tad light-headed. Well, this was Ostia. Maybe they did things a bit different here from in Rome.

'Who was he? Do you know?'

'Yeah. A guy by the name of Sextus Nigrinus. We've crossed paths before.'

He grunted. 'Fine. I'll be getting back. Have a nice day.'

And he started off up the road towards town.

Fair enough. There wasn't any point in hanging around here with only an embarrassingly dead body in the bushes for company. I took a quick glance around to check that our little fracas hadn't been observed – no one in the offing apart from a very phlegmatic goat who'd obviously decided to take a constitutional of its own and was watching me with its jaws going – and carried on towards the villa.

Perilla was sitting on the terrace with a book unrolled in her lap. She looked up when I came over.

'Marcus! You're back very early,' she said.

'Yeah, I—'

'What've you done to your hand?'

'Ah. Right. Well, it was like this—'

She set the book down, stood up, took hold of my wrist, and turned the hand over. The cut had stopped bleeding, sure, but it was still pretty noticeable, and the part of the tunic I'd been holding it against wasn't looking too healthy, either.

'Oh, *Marcus*!'

'Just a slight brush on the way back with Sextus Nigrinus, lady. Nothing to be concerned about.'

'Damn that. What happened?'

I told her.

'And Nigrinus?'

'Uh . . . he didn't make it. Agron's pal left his body in the bushes. He said he'd clear up later.'

'He said *what*? Marcus, a man has been killed. You have to report it.'

'He started it. And the other guy just punched him. The rest was pure accident.' The lady didn't look convinced. 'Come on, Perilla! It could've been me lying in those bushes.'

'Yes, I know. Do you think that makes it any better?'

'Yeah, I'd say so. From where I'm standing, anyhow.'

She turned aside, and sat down again.

'One of these days, dear,' she said quietly, 'it will be you lying in the bushes. You understand that, don't you?' I didn't answer. 'Very well. There's no point in talking to you, is there? I don't think it needs stitching. Just go inside, get cleaned up, and have Bathyllus bathe it in vinegar and put a bandage on.'

I did. When I came back out again she was a bit more like herself. She hadn't picked up the book, though.

'So,' she said. 'Sextus Nigrinus.'

'Yeah, well, he was persistent, anyway.' I sat down and took a mouthful from the full wine-cup that Bathyllus had poured for me after doing his patch-up job. 'And it's a reminder. If I needed one, which I didn't.'

'A reminder of what?'

'That the key to all this – to Tullius's murder, at least – is Nigrinus's brother's ship. The *Porpoise*. Oh, it's obvious there's some sort of trading scam involved, no mystery there; the details don't particularly matter, and I'm no expert where these things go, but it's pretty clear that the Nigrini brothers were in it with Correllius: they provided the ship, he provided the merchandise, and whatever the set-up was or is it was important enough for Sextus to be seriously interested in taking out anyone who shows unwelcome curiosity.'

'You think he could have been the original killer? Tullius's, I mean?'

'He fits the maid's description as well as Doccius does. And we don't know the full circumstances of what happened that day at the quay, when Tullius was almost beaned by the falling amphoras.'

'Marcus, you do realize that, as things stand, none of this makes any kind of sense, don't you?'

'How so?'

'First of all, you can't have it both ways: either the accident on the quayside was a deliberate attempt to kill Tullius or it was just that, an accident. If it was the former, then there must have been a prior reason. Can you think of one?'

I shook my head. 'Uh-uh. Not offhand, certainly. But then I don't have to.'

She looked at me in surprise. 'Why not?'

'Because I think it *was* just an accident, pure and simple. Oh, sure, if it'd been someone at the Rome end of things who killed him – his partner Poetelius, or his wife, or her brother, individually or in any combination you like – then the earlier shot would square: any of the three of them could've known he'd be on that particular quayside that particular morning, and they'd've had plenty of time to set the thing up, no problem. *If* – and it's a major point, because it's a big "if" – they could find a suitably venal crane operator. Which I'll grant you they might've done, because Agron hasn't traced our elusive Siddius yet. Only it looks like the reason Tullius died is connected with whatever scam the two Nigrini and Correllius were involved in, and we're looking for a killer at the Ostian end. Tullius had no interest in the *Porpoise* at the time; it just happened to be berthed at the same quay as the boat he'd arranged his own shipment for. Pure fluke. My bet is that, as a result of the accident, Tullius suspected that something screwy was going on and decided there was money to be made.'

'Blackmail, you mean?' Perilla was twisting a lock of her hair.

'Yeah. Or something like it. Again, the details aren't important, but I think that's a fair assumption. Remember what Annia said: when he told her about the accident and she responded that he might've been killed, Tullius laughed the thing off and said he'd just been lucky. Strange thing to say, right? Particularly the way she told it. The guy sounded actually pleased about what had happened.'

'Hmm. Yes.' She was looking thoughtful. 'Yes, it is strange, at that.'

'OK. So the theory is that after the accident Tullius made enquiries and put the bite on. Or he may even have put the bite on there and then, if Nigrinus Senior was on board. Whichever it was, it got him stiffed, PDQ; Agron's right, these are not boys to fool around with.'

'The actual killer being Nigrinus?'

'Yeah; my money would be on him rather than Doccius, if only because he's already shown form. And if so then Nigrinus would've been a natural for the phantom Pullius too, always assuming Correllius himself had never met the guy. Which is a distinct possibility if he'd run to type and left the piddling day-to-day admin details such as contracting hitmen to his subordinate.' I took a smug mouthful of the wine. 'So. What other aspect of the case are you having problems with, lady?'

'Mmm?'

'You said, "First of all". When you told me none of it makes sense.'

'Oh, yes. Correllius's stabbing itself. I'm sorry, dear, but that doesn't seem to fit in in any way whatsoever. Not with the *Porpoise* business, certainly, because if Correllius was part of the scam, as he would have to be, then why on earth should Nigrinus kill him? Or Doccius, or any of them?'

I frowned; yeah, she was absolutely right, and to be fair I'd been dodging the issue myself. If the guy's death – or at least planned death – was connected with the trade scam, and so with Tullius's, then I couldn't for the life of me see why or how.

'Maybe it isn't connected,' I said. 'Not with the Tullius side of things, anyway. It could just've been a coincidence of timing.' Then, when she opened her mouth to say something: 'Oh, sure, my money's still on Nigrinus as being the hitman, because it keeps things nice and tidy, but I reckon we have a parallel plot here. For whatever reason – sexual attraction or good business practice – the guy's wife and his rival Fundanius decided that the guy had outlived his usefulness, and like I say these people play rough. The original plan is to set him up – probably through Doccius – with a phoney business meeting where Nigrinus can take him out; minimum risk, because the thing's done well away from Ostia and the phantom Pullius can disappear into the long grass, while everyone concerned can hold up their hands and deny all knowledge. Only then things go wrong: the killing turns out not to have been necessary after all, but the result is that shortly afterwards a nosey Roman shows up at the door and insists on an investigation. Complicated by the fact that there is an eyewitness who can give a description, and that the nosey Roman in question is also the guy shoving his nose into the other killing their hitman's recently been involved in. Hence Nigrinus's orders to take me out. That make better sense to you?'

'Yes, actually, it does. Complete sense.'

'No comeback?'

'No. None whatsoever.'

Glory and trumpets! Well, there was always a first time. I grinned and finished my wine.

'So. What's the next step?' she said.

'Perilla, I don't know,' I said. 'If the theory holds good then like it or not the case is stitched up as far as I can take it. Nigrinus is dead, so if he was the actual perp in both instances then he's out of things. The same goes for Correllius, if he was the one who gave the original order to kill Tullius. Mamilia and Doccius could well have been involved, sure, they probably were, particularly him, but how I'd go about proving that I've no idea.'

'There's still the other Nigrinus brother. Titus, was it? The captain of the *Porpoise*.'

I blinked. Hey! Right! I'd mentally factored him out of things, because he wasn't in Ostia to talk to, and if anyone still above ground knew the ins and outs of the Tullius business, then Titus Nigrinus was the lad. The *Porpoise* had been headed for Aleria in Corsica, or so the clerk in the shipping office had told me. No great distance, in other words. It could've been a blind, of course, on the captain's part – like I say, I didn't have any details, yet, of what the trading scam involved, so he could've given a false destination – or Corsica might only have been an intermediate stop; but if not, and it was a round trip, then he might well be back in Ostia by now. I doubted he'd be very cooperative, quite the reverse, particularly after his brother's death, but beggars can't be choosers, and he was the only game left in town. Maybe I could lean on him a little.

Clearly, another chat with the harbour-office clerk was in order.

I stood up and kissed the lady full on the lips.

'Perilla, you're a genius!' I said. 'I'll find out tomorrow if he's around yet. Meanwhile, you fancy a walk?'

'Where to?'

'Just a bit down the coast road. Fundanius mentioned a villa that was up for rent. I thought we might take a look at it.'

'Marcus, what is going on?' she said suspiciously. 'Does this have anything to do with the case? Because if so—'

'Uh-uh. Cross my heart, absolutely nothing whatsoever. I just thought you might be interested, that's all. Plus it's a nice day, there's still plenty of it left, and you could do with the exercise.'

She laughed, and stood up. 'Very well. But what brought this on?'

'It just seemed a good idea, that's all. And it'd be nice to have somewhere of our own to go when Rome gets too hot.'

'It's an excellent idea. Marcus Corvinus, you're getting old and staid.'

'Bugger that.'

'True.'

We went to see the villa.

TWENTY

I set out for the port the next day.

If it came to twisting arms, I was in a better position with Nigrinus Senior than I would've been with Mamilia, or even Doccius: Tullius's death had definitely been murder, it was being officially investigated by the Watch in Rome, and I could make a reasonable prima facie case to link it with the Nigrini brothers. Besides, there was the almost certainty of the trading scam, whatever form it took; that, I could use the threat of as well if a little extra muscle was needed. I just hoped that I'd have the opportunity.

The walk from the Laurentian Gate took me up the Hinge and through Market Square, passing Vinnia's wineshop on the way. I'd got pretty much all I needed to know in that direction from old Cispius, sure, and it'd been a red herring in the end, at that, but the wine had been good – like I said, you didn't see Veian all that often – and a quick stopover while I was in the neighbourhood wouldn't do any harm.

I opened the door and went in. No Vinnia this time, just a big guy his late forties with short-cropped hair greying at the temples, sweeping the floor with a broom.

He leaned the broom against the wall and went behind the counter.

'Yes, sir, what can I get you?' he said. His eyes flicked to the stripe on my tunic, and I saw them narrow.

Uh-huh. Interesting; very interesting. And I could see the family resemblance; he and his sister were alike as two peas. If she'd been built like a carthorse and had muscles like ship's hawsers.

'A cup of your Veian would be fine, pal,' I said easily, going over to the counter and taking a few coins from my belt-pouch.

He reached for a cup, hefted the wine flask, and poured in silence. I laid the coins down.

'No Vinnia today?' I said.

'No.' Nothing else, just that; chattiness clearly ran in the family. His eyes were still fixed on the purple stripe.

I picked up the cup and sipped.

'You'll be her brother, right?' I said.

'Gaius Vinnius. Yeah.' He turned round and replaced the flask in its rack. Obviously I was being left to make the running here.

'I heard you were in Germany,' I said. 'Serving with the Second Augusta.'

'That's right.' He turned back. This time the eyes looked straight at me, challenging. 'I was. Centurion in the Third Cohort. Got my discharge a couple of months ago.'

'Back here for good?'

'No. I've a family over there, in Belgica; Augusta Rauricorum. Wife and two kids, German girl; we got married properly after I was discharged. I'm just back on a visit.'

'A long way to come just for a visit, isn't it?' I took another sip of my wine.

He shrugged. 'I haven't seen my sister for over twenty years. This was the only chance I'd get. Besides, I'm taking her back out with me when I go. We've got the room, and there's nothing to keep her here.'

'True,' I said. I was still holding the cup. 'Particularly when the guy responsible for killing her husband is dead.'

Our eyes locked, and for a moment I thought he'd go for me. I'd kept my voice neutral, and my other hand was resting in full sight on the counter top. Then he dropped his gaze, shrugged again, reached for a cloth, and began drying the already-dry wine-cups.

'Vinnia told me there'd been a purple-striper from Rome in asking questions,' he said.

'Yeah, that's me. So. You were the one who stabbed him, right?'

'I've no regrets. The bastard deserved to die. Manutius wasn't much, but he was Vinnia's husband and my brother-in-law. It was a matter of honour, someone in the family had to do it, and there was only me. Once I was free of the legion I had my chance. I'd've had that bastard Doccius as well if he'd given me the opportunity, but I'll settle for the man who gave the order.'

'You know Correllius was dead before you stuck the knife in?'

The dishcloth paused, and his eyes came up.

'*What?*'

'Sure. Dead as mutton. Natural causes, my son-in-law said, and he's a doctor, so he should know.'

'No,' he said slowly. 'No, I didn't know that.'

He was telling the truth, that was plain enough. No one was that good an actor, particularly an ex-legionary centurion.

I took another mouthful of wine and set the cup down. 'So,' I said. 'If you think you're a murderer you can think again.'

'Gods!' He reached behind him, picked up a wine flask at random, poured some into an empty cup, and downed it in a oner. 'Gods!'

'You want to tell me exactly what happened?' I said gently. 'Purely for the record.'

He refilled the cup and replaced the flask.

'How much do you know?' he said.

'That you pretended to be a businessman by the name of Marcus Pullius. That you arranged to meet Correllius outside the Pollio Library in Rome. And that you stuck a knife into him while he was sitting on one of the benches then disappeared off the map. That's about the sum of it.'

'I thought he was asleep.'

'Uh-uh. I said: he was dead as a doornail. So what's the full story? From the beginning.'

'From the beginning?' He took another swallow of wine. 'Like I say, killing Correllius was the point of the visit, the first chance I'd had to out the bastard since Manutius died ten years back, and I wasn't going to bungle it. I'd written to Vinnia telling her I was coming, sure, but no one else knew, and I'd told her to keep her mouth shut. She wasn't even to mention I'd left the legion.' He drained his cup, then refilled it from the flask of Veian and topped mine up at the same time. 'We didn't meet, either. All the arrangements'd already been made by letter, and although I'd never been to Ostia in my life – never been outside Gaul and Germany, for that matter – we thought it'd be safer. Besides, we look pretty much alike, her and me. Enough to be taken for brother and sister, anyway.'

'Yeah,' I said. 'Yeah, you are. I spotted that straight off.'

He grunted. 'So. I kept well clear of this place, took a room in town under the name of Marcus Pullius, and had a message delivered to Correllius. To Correllius, personally; that was important. I'd a good mate in the legion, came up the ranks with me; he's in line for First Spear now. He was originally from Massilia, tough background, grew up round the docks. He knew the set-up there where the shady side of things was concerned, and he clued me in, gave me a few names to drop. People and places. I was betting Correllius'd never been to Massilia himself, but I wasn't taking any chances. I did my homework before I came.' His lips twisted. 'Well enough to pass on short acquaintance, anyway.'

'Doccius didn't know anything about this? Or Mamilia?'

He frowned. 'Who's Mamilia?'

'Correllius's wife.'

'Nah, not a thing. I told you, I sent the message to the bastard personally. I needed to keep things simple, and the fewer people on his side who knew the better.'

'So.' I sipped my wine. 'What was the message?'

'I told him I represented one of the local Massilian organizations in the same line of business as he was. Not the legit side of things, naturally. Gave him a name that I knew he'd recognize; it was real enough, thanks to my pal, and the guy it belonged to had serious clout. The idea was, I said, that the two of them would set up a working partnership, the Ostian side and the Massilian. One hand washes the other, you know what I mean?'

'Yeah,' I said.

'Only I said it was strictly hush-hush at present. My boss didn't want anyone else knowing about it until it was a done deal. So it would just be me as the rep and him, settled on a handshake, details to follow after I'd reported back. That was the reason for choosing Rome for the meeting, as well. Neutral ground, anonymous as we could make it.'

'Why the Pollio?'

He shrugged. 'Vinnia'd suggested it in her last letter. Me, I didn't know Rome from Sardis, but she said she'd overheard a couple of customers talking about it as a good place to meet in the middle of the city. Not that I ever intended to kill the bastard there, it was too public: I travelled up from Ostia a couple of days beforehand and found a room to rent in a tenement building not far away, near the Circus. The plan was that once we'd made contact I'd take him there for the confab and do the job at my leisure.'

Yeah, I could see all this working. And Corellius would've jumped at it; the guy had been running his own organization for years, and I would guess that, suspecting he was being edged out, he'd grabbed the chance of putting one over on Doccius, and probably Mamilia, by cutting a prime deal off his own bat. This Gaius Vinnius was no fool. Mind you, if he'd got to be a centurion in a crack legion then he wouldn't be.

'So,' I said. 'When you turned up for the meeting you found him asleep on the bench.'

'That's right. It made things a lot simpler. There was no one around, no reason to wake him, so I just stepped behind him and let him have it in the back there and then.' He frowned again. 'Which was when the girl came round the corner and spotted me. You talk to her?'

'Yeah. She didn't think anything of it at the time.'

'Well, I wasn't hanging around to find out, that was for sure.' His lips formed a wry smile. 'I'd done what I came for and I got the hell out of it. I couldn't go back to the original tenement room – too risky, as Gaius Pullius – but I found a shakedown near the Tiber wharves where they don't need names or ask questions so long as you pay up front. Then, when I reckoned I'd be safe enough, I cadged a lift to Ostia and walked through that door there as the long-lost brother home from the wars, just off the boat and with the Belgic mud still on my sandals. That was yesterday evening. Only it seems I was wrong about the safety part of things, doesn't it?' I didn't reply. He shrugged, drank the rest of his wine, and set the cup down on the counter with an audible *click*. 'So. That's it, the whole story, first to last. I've no regrets, either way. What happens now?'

It was my turn to shrug. 'Nothing.'

He looked at me in surprise. 'Nothing?'

'Not as far as I'm concerned. I told you: there's been no crime, you're no murderer, I've got no authority anyway, and the Watch in Rome couldn't care less.' A slur on my pal Watch Commander Decimus, but I was sure he'd understand if I told him. Which, just in case, I'd no intention of doing. 'So nothing. What had you got planned yourself?'

'Go back home, taking Vinnia with me. Like I said.'

'Fine with me, pal.' I finished my own wine and stood up. 'Safe journey, and have a good life. Give my regards to your sister.'

I held out my hand, and he shook it, automatically. Then I walked out, leaving him staring.

Well, so much for that aspect of the case. Rubrius would be disappointed, mind.

So. Onward and upward. We'd cleared up the Correllius side of things, at least where the stabbing was concerned, although naturally there was still the far more important matter of the scam. Over to the harbour offices for my chat with the clerk re the *Porpoise* and her captain.

I'd have to fit in another visit to Mamilia as well, of course. Not that I'd blow the whistle on Gaius Vinnius; there was no point, because for one reason or another the lady clearly couldn't care less who'd stuck the knife into her husband, and I reckoned I didn't owe her anything along those lines. But however she figured otherwise in this case – and she wasn't off the hook yet, let alone Doccius and Fundanius, not by a long chalk – I owed her a mental apology: in part, at least, the theory about what was going on was out the window.

I carried on up Tiber Gate Road and through the gate itself to the main docks and the harbour office. The same freedman clerk I'd talked to on the other two occasions was on duty behind the desk. He gave me a rather strained smile.

'Ah,' he said. 'The gentleman who was asking about the *Porpoise*.'

'Yeah. You've got a good memory, pal.'

'Never forget a face, sir.' The brittle cheerfulness in his voice suggested that he'd gladly forget mine, given the chance. 'How can I help you this time?'

'Same subject, really. She back in port from Corsica yet?'

'No. Nor likely to be. She went down just off Palla, in the south of the island.'

I stared at him. 'She did what?'

'Sank, sir. The crew, I understand, all managed to reach land safely, but the ship herself was lost. It happens, even at the best time of the sailing year.'

'How do you know?'

'Another ship calling in at Aleria brought the news a few days ago. I forget the name. Faces, yes; names, no.'

Gods! 'What about the captain? Titus Nigrinus?'

'I told you, sir.' The clerk was getting just a little tetchy. 'He made it to shore along with the rest of the crew. I'd imagine that he's still in Corsica, because he'd have to notify whoever was taking delivery of the cargo and make his own report. No doubt he'll get passage on another ship when he's completed the formalities at that end, if he hasn't already done so, but that's his own affair. I have and would have no knowledge of the matter.'

'Those are all the details you have?'

'For the present, yes. But as I say it's no business of mine.'

'You have an address for him? Just in case he is back?'

'No, sir. That's not information that we keep on record. I'm sorry.'

Jupiter on wheels! 'Fine,' I said. 'Thanks for your trouble.'

'No trouble, sir. Any time.'

I left. So, that was that. The question was, was the sinking part of the scam, or was it a genuine accident? Like the man had said, these things happen, and I didn't know enough about the ins and outs of the shipping trade or the dangers involved in that part of the Med to know how likely an accident was. The fact that the entire crew had escaped drowning, mind, was more than a tad suspicious: a lot of sailors, I knew, made a point of not learning to swim, because then if their ship went down at least they'd die quickly.

Complication on complication. It meant that I wasn't going to be having my little talk with Titus Nigrinus in the near future, anyway.

So. Since there didn't seem to be all that many options

available I might as well pay my call on Mamilia. I retraced
my steps to Tiber Gate and the centre of town.

The big bouncer was still on door duty at the house.

'The mistress at home, pal? I said.

'Yeah. You want to see her?'

'That's the general idea, yes.'

'What was the name again?'

'Corvinus. Valerius Corvinus.' Then, as he turned to go in:
'Hang on a minute. Publius Fundanius. He been round again
since I was here last?'

He gave me a look like he was a septuagenarian spinster
I'd shown a dirty picture to. 'No. Orders from the mistress
was if the bastard showed his face I was to laugh in it and
tell him to piss off.'

Interesting. And it didn't sit well with what was left of the
theory, either. I was getting the distinct impression that we'd
been ploughing the wrong furrow here altogether. 'Fair enough,'
I said.

'Business, was it?'

'Business'll do.'

'OK. Wait there.'

I waited there. Five minutes later, he came back out.

'The mistress'll see you,' he said, and stepped aside.

She was sitting in the atrium. Not quite so dolled up
this time, but still wearing a mantle that was the height of
fashion.

'Well, Valerius Corvinus,' she said. You could've used the
tone to pickle eggs. 'You're still here, I see.'

'Yeah. Evidently. In fact, we're thinking of taking the let of
a villa of our own along the coast. The Rusticellius place. You
know it?'

'Not offhand, no.' She didn't sound exactly thrilled with the
prospect.

'Your friend Fundanius recommended it to me when I
dropped in on him yesterday morning,' I said.

That got me a glare. 'Publius Fundanius is no friend of mine,'
she snapped. Forget the pickled eggs; make that mummies, with
an extra dose of natron thrown in for good measure.

'Business associate, then.'

'Not that either. And if he told you, or implied, any differently then it was an outright lie.'

Hmm. That came across as genuine, particularly after what I'd heard from the Last of the Titans at the front door. Either she was playing a very close game really, really well or the theory – what poor ragged tatters were left of it – was definitely up the creek. 'Strange,' I said. 'I could've sworn I saw your man Doccius on the premises as I was leaving. I wondered if you'd maybe sent him over there for some reason.

Her face . . . *set*. That was the only word for it. The expression on it was pure concrete. 'Publius Doccius,' she said, 'is no longer in my employ, or a member of this household. You may well have seen him at Fundanius's, since I know nothing of his whereabouts. He may just as well be there as anywhere else.'

I tried not to let the surprise show on my face. 'Your doing, or his?' I said.

Another glare, hundred-candelabra strength. 'Valerius Corvinus, that is absolutely none of your business,' she said. 'But since you ask, at mine. I found that he had been . . . not strictly honest.' I had to stop a smile. 'Over a considerable period.'

'You care to give me some examples?'

'I most certainly would not. I told you, it is no business of yours. However, it involved the company's finances.' She straightened her mantle with a savage jerk of her hand. 'Apropos of which. Why exactly are you here? I said: my husband was not murdered, and I regard the matter of his stabbing as closed. I can't see what other business you'd have with me.'

Couldn't she? Well, maybe not after all; that news about Doccius leaving had been a facer, and no mistake. At the very least, it needed thinking about.

Unless, of course, he hadn't left at all, as such, and she was still playing games . . .

'Actually, Mamilia, I came to tell you just that,' I said mildly. 'I know now who stabbed your husband and why.'

She was rocked, I could see that. And, despite herself, curious.

'Tell me,' she snapped.

'Uh-uh.' I shook my head. 'That wasn't part of the deal. Quite the reverse. But I didn't think it was altogether fair just to go back to Rome and leave you thinking the mystery was unsolved.'

'Was it Fundanius?' Then, when I shook my head: 'Doccius?'

Interesting again; she was no fool, this lady. And it suggested that she'd been up front about the bastard having been got rid of. I added it to my list of things to think about.

'No,' I said. 'Believe me, you wouldn't know the guy, or even recognize his name, so that side of things isn't important. Like you keep saying, there was no murder, your husband was dead already. All I'll tell you is that, yes, the man thought at the time he'd murdered him, he even thought so when I faced him with it, but it wasn't a killing for . . . well, call them for the sake of argument business reasons.' She had the grace to blink. 'It was purely personal. He did it out of revenge. Not for something that your husband did to him but on behalf of one of his family.'

I'd used the feminine form, of course, and she was staring at me.

'A woman?' she said.

'Uh . . . yeah,' I said cautiously. 'His sister, as it happens. But it wasn't what—'

Completely unexpectedly, Mamilia laughed, and she went on laughing. All I could do was look on amazed until she finally stopped.

'I'm sorry,' she said when she'd finished and dried her eyes with her mantle. 'That was quite unforgivable. But *Marcus*? You never knew my husband, Corvinus, so you won't see how funny it is. I never knew he had it in him. And there was always such a lot of Marcus for something to be in. Such a terrible lot, even when he was younger.' She giggled again; it was like watching a caryatid have hysterics. 'I am *so* glad you told me. That is possibly the first laugh I've had out of the man since I married him. Thank you.'

'Uh . . . you're welcome,' I said, getting up. Strange woman, Mamilia. Well, if she got a kick – in whatever form – out of the thought that her husband had been a philanderer and been murdered, or practically murdered, as a result, then who was I to disillusion her?

On the other side – the black side – she must've really hated the guy. Or no, not hated; hated was too positive. Despised came close, but I wondered if even that was too strong. I suspected that Mamilia hadn't been totally conscious of her husband's existence as part of her life. Which was sad, but it explained a lot. It explained everything, really.

Mamilia had stood up too. 'So you're off back to Rome?' she said; she was almost chatty now.

'No, not straight away,' I said cautiously. 'I've got one or two other things to see to before that happens.'

'Oh, yes, the villa. Of course. I hope you find it suits. And naturally, if you do find yourself an Ostian resident, albeit a part-time one, you must let me know. I think we might come to like each other.'

'I'll do that,' I lied; caryatids have never been my bag, particularly ones prone to sudden giggling fits or bouts of hysteria. And I still wasn't hundred per cent certain of Mamilia's bona fides where the case was concerned. Eighty per cent, sure, but still.

She saw me out.

TWENTY-ONE

S o; a fairly short morning, but one full of incident. And if we had to do a drastic rethink where the overall picture of things was concerned, at least we'd got some of the dead wood cleared away.

I went back to the villa, where Bathyllus's minions were just laying the outside table for lunch. Me, if I'm out and about, I usually settle for a quick snack at a wineshop counter, and because lunch is made up of cold leftovers from dinner the day before, Meton's perfectly OK about that. Perilla, though, tends to go for the sit-down variety. When I came through onto the terrace she was ensconced in her favourite wickerwork chair with her book and a stiff pre-lunch barley-water and honey.

'Back early again, Marcus,' she said when I'd kissed her. 'This is getting to be a habit.'

'I've got news,' I said. 'The stabbing business is solved.'

She laid the book down on the side table. 'Really? That's marvellous! You're certain?'

'Hundred per cent cast-iron sure. I've seen the guy himself, our elusive Pullius, and he gave me the whole story.' I told her about Gaius Vinnius. 'So we can forget about that aspect of things. The shipping scam, though, that's another matter. There've been developments there too. I called in at the harbour office and seemingly the *Porpoise* went down before it reached port.'

'Did it, indeed?' she said. 'Interesting. You don't think it was an accident?'

'The jury's out on that one, but my gut feeling says no. Absolutely, no. According to the clerk, the ship sank just short of the Corsican coast and all the crew made it safely ashore.'

'Convenient.'

'Right. The only problem – and it's a clincher – is that if the sinking was done deliberately then it makes no sense.'

'Why not?'

'Come on, Perilla! Nigrinus owned the ship and Correllius owned the cargo. The whole cargo. When the *Porpoise* went down they'd both've lost out in spades, however you slice it. Nigrinus would've lost his ship and Correllius would be down the value of eight hundred amphoras' worth of wine and oil. That's no fleabite, however big a businessman you are.' Something was niggling at the back of my mind; I reached for it, but it wouldn't come. 'Just the idea of it's silly. As things stand, they'd be cutting their own noses off for no reason.'

'So if they did do it, then why?'

I sighed. 'Search me. Maybe the sky is full of flying pigs and it was a genuine accident after all. We'll just have to—'

'Hey, Corvinus. I was hoping I'd catch you.'

I looked round. Agron was coming through the peristyle opening towards us, Bathyllus hovering behind him.

'Oh, hi, pal,' I said. 'Yeah, well, you have. Sit down, take the weight off your sandals. Bathyllus? The wine, little guy.' He buttled out. 'You staying for lunch?'

'Sure.' He pulled up another of the wicker chairs. 'Hi, Perilla.'

'This a social visit?'

'Partly,' he said. 'I wanted to see for myself how the other half live.' He looked around. 'Nice place.'

'Yeah, it is. Only partly?'

'Uh-huh. You'll be glad to know I've finally managed to trace your Gaius Siddius for you. The crane operator.'

I sat up straight. 'Have you, indeed?'

'Yeah. Turns out he's working for one of the local stone-masons. Just along the road from my yard, as it happens, so I'm kicking myself I didn't find him sooner.'

'That's OK.' Great! Siddius was someone I really had to talk to. 'Absolutely OK. If you give me directions, I'll go and see him this afternoon.'

'No problem. In fact, I'll take you there myself when I go back. I left Sextus minding the store, but like I told you we're pretty busy at present, so we're working flat out.'

'Right.' Bathyllus came back with the wine, and two cups. I waited while he poured. 'By the way, I should've thanked you for the babysitter. You were right; it could've been nasty.'

He shrugged. 'Don't mention it. Big Titus enjoyed the break. He said it made a change from hefting cement bags. And at least it meant that that bastard Nigrinus is off your back permanently.'

'Yeah.' I glanced at Perilla; she was looking pretty tight-lipped, but she didn't say anything. 'True.'

Agron took a sip of his wine. 'So. How's the case going?'

'Not too badly. You interrupted a bit of head-scratching; we're not there yet, not by a long chalk, but things are moving. And a chat with this Siddius character should help a lot, or I hope it will, anyway. At least quite a slice of the Correllius side of things has cleared itself up. Just this morning, in fact.'

His eyes widened. 'Is that so, now? Turf war?'

'No. Long-standing personal grudge.' I gave him the details, while round about us the minions set the cold bits and bobs on the table and laid an extra place. 'There was no point in taking things further, because in the event whatever the original plan was Vinnius didn't kill the guy, and like I say the widow's pretty blasé about the whole thing. Ask me, she's either happy enough on her own or she's got another likely prospect already lined up.'

Perilla sniffed. 'Marcus, that is pure unwarranted speculation,' she said. 'And it comes very close to muck-raking.'

Agron grinned.

'Yeah, well, you haven't met her, lady,' I said. 'She dresses to kill and she takes no prisoners.' I refilled my wine-cup and offered the jug to Agron. 'You want a top-up, pal?' He shook his head. 'Anyway, we thought – Perilla and me – that Mamilia might have a thing going with Publius Fundanius, business or pleasure or both, but that horse is a non-starter. Or I'm fairly sure it is.'

'Glad to hear it,' Agron said. 'You've almost been knifed once in the past couple of days already. The less you mix yourself up with Fundanius the better.' He reached for the plate of cheese and pickles. 'I'll tell you again: you want to stay clear of that guy.'

'That might be tricky,' I said. 'Chances are, he's still mixed up in things somewhere along the line. Where exactly or how deeply he's involved I don't know, but lily-white he isn't, nor is Correllius's erstwhile second, Publius Doccius. That crooked bastard's in it up to his eyeballs, that's for sure. I'd bet my sandal straps.' I helped myself to some of the cold chicken stew. 'Anyway, leave it for the present. Eat your lunch, I'll give you the tour, and then you can—' I stopped. 'Shit!'

'What is it, Marcus?' Perilla said.

The niggle at the edge of my mind was back, and this time it'd had something to say for itself. I shook my head. 'Nothing. Just an idea. Or half of one, if that. Forget it; it'll wait until I've talked to our cack-handed crane operator.'

Fundanius and Publius Doccius, eh?

Hmm.

There was still plenty of the afternoon left when we arrived at the stonemason's yard. Like Agron had said, it was just down the road a shade from his place, in the town's top right-hand corner near the river, where a lot of the commercial enterprises are located: handy for trans-shipping the stone, and not all that far from the Roman Gate and the Appian Road beyond with its flanking line of roadside tombs where most of it would finally end up.

'You need me any longer?' Agron said.

'No, that's OK, pal.' He was obviously anxious to get on, and unlike me he had a living to earn. 'Thanks a lot. Dinner in a couple of days, all right? I'll ask Meton to do fish.'

'Great.' He walked off, and I went through the yard gates.

Obviously a thriving business, this: there were at least half a dozen workmen busy on pieces of stonework in various shapes and sizes and a good few finished slabs and pillars waiting for delivery or purchase by the end-users' heirs. Monumental sculptors' yards have always seemed pretty sad places to me; your average concern is stocked with ready-made tombstones showing tradesmen or shopkeepers going about their everyday business or kids playing with their goat-carts, with an empty space underneath for the inscription to be added. The thing is, said tradesmen and kids are currently still alive and breathing, not knowing that their own personal tombstone is sitting there waiting for them.

Sad, like I say. Sad, and just a smidgeon eerie. The thought of it sends a shiver down my spine every time.

Still, the guys who work there don't seem to mind. I buttonholed the nearest workman, who was chipping out the already-lined-in inscription on a tombstone showing a cutler standing in front of a rack of his wares. He was humming to himself while he did it; evidently a man happy in his work.

'Excuse me, friend,' I said. He stopped humming and looked up. 'You happen to have a Gaius Siddius working here?'

'Siddius?' he said sourly. 'Sure. If you can call it working. That's him over there.' He nodded in the direction of a weedy unshaven runt in a threadbare tunic who was sitting on a block of dressed stone drinking from a leather flask. 'Skiving off like he usually does when the boss isn't around.'

'Thanks,' I said. I went over. The guy looked up and lowered the flask.

'Your name Siddius?' I said to him.

He wiped his lips with the back of his hand. 'What if it is?' he said.

'No hassle, pal. I just wanted to ask you a few questions.'

'I'm on my break.'

I sighed. So, it was going to be like that, was it? I pulled out my purse, opened it, and took out a couple of silver pieces. His eyes followed every move, and he put the flask down.

'OK,' he said. 'I'm Siddius. Questions about what?'

'You used to work as a crane man at the docks, right? Until twelve or thirteen days back. Quay Twenty-five.'

'Yeah, I did. So?'

I added another silver piece. 'There was an accident the day before you left. You dropped a load of amphoras.'

He scowled. 'What the hell is this?' he said. 'You from the port office? Because if you are, you can—'

'No. I told you. No hassle. I'm just checking something out privately. Someone almost got hit. Name of Gaius Tullius.'

I was watching his expression. Wary; definitely wary, and his eyes flickered. Then he laughed. 'Almost hit, nothing,' he said. 'The bastard was nowhere near me. He was a dozen yards up the quay.'

Uh-huh. 'You're sure?'

'Sure I'm sure. The accident happened, no point in denying it, it's no skin off my nose now, but if he's a friend of yours trying it on with a claim then he's lying through his teeth.'

'The ship you were loading was the *Porpoise*. Master Titus Nigrinus.' This time the flicker was unmistakable. 'You know him?'

'Yeah,' he said grudgingly. 'I know Nigrinus. He's a regular. And it might've been the *Porpoise* right enough, for all I remember.' His eyes went to the purse, and to the silver pieces I was holding in my other hand. I added another couple. 'So what?'

'So there's one thing puzzling me, pal,' I said. 'According to the clerk in the harbour office the *Porpoise*'s cargo was oil and wine. Drop a few amphoras of that on the quay and it'd make quite a mess. Only I talked to the quay-master and he said there was no sign of one. And that there'd been no accident at all, at least none that was reported, either by you or by Nigrinus. You care to explain, maybe?'

Siddius licked his lips. He looked round nervously. 'That depends,' he said.

'Depends on what?' I tipped out more coins into my palm. One of them was a half gold piece. His eyes went to it and stayed there, and he licked his lips again.

'No hassle, you say?' he said.

'None at all. Cross my heart.' I jingled the coins absently. There was enough money there to keep him drunk for the rest of the month. Even so, he was hesitating, which, if my theory was right, made a lot of sense.

'OK,' I said. 'I'll make it easy for you. I'll tell you what I think the explanation was. All you have to do is say whether I'm right or wrong, and we'll take it from there. Deal?'

He swallowed. 'Deal.'

'There was no mess because there was nothing to make it. The amphoras were empty. Throw the broken bits over the side, and everything's neat and tidy again. And Captain Nigrinus wasn't likely to kick up a fuss with the authorities, was he, because he knew damn well that there was no oil or wine there to begin with.'

Another swallow. Then, slowly, Siddius nodded. 'That's more or less it, yeah,' he said. 'Not spot on, but more or less.'

Glory and trumpets! I kept my face straight.

'Only,' I said, 'you'd've had to know that too, wouldn't you? A load of empty amphoras hanging at the end of your crane-hook'd feel a lot different from a load of full ones.'

'Yeah, they would.' He grinned. 'Only the buggers weren't empty, were they? They'd been filled with water. So I didn't know they was dodgy until they smashed, did I, clever Dick?'

Well, at least he was talking, and the precise detail didn't matter much; in fact, if the amphoras had been full it made more sense. At any rate, the theory held good, in spades.

'What about the water?' I said. 'Wouldn't somebody notice that?'

He shrugged. 'Been raining that morning, hadn't it, so the quay was wet in any case. Nothing to notice, except if you were there at the time. I had that crooked bastard Nigrinus over a barrel. How he managed the switch or swung things in the first place, I don't know and I don't care, but it was a pretty good scam. Contract for a big consignment, swap the amphoras for ringers, load them onto a leaky tub like the *Porpoise* that's long overdue for the breaker's yard, stage a fake accident, and you're laughing.' He gave me a sharp look. 'The *Porpoise* went down, didn't she?'

'Yeah. Just off the Corsican coast.'

'And the crew got ashore safe?'

'Yeah, they did.'

He nodded with satisfaction. 'There you are, then. The perfect scam. No one's crying but the guy who owned the original cargo, and you may be down one leaky old tub but you're up eight hundred amphoras' worth of oil and wine.' He frowned. 'Mind you, it'd take a lot of organizing. Just the shifting and storing would be a major job, big-time stuff. I wouldn't've thought Nigrinus'd be up to that. You live and learn.'

Yeah, I'd agree. Still, I had my own thoughts on that score.

'The cargo's owner was Marcus Correllius, right?' I said.

'Yeah. He didn't handle things himself, mind. Guy's too ill

to involve himself much with everyday business these days, or
so I hear. He left the nitty-gritty to his manager, Publius Doccius.
Now there's a real hard bastard. If Nigrinus was putting one
over on him then no wonder he was sweating when I dropped
the load.'

Bullseye! 'Doccius wasn't there himself at the time?'

'Nah. Saw the loading started, then buggered off to the
nearest wineshop for a drink.'

'The guys doing the loading. They were Correllius's?'

'Sure. Doccius always uses a company team. It's cheaper
that way.' Yeah, Cispius had told me that was how it worked.
'He would've used one of his own men for the crane, too,
but he'd broken his wrist.' He laughed. 'Bad luck on Doccius's
part, of course, because then the accident might not've
happened. I was pretty hungover that day.'

'And none of the team – the loaders – noticed that there
was something funny going on?'

'Must've done. But they weren't going to get involved,
were they? That might just lead to trouble.

Uh-huh; Cispius again. He'd said that shoving your nose
in and asking questions when you worked for Correllius was
a bad idea. And given my suspicions – more than suspicions,
now – where Doccius was concerned they'd probably have
been right.

'So,' I said. 'What happened then?'

'I finished the loading, nice as pie, and then went to Nigrinus
to put the bite on. Like I say, the guy was sweating. He grum-
bled, sure, but when I threatened to take the story straight to
Correllius he paid up like a lamb. Five gold pieces I got from
him for keeping my mouth shut, and cheap at the price. They
came in handy, as well, because next day that bastard of a
quay-master Arrius sacked me.'

Which had probably, in fact, saved his life: me, I
wouldn't't've given a copper quadrans for it once he'd told
Nigrinus what he'd seen. The sacking had been lucky for
both of us.

'The other guy who witnessed the accident. Gaius Tullius,'
I said. 'You happen to know what he did then?'

'Nah. Not a clue. I hardly even noticed him, and like I say

he was nowhere near me when I dropped the load. Probably just went about his business.'

Yeah; that I'd believe. Only Tullius's business, I'd bet, had comprised putting the bite on himself. Which, if I was right, was exactly why he'd ended up dead.

'It doesn't matter,' I said. 'Forget it.' I handed over the coins. 'Thanks, pal. That's been a great help.'

He pocketed them. 'Any time.'

TWENTY-TWO

S o; next major port of call, as it were, Publius Doccius.
Only before I did that I needed a little insurance of
my own.

Siddius was right: disappearing eight hundred amphoras
and selling on their contents would take organization and
manpower, and if Nigrinus didn't cut the mustard in that
department then I'd bet Doccius couldn't've managed it either;
not off his own bat, at least. For a heist like that, he'd've needed
a partner with real clout, and there was only one obvious
candidate; Publius Fundanius. Fundanius made all kinds of
sense: he'd have the organization that could cope with something on that scale, he'd've jumped at the chance to do the
dirty on his long-time business rival, and – which was really
the clincher – I'd seen Doccius at his villa, where presumably
he'd gone straight off when Mamilia threw him out on his ear.
Where, again presumably, I'd find him now.

Only, especially after Agron's repeated warnings, I wasn't
going to walk in blithely and accuse them both to their faces,
was I? Oh, sure, I was a Roman purple-striper, with all that
entailed where the authorities were concerned, but that hadn't
seemed to cut much ice with the bastards so far, had it? Not
when their hitman of choice Sextus Nigrinus had tried to zero
me on at least two occasions. So insurance of a very physical
kind it had to be, plus an ally who had the same kind of clout
that Fundanius had; and my best bet on that score was the
injured party, Mamilia. Persuading her re the whys and wherefores shouldn't be difficult, given that she already knew that
Doccius had been on the fiddle. And as far as Fundanius
himself was concerned, if she had an axe to grind it was
one I'd bet she would cheerfully have smacked him between
the eyes with. So Mamilia it was.

No time like the present. I headed across town in the
direction of the Hinge.

The Tullius side of things was obvious, too. If Gaius Siddius, coincidentally and fortunately for him, had disappeared into the woodwork after conducting his business with Nigrinus, Tullius hadn't been so lucky. He wasn't to know, of course, that he was messing with some pretty hard guys, or he might've thought twice about trying on a bit of blackmail, but the whole thing had been done off the cuff; he'd seen a chance to make a dishonest silver piece or two, and he'd taken it. Who exactly had done the actual killing – the captain's brother Sextus or Doccius himself – I didn't know, and it wasn't crucially important at this stage; nor were the precise circumstances of how he'd been lured to an out-of-the-way spot like the Shrine of Melobosis off Trigemina Gate Street. What was important was I knew now who was behind the murder, and why.

Case solved. Or almost, bar the shouting.

'Valerius Corvinus! This is a surprise!' The lady actually gave me a smile; clearly our relationship had moved up a notch, which was all to the good under the circumstances. 'What brings you back so soon? I was just about to go out, but I can spare you a few minutes.'

We were in the atrium again, and the lady had obviously just been having her make-up freshened: the maid was putting away the bits and bobs, and Mamilia herself was done up to the nines.

'It, uh, might take a little longer than that,' I said. 'But it's important.'

That got me an interested look. 'Really?' she said. 'How intriguing. In that case you had better sit down and we'll take it from there. That's all, Chloe. You can go.'

The maid left.

I sat. 'Your husband sent a shipment of wine and oil to Aleria shortly before he died,' I said.

'Yes, that's right. We did.' Uh-huh; no pretence, this time, of being ignorant of Correllius's business affairs, I noticed. And the 'we' didn't escape me, either.

'You know the ship – the *Porpoise* – sank just short of the Corsican coast?' I said.

She frowned. 'Yes, I did, as a matter of fact. The news came a few days ago. Unfortunate, but these things do happen, and we can stand the loss. So?'

'There was no wine or oil on board. The amphoras were filled with water.'

'What?' She stared at me. 'You're sure?'

'Hundred per cent certain.' I told her the whole story, barring a mention of Tullius. 'It was a scam. The cargo had been switched.'

She was quiet for a long time. Then she said, and I could hear her teeth grind: 'That bastard Doccius.'

Right; no fool, Mamilia. And there was no fluffy softness there, either, none at all. Not a comfortable lady to cross, this one.

I almost felt a pang of sympathy for Publius Doccius. Almost.

'That was my guess, yeah,' I said. 'Him and Publius Fundanius, working together.'

'Fundanius.' She sat back in her chair. I could see her thinking. 'Yes,' she said slowly. 'Yes, that would make perfect sense. I'm in your debt, Corvinus. Thank you for telling me.'

'Actually, Mamilia, I've business of my own with Doccius. Not immediately connected with the scam, or not directly. But he has other questions to answer.'

'Has he, indeed? Then he had better answer them.' She smiled, and it wasn't a nice smile, either. She got up. 'Excuse me a moment. I'll be right back.'

She went off through the peristyle, and I twiddled my thumbs. A few minutes later, she was back with a couple of heavies who could've been brothers to the guy on the front door, and probably were.

'These two gentlemen are Marcus and Quintus,' she said. 'They have my every confidence, and they are fully apprised of the situation. If you were thinking of paying a call on Publius Doccius, who, I understood from what you said during your last visit, is currently with Fundanius at his villa, then they would be delighted to accompany you. I don't think you'll have any trouble either getting in or leaving.'

Yeah, I'd believe that: the pair of them looked like they'd stepped straight off a temple pediment showing the Battle of the Titans. The marble aspect of things was about right, too.

'They have their own instructions, naturally, since I have reasons of my own to make contact with Doccius. But since our interests seem to coincide at this point you're very welcome to make use of them. Clear, gentlemen?'

'Yeah, madam. Clear.' The guy on the right flexed his hands. I could hear the knuckles crack.

'Off you go, then. As I said, I was just about to go out myself. You'll forgive me, Corvinus.'

'No problem,' I said.

'Goodbye. And thank you again.'

'You're welcome.'

She left, and I looked at the two fugitives from the pediment.

'Which of you is which?' I said.

'I'm Marcus,' the hand-flexer said. 'Pleased to meet you.'

'Yeah. Likewise.' Well, at least they'd been nicely brought up. 'Shall we go?'

'After you.'

We went.

'We're here to see Publius Doccius,' I said to the old guy on the gate.

He looked doubtfully at my two tame Titans.

'I'm sorry, sir, I don't think we have a—' he began.

I held up a hand. 'Don't even think of it, sunshine,' I said. 'Just go and tell him. And if your master's at home then we'll see him at the same time. Off you go, spit spot.'

He opened his mouth to say something, took another look at Marcus and Quintus standing – looming – behind me, and wisely decided to close it again. Then he hobbled inside, closing the gate behind him.

He was away for a good ten minutes, by which time Mamilia's lads were definitely chafing. Finally, though, he reappeared.

'They'll see you, sir,' he said. 'On the terrace, as before. Would you like me to show you the way, or can you find it for yourself?'

Delivered in the most unpressing tones, which was fair

enough: I had the distinct impression that Tithonus here would be glad to get shot of us and take up his afternoon snooze where he'd left off.

'No, that's OK, pal,' I said. 'I think I can remember.'

We went round the corner of the villa. Fundanius and Doccius were sitting at the terrace table, on two of the three chairs; at least, Fundanius was sitting, and Doccius was sprawled, his arm across the chair-back and his feet resting on the third chair, completely at his ease. He grinned and gave us the high wave as we came in sight. Behind me, I heard one of the minders growl softly.

'Corvinus,' Fundanius said, and you could've used his tone to saw marble. 'What exactly is the meaning of this, please?'

Not a happy bunny, evidently. Still, I hadn't expected to be welcomed with open arms, so that was absolutely fine by me.

'Oh, I think you know,' I said. 'To begin with, the little matter of eight hundred amphoras filled with wine and oil belonging to Marcus Correllius, that should be under several fathoms of seawater but aren't.'

'I have not the slightest idea what you're talking about.'

'You,' Marcus pointed at Doccius, 'are dead, pal.'

Doccius's grin slipped just a little, and he took his feet off the chair.

'Come on, Fundanius!' I said. 'We've got Doccius here cold. He arranged the shipment on a boat called the *Porpoise*, captain Titus Nigrinus, that went down just short of the point of delivery. That should've been the end of it with no one any the wiser, only I've talked to the crane operator who did the loading. According to him, he dropped some of the amphoras on the quayside and they were full of water.'

'He's lying,' Fundanius said; he hadn't even blinked. 'Besides, even if they were, what business is it of mine? Or of yours, for that matter?'

'Yeah, well, as far as the first bit's concerned, squirrelling away eight hundred amphoras takes a bit of doing. Laughing boy here's a natural second-stringer, and I doubt if he could hack it on his own.' Doccius scowled, and he took his arm from the back of the chair. 'As for the second part, there was a witness. A guy by the name of Gaius Tullius, an import-export merchant in Rome, who is definitely my business, because he was murdered twelve days back. You heard of him, maybe?'

I could feel them stiffen, and Fundanius's eyes flicked towards Doccius.

'No,' Fundanius said. 'At least, I haven't. Publius?'

'He's a new one on me,' Doccius said. 'And last time I looked this was Ostia, not Rome. Murders in Rome are no concern of ours.'

'I said he had his business in Rome, pal, not that he was killed there. But then you knew that already, didn't you?'

Doccius shrugged. 'It was a logical assumption. Why should I have heard of him? He isn't anyone I ever had any dealings with.' He gave Marcus and Quintus a level look. 'When I worked for that fat slob Correllius, that is.'

'Yeah, well, that's just the point, isn't it?' I said. 'The time your paths crossed you weren't working for Correllius, were you? You were working for Fundanius here, or at least the two of you were partners in the wine and oil scam along with the *Porpoise*'s owner, Titus Nigrinus.'

Doccius smiled. Then he laughed and set his feet back on the spare chair. 'Corvinus,' he said, 'you are so full of shit it's unbelievable. I told you: I've never even heard of this Tullius guy, let alone met him. And if he claimed that there was any funny business with the consignment then he was lying for reasons of his own, just like that crane operator of yours. As for Nigrinus, well, there was no scam to begin with, so there couldn't've been a partnership, could there? I'm sorry for the man, he's down one ship, but that's one of the risks you take in this business, and at least if I've heard rightly he survived the accident.'

'Publius is quite correct.' Fundanius was smiling too. 'I'm sorry, gentlemen' – his look included the heavies standing behind me – 'but all this is complete nonsense. As far as your accusation concerning the shipment is concerned, Corvinus, your only proof, correct me if I'm wrong, is the word of a drunken crane operator and an obscure Roman trader of whom neither of us has any knowledge and who is in any case now dead. As for the trader himself' – he shrugged – 'well, what more can I say? I know nothing of him whatsoever. Now if that's your only business here—'

'Fuck that.' Marcus – obviously the spokesman of the duo – pushed in front of me. 'You' – he levelled a finger at Fundanius – 'are going to be one sorry cheating bastard before much longer. The mistress told me to promise you that; she'll see to it personally. And you' – the finger shifted to Doccius – 'I've already told you; you're a dead man walking. Buy yourself an urn.'

Doccius was looking queasy again, but Fundanius hadn't moved.

'How fascinating,' he said equably. 'But Publius Doccius works for me now, and I look after my own. Do be sure to give my regards to Mamilia, won't you? I think you know your way out.' He nodded to me. 'Corvinus.'

I nodded back, and we left.

'We're stymied,' I said to Perilla when we'd settled down later that afternoon on the terrace with a pre-dinner drink. 'The bastards just sat there and laughed in our faces.'

'It can't be as bad as all that, dear,' Perilla said. 'There must be something you can do.'

'Like what, for example?' I took a morose swallow of wine. 'They know I know the whole story, no argument, but they also know there isn't a blind thing I can do about it. Not without some solid proof; Fundanius pointed that out, and he was right.'

'But you have it, surely. As far as the scam aspect of things goes, at least. Your crane operator, what was his name, Siddius, confirmed that the accident on the quayside happened, and that the amphoras he dropped were filled with water. That's confirmation in itself.'

I sighed. 'Perilla, I haven't a hope in hell of getting a signed statement from the guy, which is what it'd need. How long do you think he'd survive if he crossed Publius Doccius, never mind Fundanius? He'd be signing his own death warrant, and he'd know it. Plus the fact that, a), it'd be his word against everyone else's, and b), as far as the port authorities are concerned there was no accident to begin with because he didn't fucking report one at the time.'

'Gently, Marcus.'

I took another swig of wine. Not that it did any good, mind.

'Well, he didn't,' I said. 'And the reason he didn't was, he was paid to keep his mouth shut. You think he'd change his story now, in public, anyway? Why should he? What's in it for him, barring a slit throat down an alley?'

'You're certain that Fundanius was in on the fraud?'

'Absolutely; one hundred per cent. He knew about Siddius, for a start, and he couldn't've done that if he wasn't involved up to his eyeballs.'

'What makes you so sure?'

'Because when he mentioned the crane operator he used the word drunken. Which I hadn't done. Oh, sure, clumsy, incompetent, cack-handed, any appropriate term you like given the circumstances; but the only way he could know Siddius had a drink problem is if Doccius had told him. QED.'

'That isn't much to build a case on.'

'It's good enough for me, lady. But with the only other witness being oh-so-conveniently dead unless by some miracle I can twist Nigrinus's arm when he shows up and get a confession out of him we are well and truly screwed.' I refilled my wine-cup. 'The only consolation is that if I'm any judge of character Mamilia won't let them get away with it. That is one very ruthless lady. Me, I wouldn't be in Publius Doccius's sandals for his weight in gold pieces, whether he has Fundanius's protection or not.'

'You can't prove a connection between Fundanius – or Doccius, at least – and Gaius Tullius? That's the other angle, surely.'

'Uh-uh. For the same reason: no hard facts. Oh, they knew the name when I brought it up, sure, I'd bet a year's income on that, because it came as a nasty facer; in fact, I thought at that point I had them. But then when I mentioned the partnership arrangement with Nigrinus, they—'

I stopped.

Oh, shit! Oh, holy gods!

'Marcus?' Perilla was frowning. 'What is it?'

'That was when the bastards relaxed,' I said slowly. 'Both

of them at once, right then and there. Grinning their heads off. They'd been on the back foot up until then, but when I brought in Nigrinus you could almost hear the sigh of relief.'

'But that doesn't make any sense! Nigrinus had to be involved for the fraud to work. Didn't he?'

'Sure he did. No argument.' I was thinking hard. There was something there; there had to be. When I'd mentioned Gaius Tullius completely out of the blue, it'd been a shock, because up to then he hadn't figured; everything I'd said, all the questions I'd asked and the accusations I'd made, had had to do with the scam itself or – previously – with the death of Correllius. Now for the first time with the mention of Tullius Fundanius and his new pal had lost control of the plot, and they were running blind. Only then they realized that I wasn't as smart or as clued-up as they thought I was. Feared. Whatever. Because I'd made a crucial mistake.

'Marcus . . .'

I waved her to silence. So what was it? I replayed the conversation in my head.

I'd said that when Doccius ran across Gaius Tullius he hadn't been working for Correllius; that he'd been in partnership with Fundanius and the *Porpoise*'s captain Nigrinus . . .

Only I hadn't said captain, had I? I'd said owner.

'Nigrinus didn't own the *Porpoise*,' I said.

Perilla was still frowning. 'But that's silly, dear! Of course he did!'

I shook my head. 'Uh-uh. Oh, we assumed he did, sure, because he was the ship's captain, after all, and that's the way these things usually work. But that's all it was: an assumption.' I was trying to remember my original conversation with the clerk in the harbour master's office, and with the quay-master Arrius. As far as I could recall, neither had said that Titus Nigrinus actually owned the *Porpoise*; like I said, that'd only been an assumption on my part, and it had gone uncorrected. 'Nigrinus was only the hired help, not the third partner per se. No wonder the bastards were laughing up their sleeves. I'd got my facts wrong, and they knew it.'

Perilla was staring at me. 'Can you check?' she said.

'Sure. Easiest thing in the world. It's too late today, but I'll go round to the harbour master's office first thing tomorrow morning.'

Perhaps we were on to a winner after all.

I walked into the harbour office bright and early next day, just after it opened. Everything hinged on the answer to one question, but I was pretty sure now what that would be. Or at least that it would be one of two possibilities.

I found the clerk I'd talked to before at his desk. The guy didn't exactly look over the moon to see me, mind. Not that I blamed him.

'Good morning yet again, sir,' he said. 'And how perchance may I help you today?'

Sarcastic as hell. But in the mood I was in sarcasm slid off me like water from a duck's back. 'It's about the *Porpoise* again,' I said. 'I was wondering if you could give me the name of the owner. If he's different from the ship's captain, that is. And an address for him, if you've got it.'

'Nothing easier, sir. It'll be entered on the file I looked out for you previously. Unless, under the circumstances, it's been destroyed, as it may well have been.' Bugger; I hadn't thought of that! Oh, gods, no; please, please, no! 'If you'll just wait a moment, I'll go and check.'

He went off, and I spent the next five minutes biting my nails. Then he came back holding the document. I breathed a sigh of relief. Thank heavens for bureaucratic inertia.

'Here you are, sir,' he said. 'The *Porpoise*, ninety tons when it was a viable proposition.' He chuckled: obviously a clerical in-joke. 'Captain, Titus Nigrinus. Owner . . .'

He told me the name. Well, well, well: bullseye!

'I've only an office address for him, I'm afraid,' the clerk said. 'Will that do? It's in Rome, naturally, the gentleman being Roman.'

'Yeah. Yeah, that'll be fine.'

He told me that, as well. Double bullseye! Case closed, barring the mopping-up.

'Thanks, pal,' I said. 'I'm grateful.' That was an understatement, if ever there was one. 'You've been really, really helpful.'

'Don't mention it.'

'You mind if I take that with me?' I pointed at the flimsy he was holding.

'Not at all. As I said, it would have been destroyed in any case.'

'Thanks.' I took it and tucked it into my belt. I was turning away when another thought struck me. 'Oh; one last question,' I said, 'and I'm out of your hair for good.'

He sighed. 'Really, sir?'

'Yeah. I absolutely guarantee it. You know if anyone else was in here after the same information? It would've been the day the ship was being loaded.'

He was frowning. 'Yes, actually, now you mention it, there was,' he said. 'I can't give you his name, though; I told you, I'm not too good with names, but faces I do remember. He was Roman, too, by the look of him. Youngish, smart dresser. The sort the ladies might take a fancy to, if you know what I mean. A friend of yours? Business colleague, perhaps?'

'No, not exactly.' I'd never seen Tullius in the flesh, so the description didn't tell me much; but it'd been him, all right, I was as certain of that as of the next day's sunrise, and it explained everything. If I needed further explanation at this point, which I didn't. 'Perfect. Thanks again for your help, friend. I'll see you around.' I caught the look on his face. 'Or perhaps not.'

'Goodbye, sir. Have a nice day.'

I left.

Back to Rome, ASAP. Perilla would be disappointed to cut short the holiday, sure, but into every life a little rain must fall. And we might well take that villa.

The case was cracked wide open.

TWENTY-THREE

Next day I left Perilla organizing her more leisurely return, sent a skivvy round to Agron's to apologize for cancelling the dinner invitation – I doubted that, under the circumstances, Fundanius's to me still held good, so that one I didn't bother about – and rode straight back to Rome.

I had a couple of bread-and-butter arrangements to make before I confronted Tullius's killer. The first of these was to call in on Gaius Memmius, the Aventine Watch Commander who'd been handling the case, explain things to him, and borrow a couple of his squaddies, including the one who'd originally been dispatched to the scene of the crime. I'd only get one shot at this, and I wasn't taking any chances.

The Shrine of Melobosis in the alleyway off Trigemina Gate Street was exactly as I'd left it the last time I'd been there; the little bunch of wild flowers – withered, now – lay undisturbed where I'd put them on her altar, and it didn't look like anyone had been inside the gate since. Not the courting couple who'd found the body, certainly: they'd've gone somewhere else for their evening meetings.

Sad.

I swept the top of the altar clear with my hand, filled the lamp from the small bottle of oil I'd brought with me, lit it with a fire striker, ditto, and burned a pinch or two of incense: there'd been a strong sea connection in this case, and who was I to say that a sea-nymph like Melobosis hadn't been helping out behind the scenes? At any rate, a drop of oil and a couple of pinches of incense wouldn't break me, and I reckoned I owed the lady something, at least. Just on the off-chance.

The two squaddies had been watching me curiously. I turned and went over to the right-hand wall, directly under one of the buildings which flanked the shrine precinct.

'This was where the body was lying, right?' I said to the guy who'd been there before.

'Yeah.' He pointed. 'Down there. Just clear of the wall.'

Uh-huh; I could still see the traces in the long, partially flattened grass. I looked up at the building; there was a window two floors directly above us. Check. It fitted, all the way along the line. Last box well and truly ticked.

'OK,' I said. 'Let's go and get it over with.'

The address the clerk at the harbour office had given me was on the second floor. We climbed the stairs. I pushed open the door and went in.

'Good morning, sir. What can I—?' The chief clerk in the outer office froze when he saw the squaddies behind me. The other clerks gaped, pens poised.

'The boss around, pal?' I said.

He swallowed. 'Yes, sir. I'll just see if he's free.'

'No, that's OK. We can manage.' I pushed past him and opened the communicating door.

Quintus Annius was at his desk in front of the window. If I'd gone over and looked through it and down, I'd've seen Melobosis's shrine.

'Corvinus, this is a surprise,' he said. He smiled at the squaddies. 'How can I help you?'

'You killed Gaius Tullius,' I said. 'Or maybe your pal Doccius did.'

The smile disappeared. He stared at me. 'That's nonsense,' he said. 'Who the hell is Doccius?'

'Uh-uh. It's not nonsense. And you know who Doccius is perfectly well.' There was a stool next to me. I pulled it up and sat down while the squaddies stationed themselves either side of the door. 'You want to tell me the story yourself, or should I save you the trouble?'

He leaned back against the wall. 'This is silly,' he said.

I shrugged. 'OK. Have it your way. Let's start with the *Porpoise*.' His eyelids twitched, but he just stared at me. 'Captain Titus Nigrinus. You're her owner, for what that's worth, because she was a worm-eaten tub that was held together by no more than spit and a lick of paint. Which, basically, was the whole idea, because the *Porpoise* is at the bottom of the sea off Corsica. Or rather, close enough to Corsica for Nigrinus to have got himself and his crew safely ashore.'

'Corvinus, this is insane!' Annius snapped. 'I've never even heard of this *Porpoise* of yours, nor of a Titus Nigrinus!' He stood up. 'Now I have business to attend to. If you won't leave peaceably, I'll call my chief clerk and have you—'

The bigger of the two squaddies moved forward and pushed him back onto his stool. I didn't move. Annius sat glaring.

'Not what the clerk in the Ostia shipping office told me, pal,' I said. I took the flimsy from my belt and showed him it. '*Porpoise*, ninety tons, registered in Ostia. Master, Titus Nigrinus, current owner, as of a month ago, Gaius Annius. You want to read it for yourself?'

He was quiet for a long time. Then he said: 'All right. I owned the *Porpoise*. I bought it from Titus Nigrinus and kept him on as captain. So what? I'm in the import-export business. Ship-owning is a natural offshoot of that. And if the ship went down then surely that's my affair, and my loss.'

'Fine,' I said. 'So. You like to explain why the cargo she was carrying at the time was eight hundred amphoras of water?'

'Again, that is sheer nonsense! The *Porpoise* was loaded with wine and oil.'

'Which you were transporting for a customer in Ostia by the name of Marcus Correllius, right?'

'Possibly.' There was a bead of sweat on his forehead. 'You can't expect me to remember the exact details of every order. If you'll let me ask my clerk—' He half-rose. The squaddie standing beside the desk cleared his throat and shifted his weight.

'Sit down,' I said.

He subsided, one eye on the squaddie. He was looking distinctly grey now.

'OK, next part,' I said. 'You heard of a guy called Siddius? Used to work a crane at the Ostia docks?'

'A crane operator? Of course not! Why should I?' A muscle in his face twitched.

'The name isn't important. But he was loading some of your wacky amphoras when the load slipped and they got broken. Oh, Captain Nigrinus paid him on the spot to keep his mouth shut, so that was all right. The problem was, though, there was someone else on the quay who just happened to be your brother-in-law. And he'd seen the whole thing as well.'

This time Annius said nothing. He just glared at me.

'Tullius is no fool, and like you when he gets the chance he isn't averse to a bit of sharp practice where it turns a neat profit. He sees the water where there should be a mess of wine or oil, and like Siddius he puts two and two together. But he's a lot cleverer than Siddius, and a lot more greedy. So instead of taking things up with the captain he checks the ship's details at the harbour office, like I did later, and he gets your name and your office address.' I paused. 'How am I doing, pal?'

Annius said nothing.

'Round he comes and you have a little chat. He wants money, of course, a lot of money, which you tell him you haven't got. Or not at present, anyway. However, the Ides're coming up, and the Ides are a holiday. The office is closed, there's no one around. If he drops by then, you tell him, you'll have the money ready and you can conduct your business with no one to disturb you. And in the interim you send word to your partners in Ostia, the other two in the scam who are doing the dirty on Correllius; Publius Fundanius, his long-term business rival, who was responsible for storing and selling on the contents of the genuine amphoras, and Publius Doccius, his deputy, who organized the switch and generally facilitated matters. Doccius – I'm guessing here, but it seems likely, because I don't think you've got the guts for murder on your own – comes through to Rome lickety-split to give you some not-so-moral support.'

I was glad I'd thought to bring the squaddies with me; the look I was getting from Annius suggested that, if he hadn't actually done the killing himself first time round, he'd happily do it now.

'OK,' I said. 'Tullius turns up for the pay-off and you – or Doccius – slip a knife into him. Then it's just a case of getting rid of the body. Easy-peasy; one heave, and the problem's solved.' I stood up, walked to the window, and looked out and down at the patch of flattened grass two floors beneath.

'As far as the Watch was concerned – as far as I was concerned, for that matter – he was killed down there in the shrine, although I did half-wonder even at the time why anybody planning to commit a murder would take the risk of being seen going into and coming out of a shrine that no one visits. Plus why once they'd done the job they didn't bother to hide the corpse properly when there was plenty of cover available. Oh, sure, it was a holiday so your office itself would be closed and the alleyway deserted, but there might still've been people passing on the main drag who might have seen and remembered.' I turned back round and gave him my best smile. 'Only in the event it turned out that there was no risk involved at all. Murdering a guy in the privacy of an empty office block, then pushing him through a window overlooking a patch of ground no one's ever in was a different thing altogether, and completely safe. Like I say, the only question is whether you or Doccius were the actual perp. Not that it matters much because in either case you, pal, are up the creek without a paddle.'

'It was Doccius,' Annius said quietly.

Glory and trumpets! 'Fair enough,' I said. 'I'm happy to go with that. For the present.'

He took a deep breath. 'Tullius was a complete bastard,' he said. 'A womanizer, a sponger, and a blackmailer. He's no great loss, and he deserved all he got. The world's a better place without him.'

'Maybe so. But then that wasn't your reason for killing him, was it?' I paused. 'Did your sister know?'

He shrugged. 'She may have suspected. She certainly knew where this office was. But she never asked me directly, and I didn't tell her.'

Yeah, I could appreciate that; they were well-matched, him and Annia, both cold fish, which was probably why they were so close. Maybe Tullius's partner, Poetelius, had had a lucky escape in the matrimonial stakes, if he had escaped. And Annius was right about one thing: Gaius Tullius was no great loss to humanity.

Still, that wasn't my concern. I turned to the squaddies.

'You can take things from here, lads?' I said.

'Uh-huh,' the guy beside the desk said. 'No problem.'

That was that, then. I left them to it.

Not that I was feeling smug; the case was finished, sure, and I'd got our killer, but it'd left a bad taste in my mouth. Why're these things never straight black and white, with the villain being really, really evil and the victim just that, an innocent shoved into an urn before his time? Despite what I'd said to him, despite the kind of guy he was, I had a lot of sympathy for Quintus Annius, and most of the people I'd been involved with would've agreed. Now all I wanted was a half-jug of wine and Perilla's reassurance, when she got back, that I'd only been doing my job.

I went home.

My neighbour Titus Petillius was just coming out of his front door. When he saw me, he froze.

The dead-cat incident. Oh, shit; I'd forgotten all about that. This I could do without.

I kept my eyes fixed on our door and made for the steps.

'Just one minute, Corvinus, if you please,' he said.

Hell. I stopped and turned round.

'Actually,' I said, 'I'm in a bit of a hurry at present. Maybe later?' Like after the Winter Festival. Preferably next year's.

'I won't keep you long.' Petillius came towards me and stood eyeball to eyeball. Or rather in his case eyeball to Adam's apple. 'And this won't wait.'

'Uh, right. Right.' I glanced up at the door. Where was Bathyllus when I needed him? Fourteen fucking miles off, in Ostia, that was where, and a distraction at this point would've been useful. Something along the lines of: *Excuse me, sir, but the kitchen's on fire, one of the maids has run amok with a cleaver, and the Emperor is waiting to see you in the atrium. Just when you're ready, of course.*

'OK,' I sighed. 'You have my full attention. What is it, Petillius?'

He was quivering with suppressed rage. 'I went down to the City Judge's office this morning to start proceedings against you,' he said. 'Killing a valuable feline, attempting to cover up the crime, and inciting a member of your household staff to engineer an assault on one of my most expensive slaves. You may expect to be notified in due course. That's all I have to say. Good day to you.'

Bugger this. 'Now look, pal,' I said. 'Don't you think you're overreacting just a little here? Not to mention the fact that I never touched your fucking cat to begin with.'

He bristled. 'That is an outright lie, and you know it!' he said. 'You were caught in the act of disposing of the body. And I intend now to add verbal abuse to the list.'

'Holy fucking Jupiter! All I did was—'

'And don't blaspheme!'

'Ah . . . excuse me, gents.'

I looked round. There was a big guy in a workman's tunic standing behind me who must've come up while Petillius was in full rant mode.

'Yeah?' I snapped.

'Only I was just wondering,' he said. 'Did one of you happen to own a cat? A Parthian male, white?'

'Uh . . . that'd be this gentleman here,' I said.

He turned to Petillius. 'Then I'm sorry, sir. Truth is, I ran the poor bleeder over a while back.' Petillius was goggling at him. 'I'm a cat-lover myself, five at the last count, wouldn't be without the little darlings. There wasn't nothing I could do. I drive a cart, see, and I was making a delivery at the house at the end of the road. They're building an extension on. Your cat run off the pavement in front of me right under the wheels, and with a load of stone and bricks in the back what can you expect?' The guy was practically sobbing. 'Sir, I've agonized about it ever since. If he'd been mine, I'd've wanted to know how he met his end, and I'm sure you're the same. Anyway, this morning the wife says, "Quintus, you go round, you find the owner and apologize." So here I am.' He took a deep breath. 'I laid him out decent, sir, on the pavement, like. That time of night, I couldn't do anything else. Now, I can see you're busy, and I won't take up any more of your valuable time. It won't help you in your grief, I know, but I'm glad I come and told you, all the same. The gods bless you, sir.'

And he left.

There was a long silence while Petillius and I looked at each other. Then Petillius said: 'Ah.'

'Indeed,' I said.

'It seems I owe you an apology, Corvinus.'

'Don't mention it.'

'We'll forget about the civil charges, then, shall we?'

'Yeah, that might be best.'

'And of course' – he indicated the writing on his wall that still read 'MY NEXT-DOOR NEIGHBOUR IS A CAT-KILLER' – 'I'll get one of my slaves to paint that over immediately.'

'Fine. Fine.'

'As for your chef and the incident with the melon . . . well, there may have been faults on both sides. Those artistic types can be so sensitive, don't you think?'

'I certainly do.'

'I'll bid you good day, then. My regards to your wife.'

'I'll tell her.'

He went back inside and closed the door.

Ah, well, life, it seemed, still had something to offer after all. I grinned and climbed the steps.